ADVENTURE TIME

WITH FIONNA & CAKE

PARTY BASH BLUES

Ross Richie..CEO & Founder
Joy Huffman ....CFO
Matt Gagnon ....Editor-in-Chief
Filip Sablik........................President, Publishing & Marketing
Stephen Christy ....President, Development
Lance Kreiter.............Vice President, Licensing & Merchandising
Arune Singh...Vice President, Marketing
Bryce Carlson............Vice President, Editorial & Creative Strategy
Scott Newman..Manager, Production Design
Kate Henning ....Manager, Operations
Spencer Simpson ....Manager, Sales
Sierra Hahn...Executive Editor
Jeanine Schaefer ....Executive Editor
Dafna Pleban ....Senior Editor
Shannon Watters ....Senior Editor
Eric Harburn ....Senior Editor
Chris Rosa ....Editor
Matthew Levine ....Editor
Sophie Philips-Roberts ....Associate Editor
Gavin Gronenthal ....Assistant Editor
Michael Moccio..Assistant Editor
Gwen Waller ....Assistant Editor
Amanda LaFranco ....Executive Assistant
Jillian Crab..Design Coordinator
Michelle Ankley..Design Coordinator
Kara Leopard ....Production Designer
Marie Krupina ....Production Designer
Grace Park ....Production Designer
Chelsea Roberts ....Production Design Assistant
Samantha Knapp ....Production Design Assistant
José Meza...Live Events Lead
Stephanie Hocutt ....Digital Marketing Lead
Esther Kim ....Marketing Coordinator
Cat O'Grady....................................Digital Marketing Coordinator
Amanda Lawson...Marketing Assistant
Holly Aitchison ....Digital Sales Coordinator
Morgan Perry ....Retail Sales Coordinator
Megan Christopher ....Operations Coordinator
Rodrigo Hernandez.......................................Mailroom Assistant
Zipporah Smith..Operations Assistant
Breanna Sarpy.......................................Executive Assistant

Designer
JILLIAN CRAB

Assistant Editor
MICHAEL MOCCIO

Editor
MATTHEW LEVINE

With Special Thanks to
MARISA MARIONAKIS, JANET NO, BECKY M. YANG,
CONRAD MONTGOMERY, KELLY CREWS, SCOTT MALCHUS,
ADAM MUTO and the wonderful folks at CARTOON NETWORK.

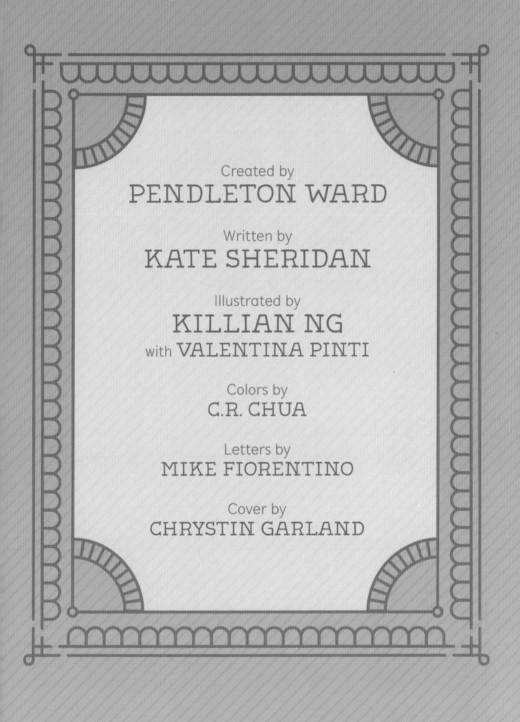

Created by
PENDLETON WARD

Written by
KATE SHERIDAN

Illustrated by
KILLIAN NG
with **VALENTINA PINTI**

Colors by
C.R. CHUA

Letters by
MIKE FIORENTINO

Cover by
CHRYSTIN GARLAND

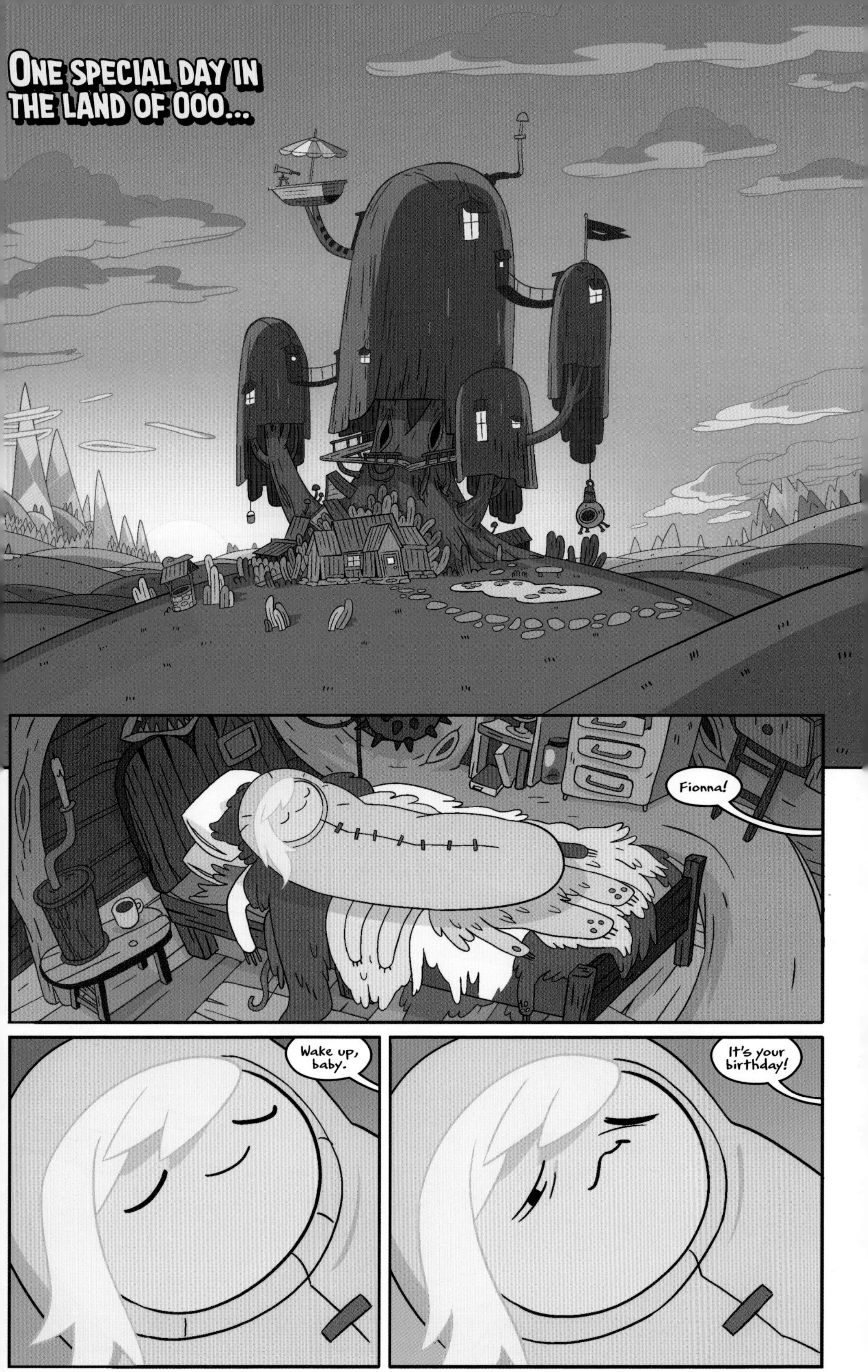
ONE SPECIAL DAY IN THE LAND OF OOO...
Fionna!
Wake up, baby.
It's your birthday!

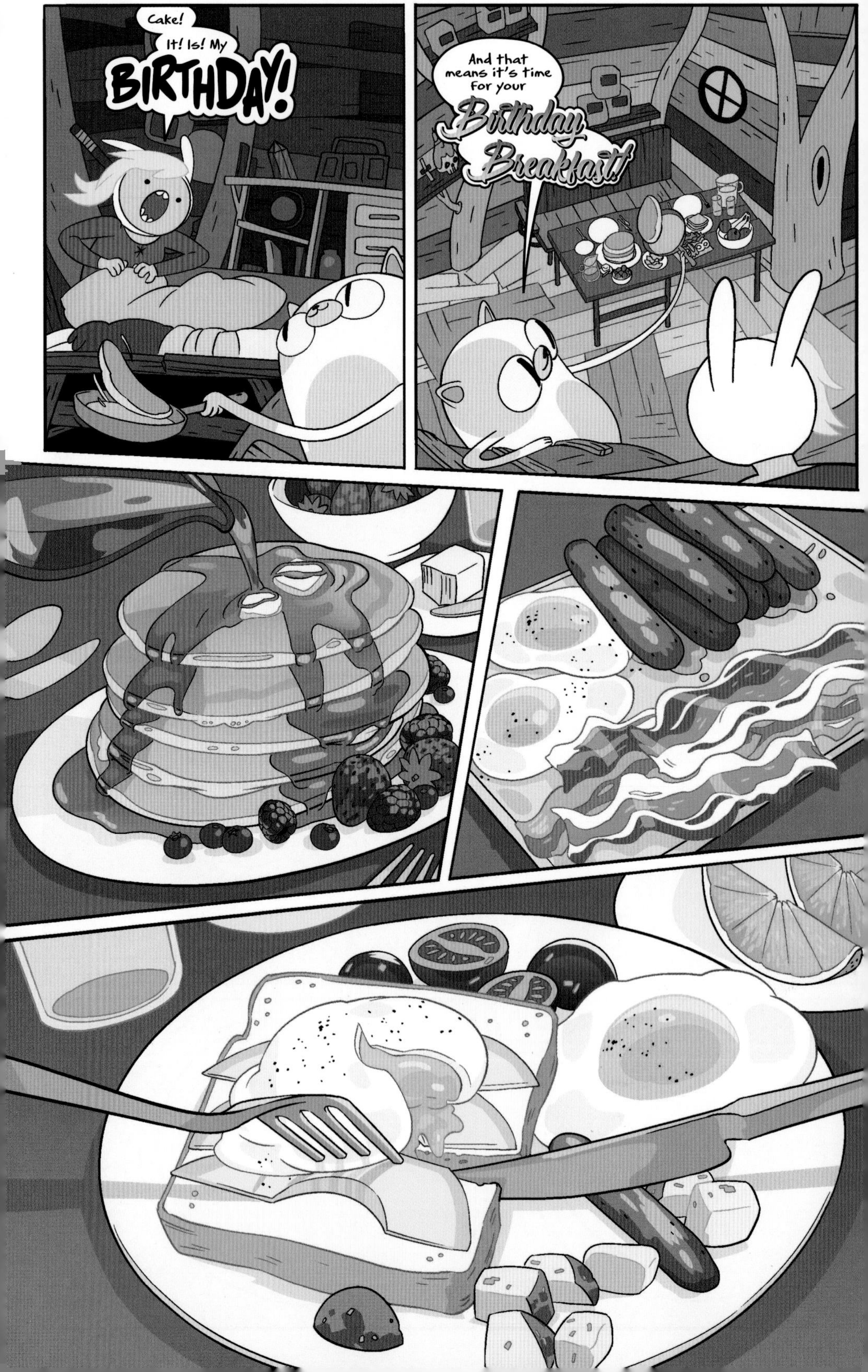
Cake!
It! Is! My
BIRTHDAY!
And that means it's time for your
Birthday Breakfast!

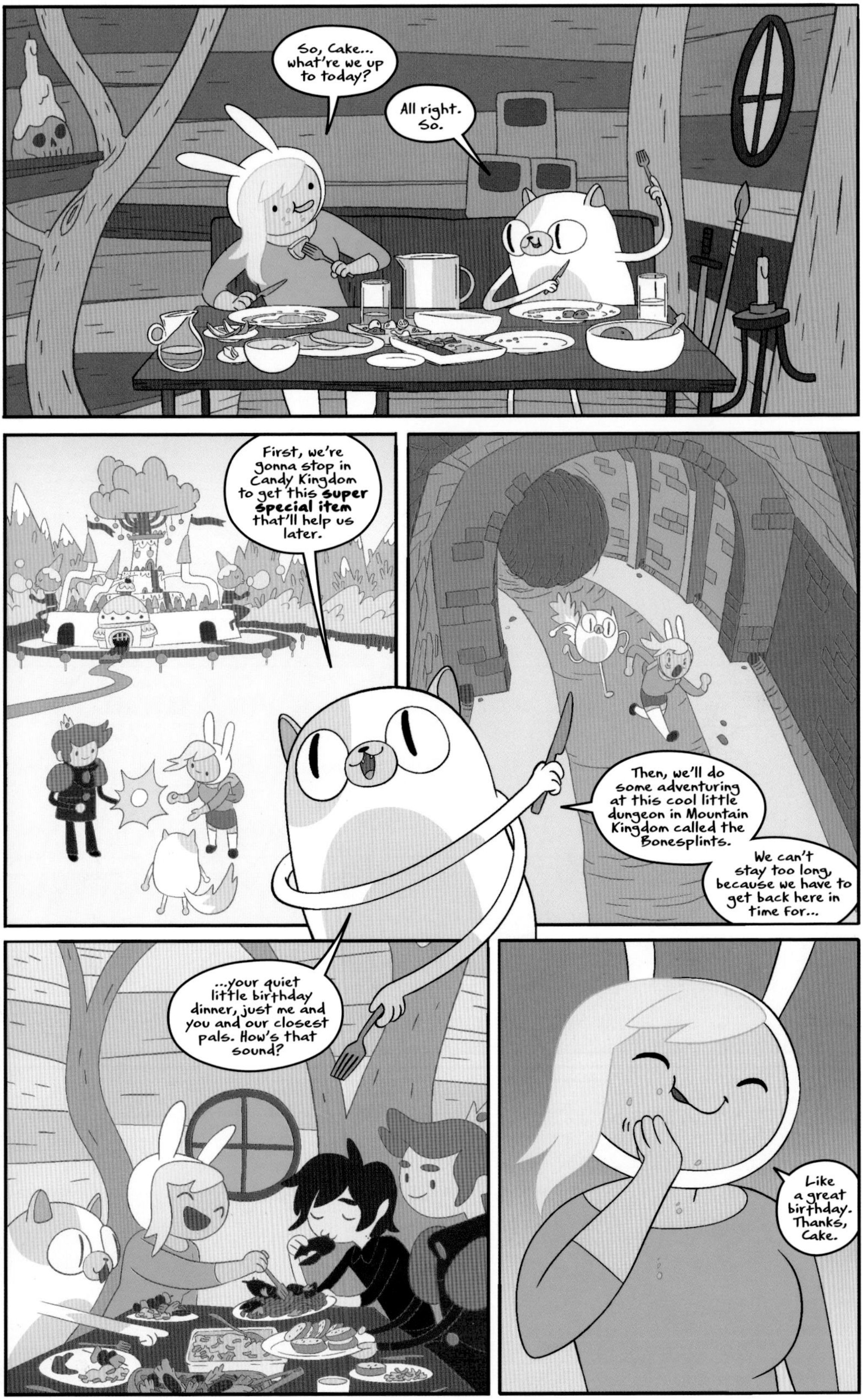
So, Cake... what're we up to today?
All right. So.
First, we're gonna stop in Candy Kingdom to get this **super special item** that'll help us later.
Then, we'll do some adventuring at this cool little dungeon in Mountain Kingdom called the Bonesplints.
We can't stay too long, because we have to get back here in time for...
...your quiet little birthday dinner, just me and you and our closest pals. How's that sound?
Like a great birthday. Thanks, Cake.

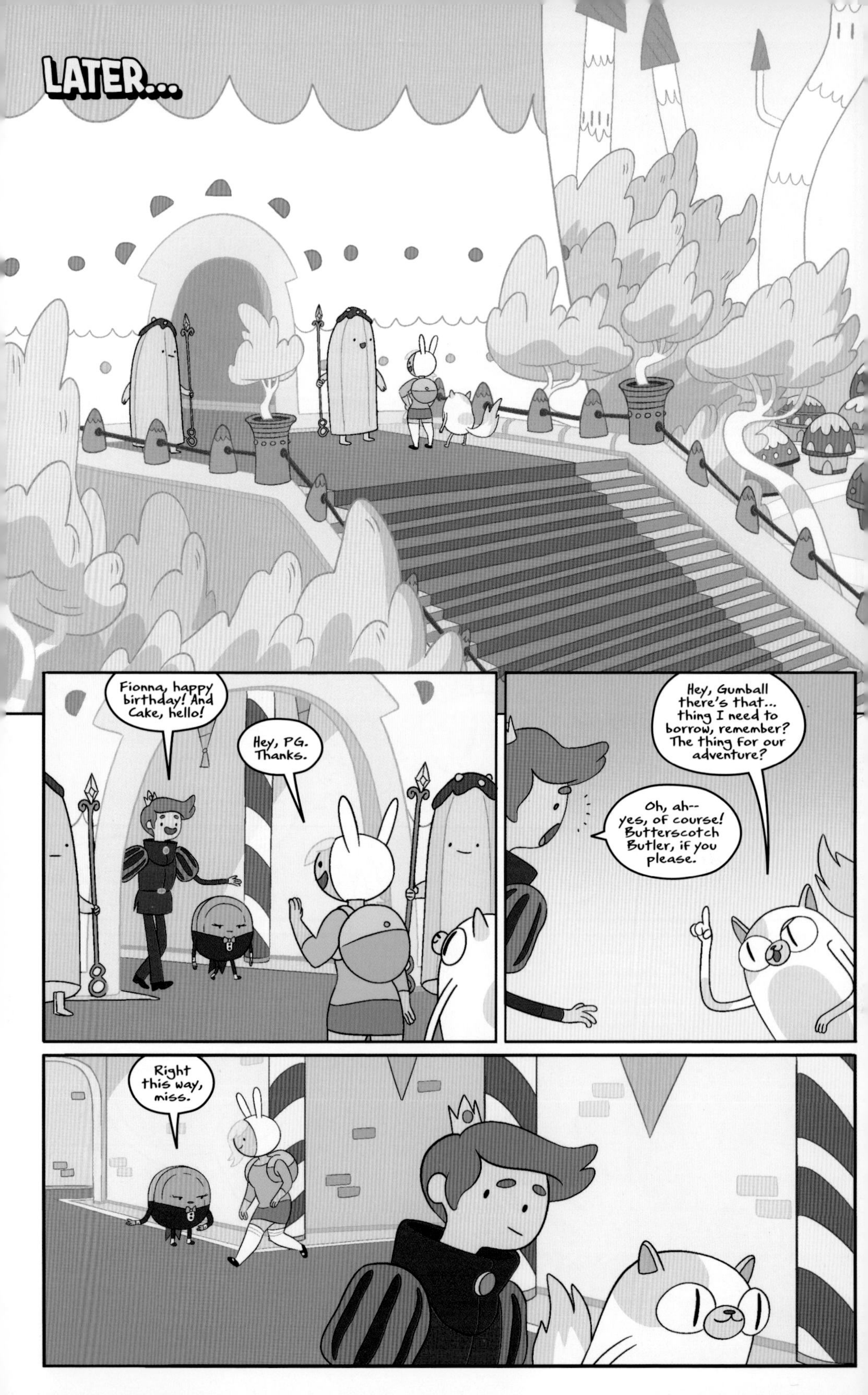
LATER...
Fionna, happy birthday! And Cake, hello!
Hey, PG. Thanks.
Hey, Gumball there's that... thing I need to borrow, remember? The thing for our adventure?
Oh, ah-- yes, of course! Butterscotch Butler, if you please.
Right this way, miss.

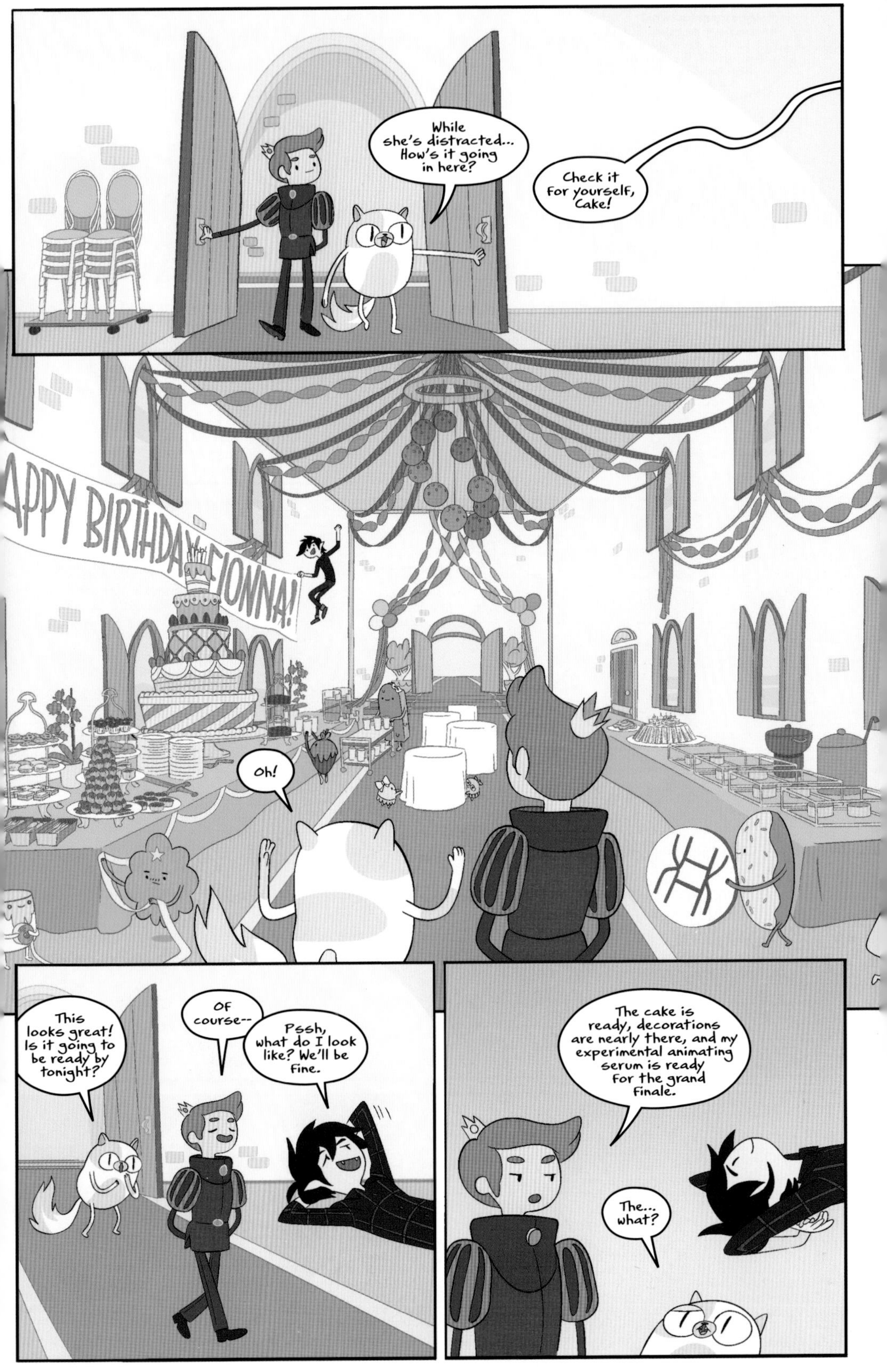

While she's distracted... How's it going in here?
Check it for yourself, Cake!
APPY BIRTHDAY FIONNA!
Oh!
This looks great! Is it going to be ready by tonight?
Of course--
Pssh, what do I look like? We'll be fine.
The cake is ready, decorations are nearly there, and my experimental animating serum is ready for the grand finale.
The... what?

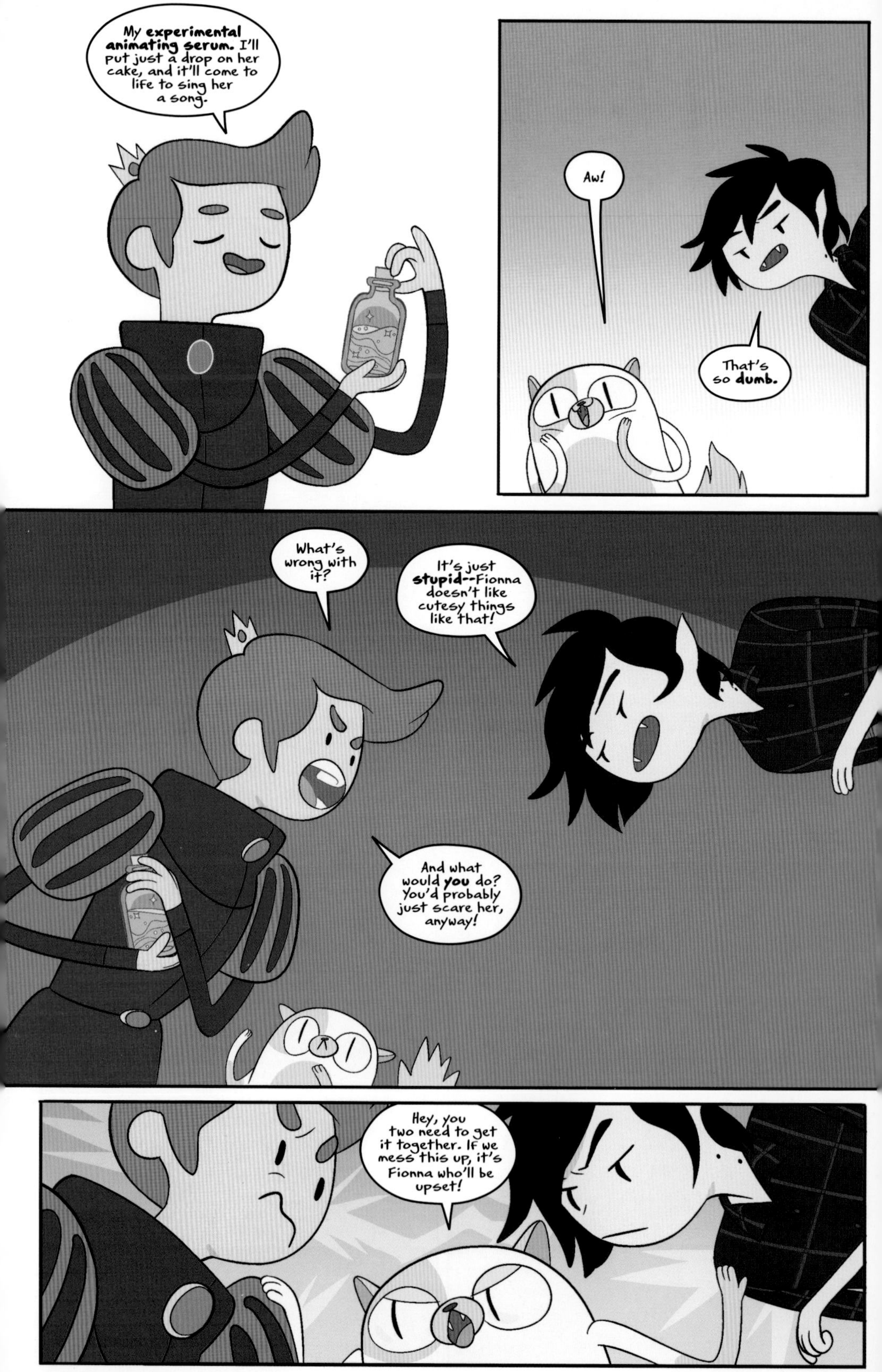

My experimental animating serum. I'll put just a drop on her cake, and it'll come to life to sing her a song.
Aw!
That's so dumb.
What's wrong with it?
It's just stupid--Fionna doesn't like cutesy things like that!
And what would you do? You'd probably just scare her, anyway!
Hey, you two need to get it together. If we mess this up, it's Fionna who'll be upset!

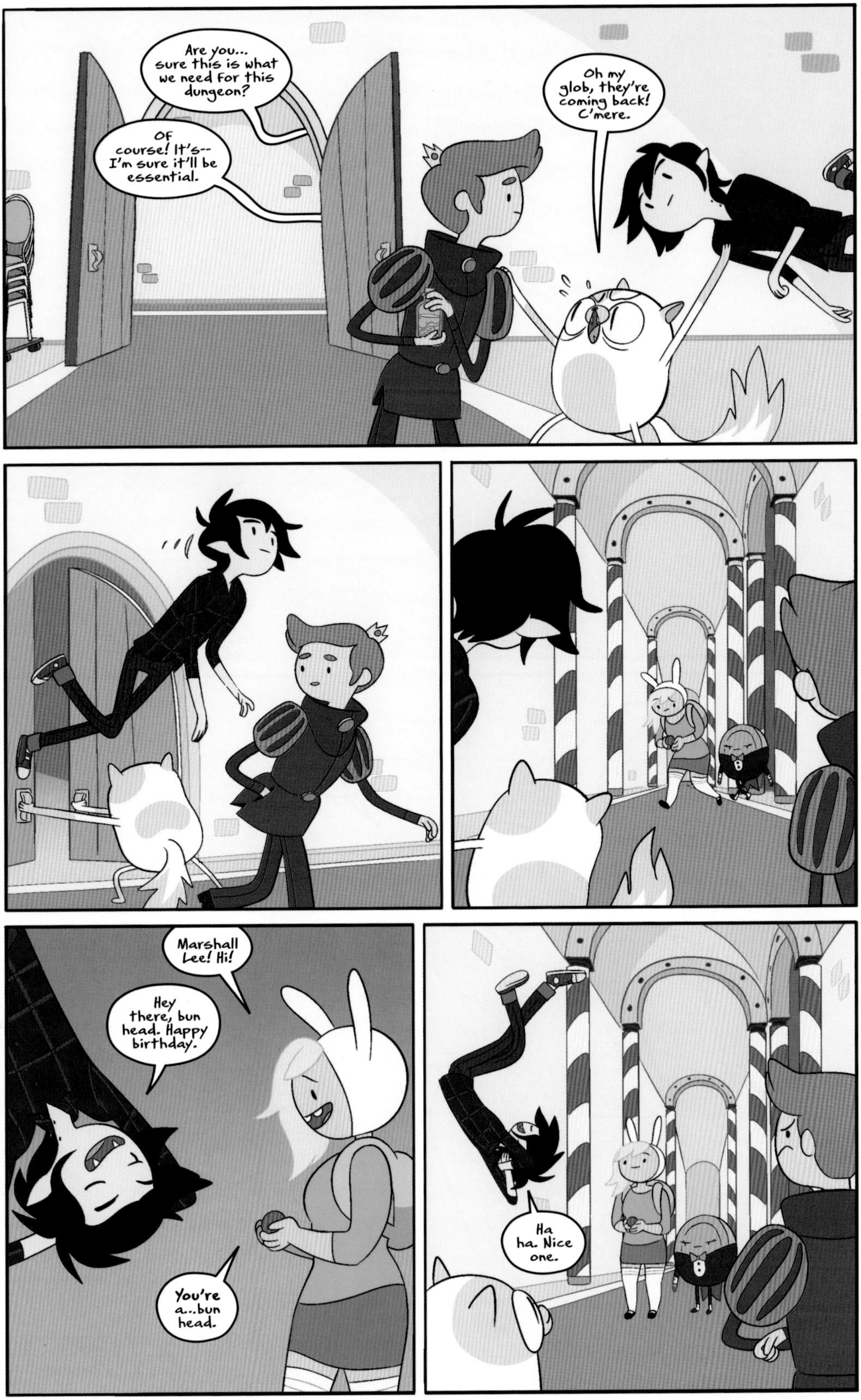
Are you... sure this is what we need for this dungeon?
Of course! It's-- I'm sure it'll be essential.
Oh my glob, they're coming back! C'mere.
Marshall Lee! Hi!
Hey there, bun head. Happy birthday.
You're a...bun head.
Ha ha. Nice one.

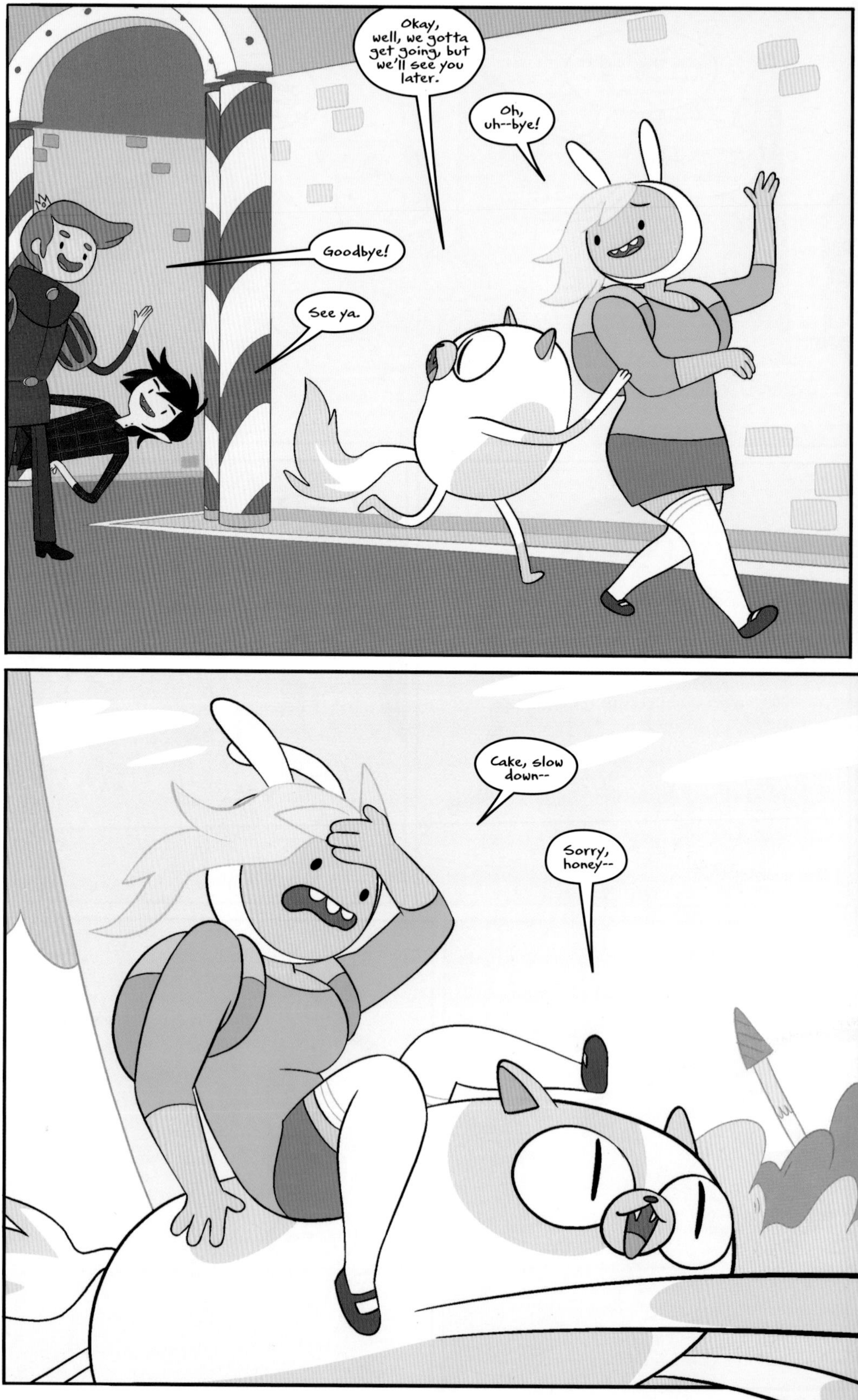
Okay, well, we gotta get going, but we'll see you later.
Oh, uh--bye!
Goodbye!
See ya.
Cake, slow down--
Sorry, honey--

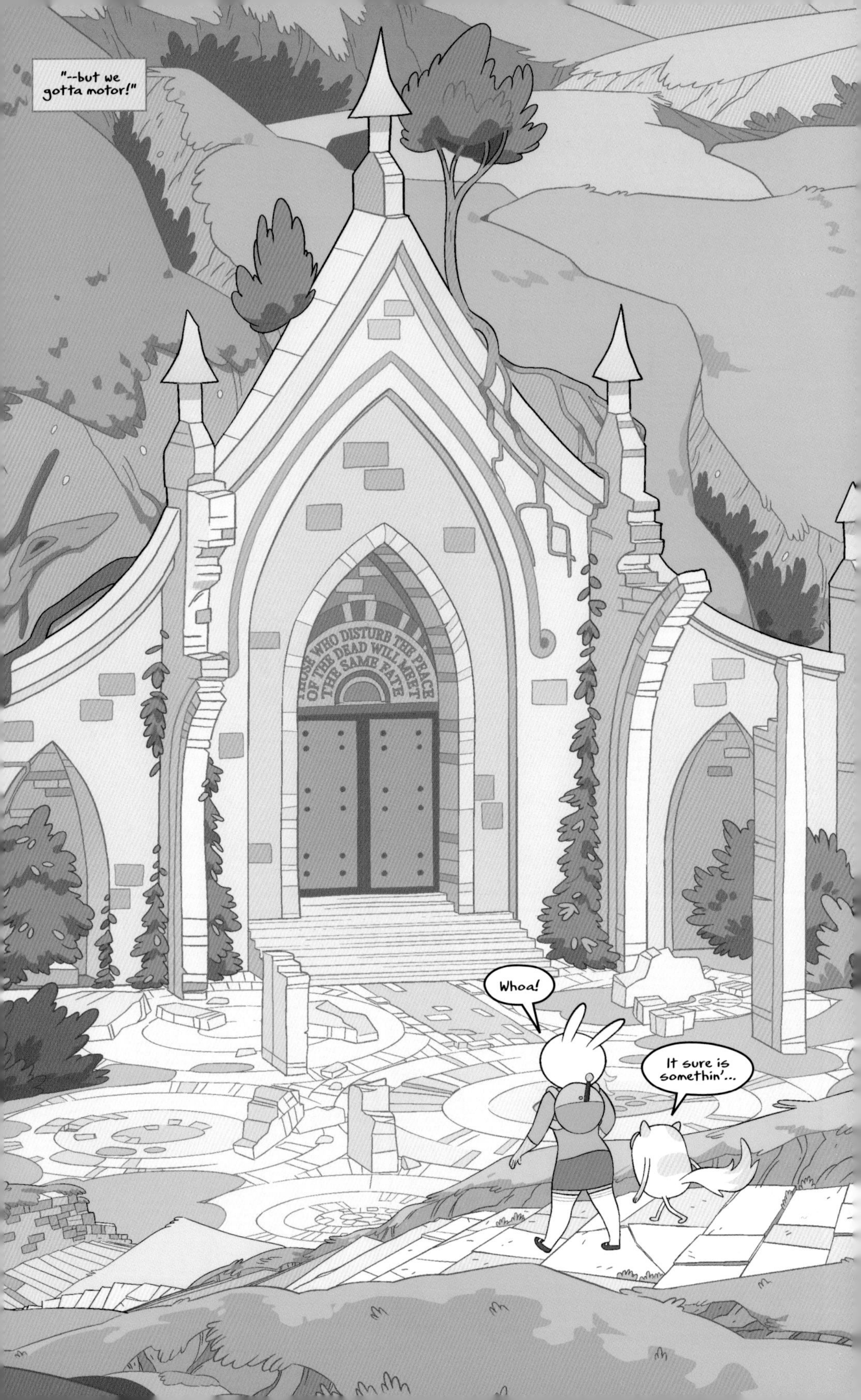
"--but we gotta motor!"
THOSE WHO DISTURB THE PEACE OF THE DEAD WILL MEET THE SAME FATE
Whoa!
It sure is somethin'...

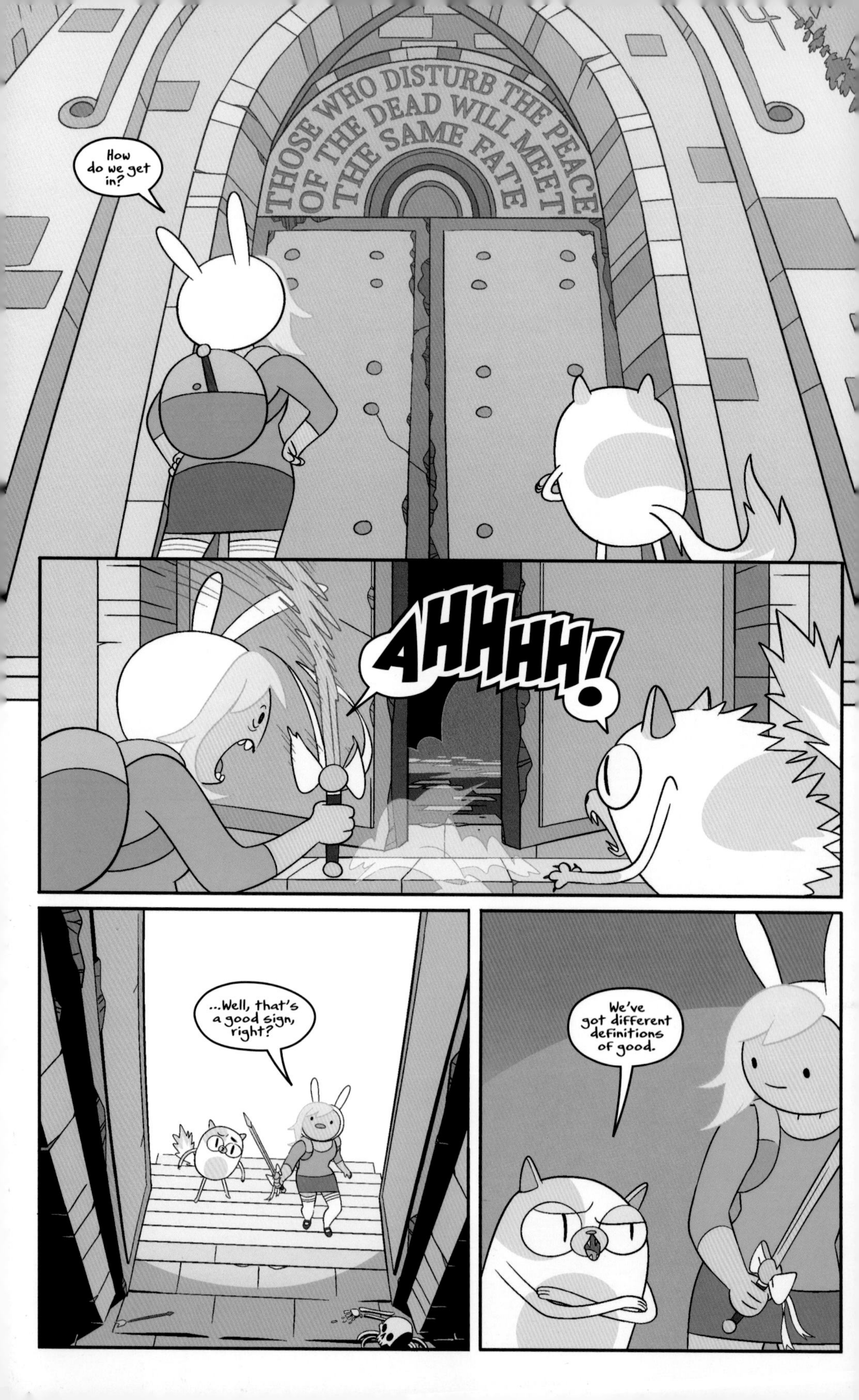
THOSE WHO DISTURB THE PEACE OF THE DEAD WILL MEET THE SAME FATE
How do we get in?
AHHHH!
...Well, that's a good sign, right?
We've got different definitions of good.

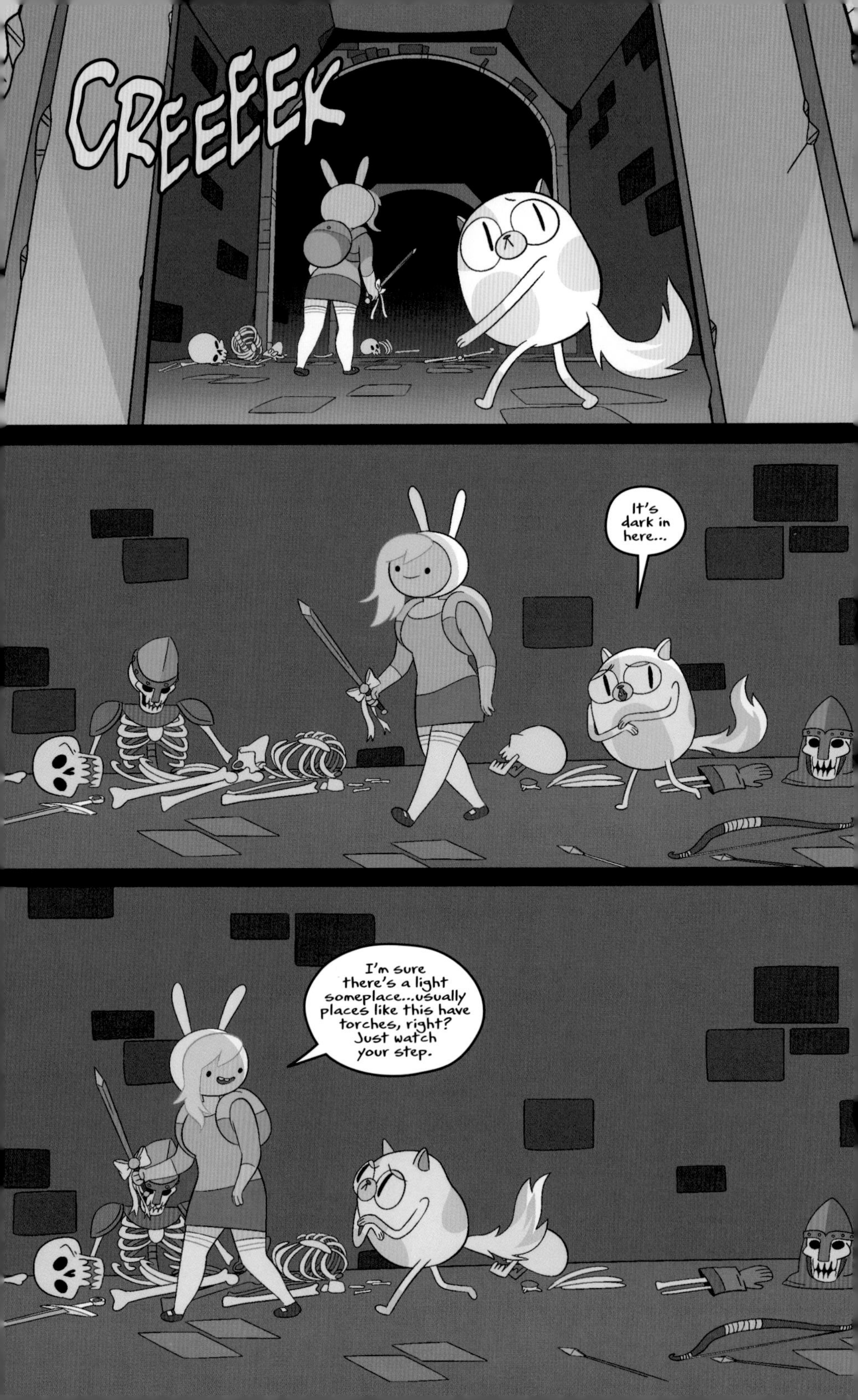
CREEEEK
It's dark in here...
I'm sure there's a light someplace...usually places like this have torches, right? Just watch your step.

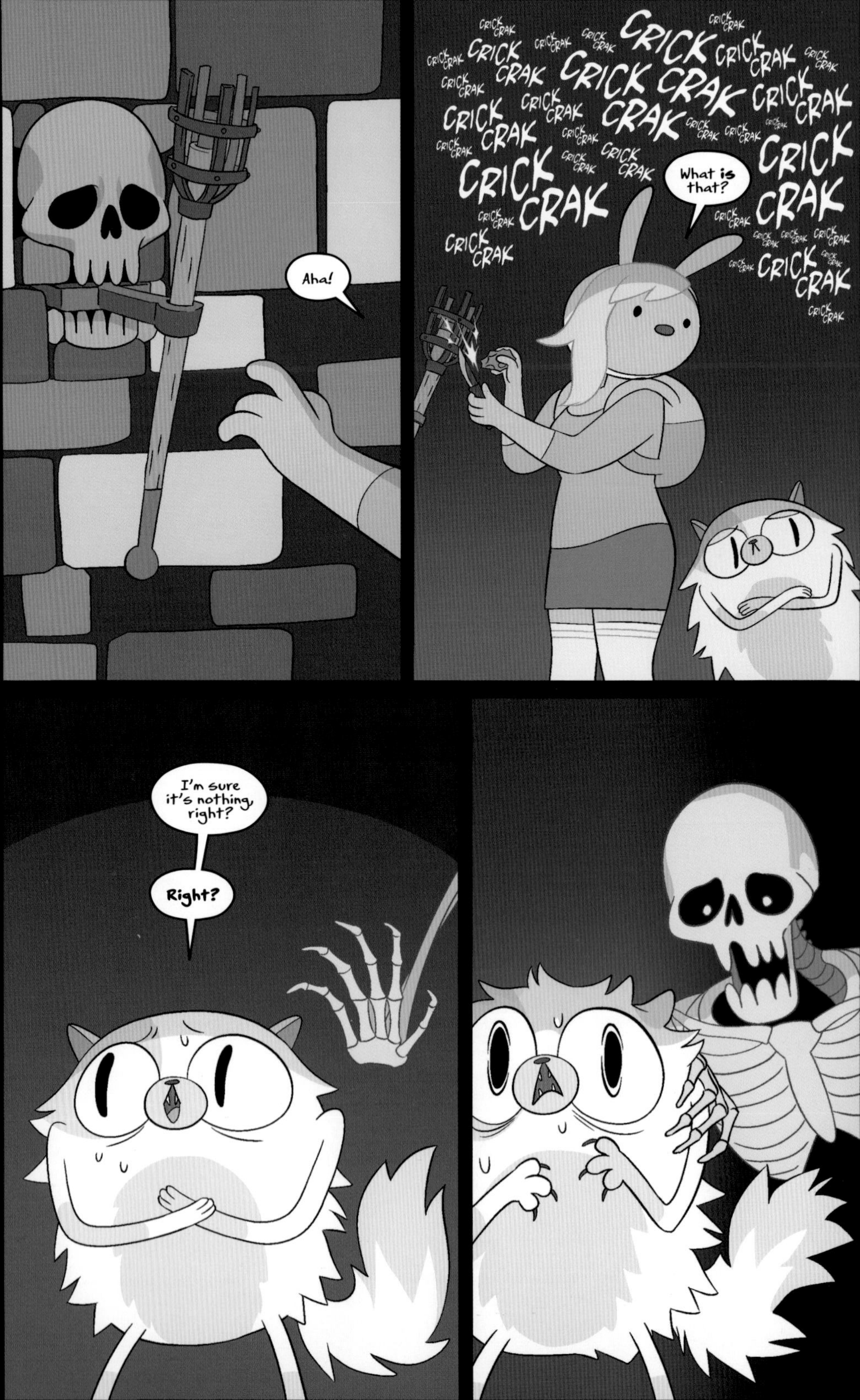

Aha!
CRICK CRAK
CRICK CRAK
CRICK CRAK
CRICK CRAK
CRICK CRAK
What is that?
I'm sure it's nothing, right?
Right?

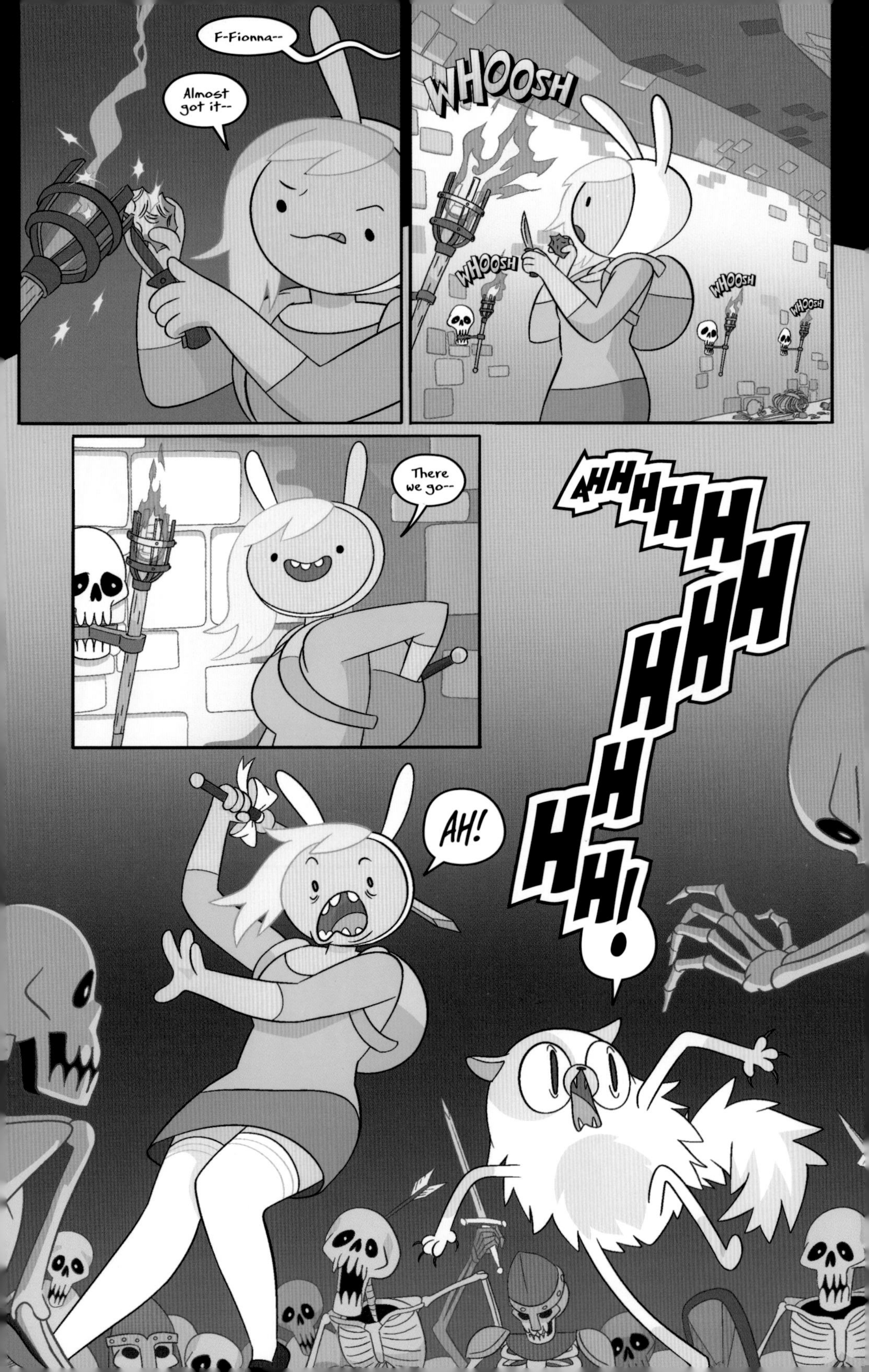
F-Fionna--
Almost got it--
WHOOSH
WHOOSH
WHOOSH
WHOOSH
There we go--
AHHHHHHHHHHHHHH!
AH!

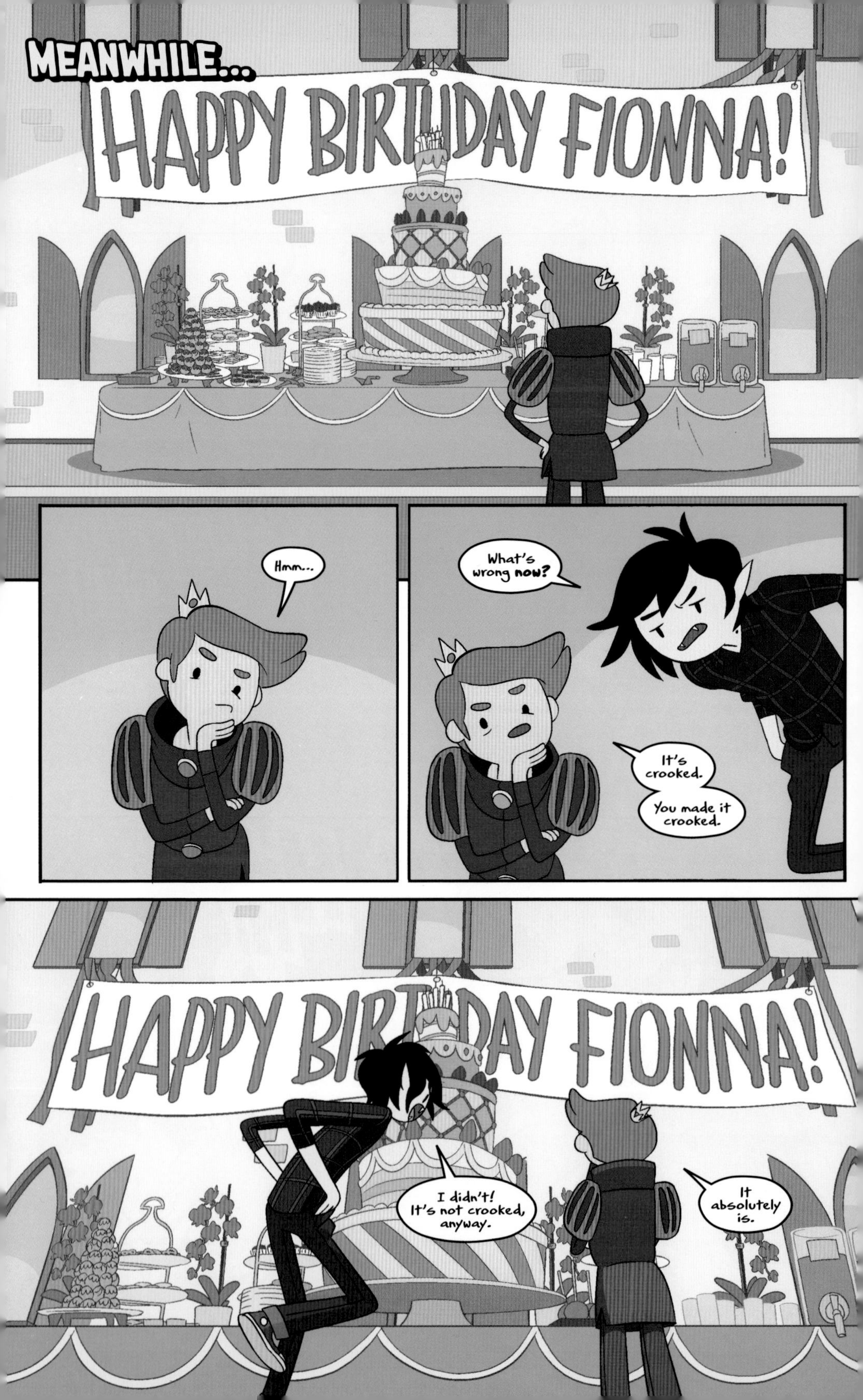
MEANWHILE...
HAPPY BIRTHDAY FIONNA!
Hmm...
What's wrong now?
It's crooked.
You made it crooked.
HAPPY BIRTHDAY FIONNA!
I didn't! It's not crooked, anyway.
It absolutely is.

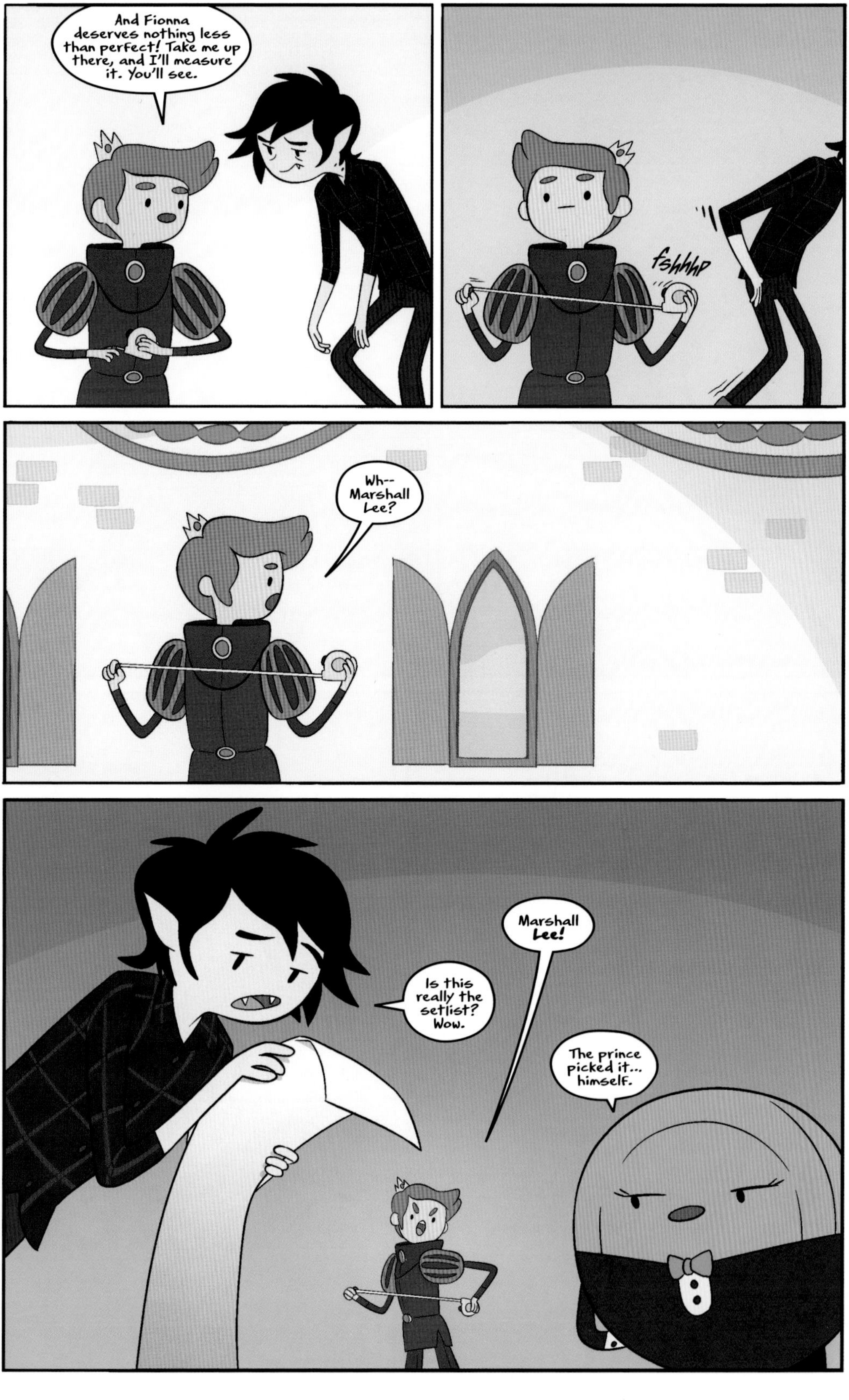
And Fionna deserves nothing less than perfect! Take me up there, and I'll measure it. You'll see.
fshhhp
Wh-- Marshall Lee?
Marshall Lee!
Is this really the setlist? Wow.
The prince picked it... himself.

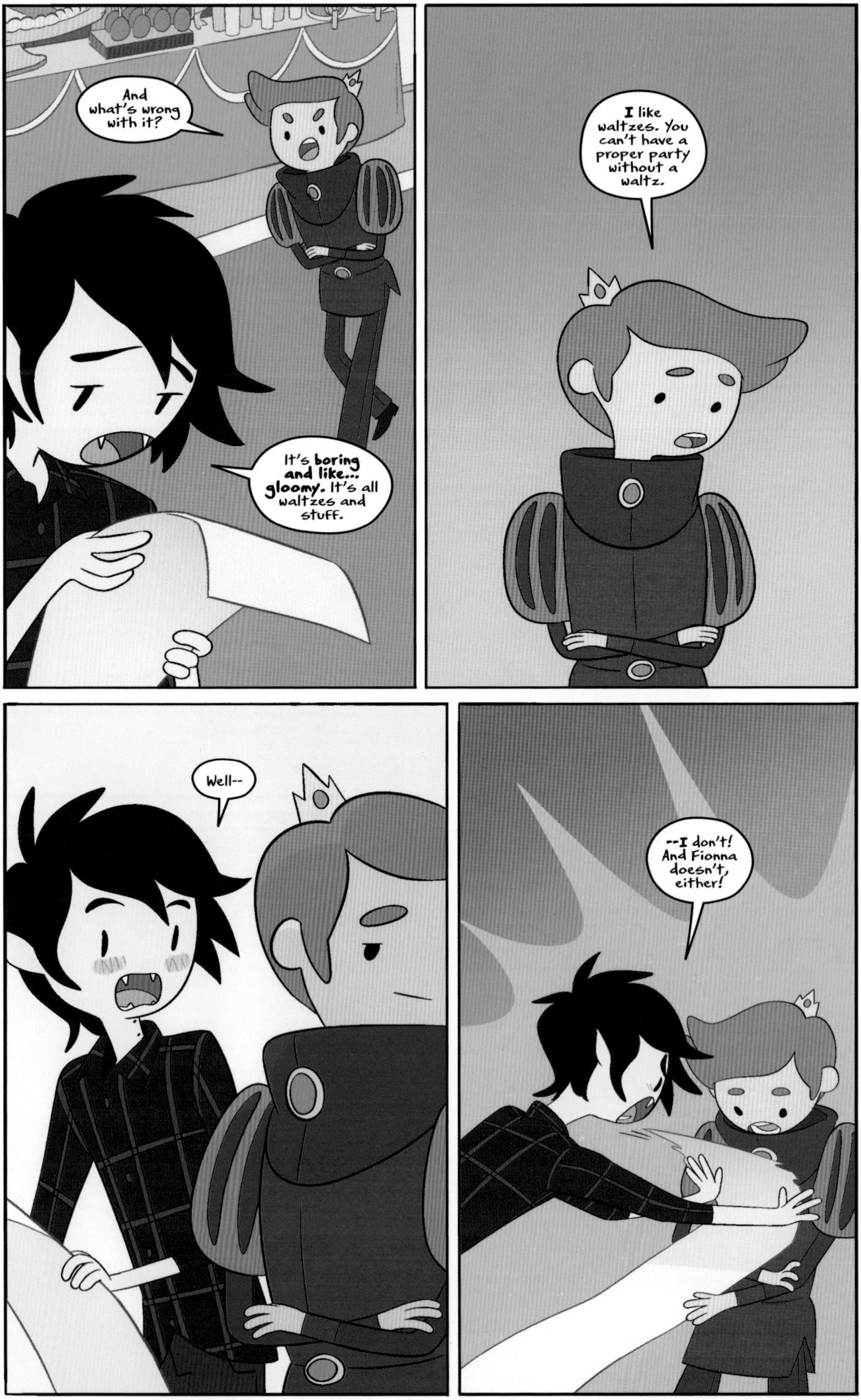
And what's wrong with it?
It's boring and like... gloomy. It's all waltzes and stuff.
I like waltzes. You can't have a proper party without a waltz.
Well--
--I don't! And Fionna doesn't, either!

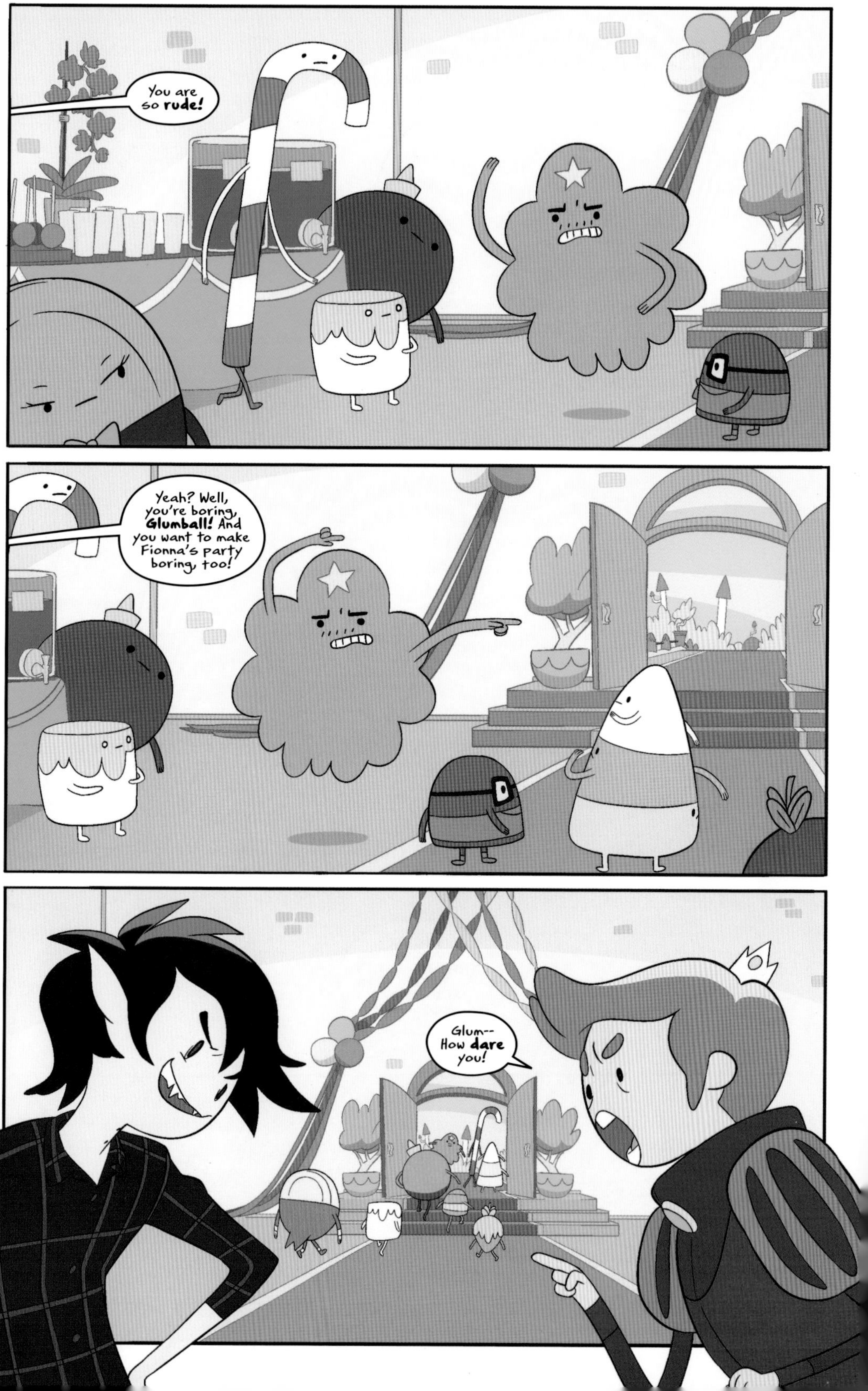
You are so **rude!**
Yeah? Well, you're boring, **Glumball!** And you want to make Fionna's party boring, too!
Glum-- How **dare** you!

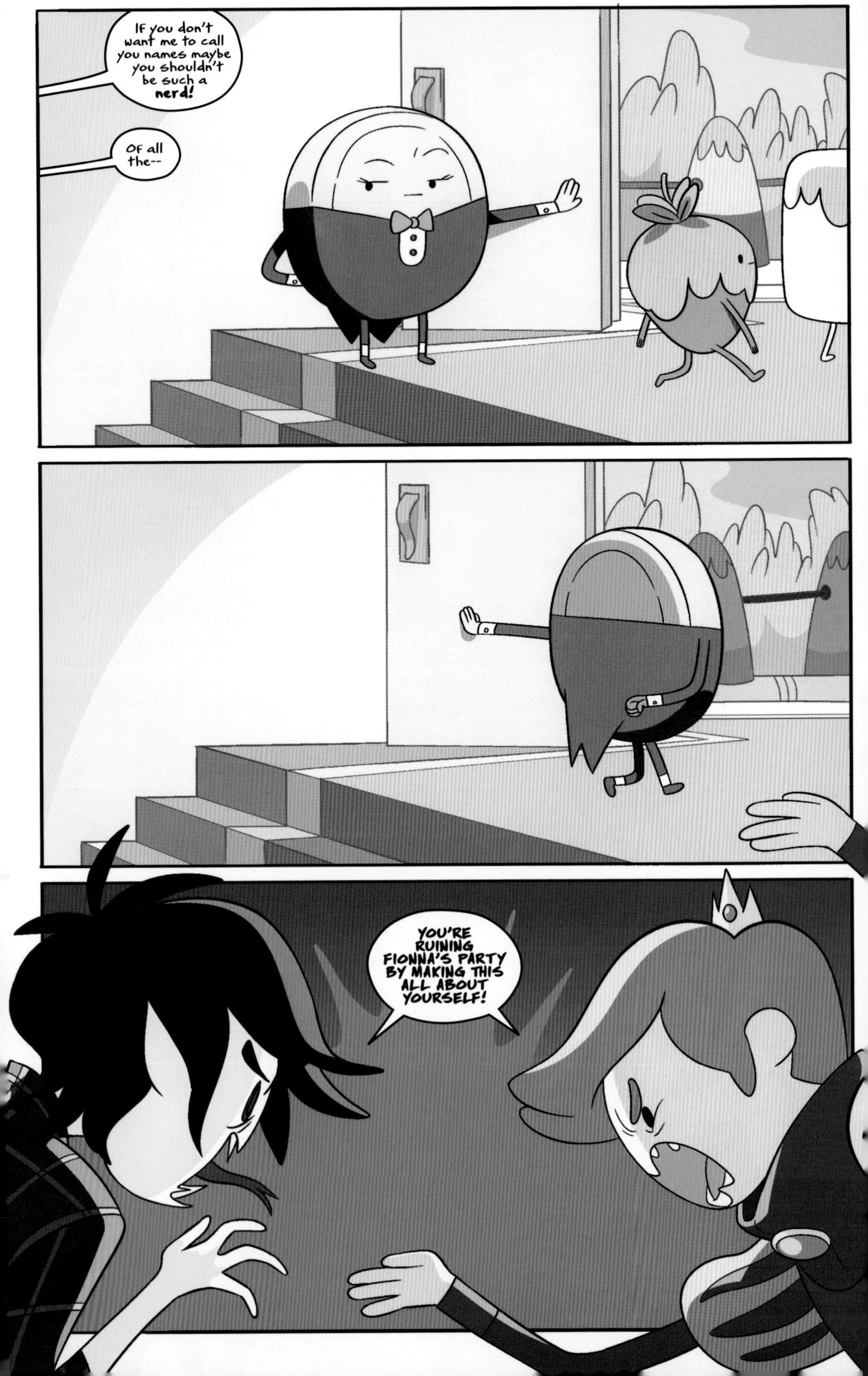
If you don't want me to call you names maybe you shouldn't be such a **nerd!**
Of all the--
YOU'RE RUINING FIONNA'S PARTY BY MAKING THIS ALL ABOUT YOURSELF!

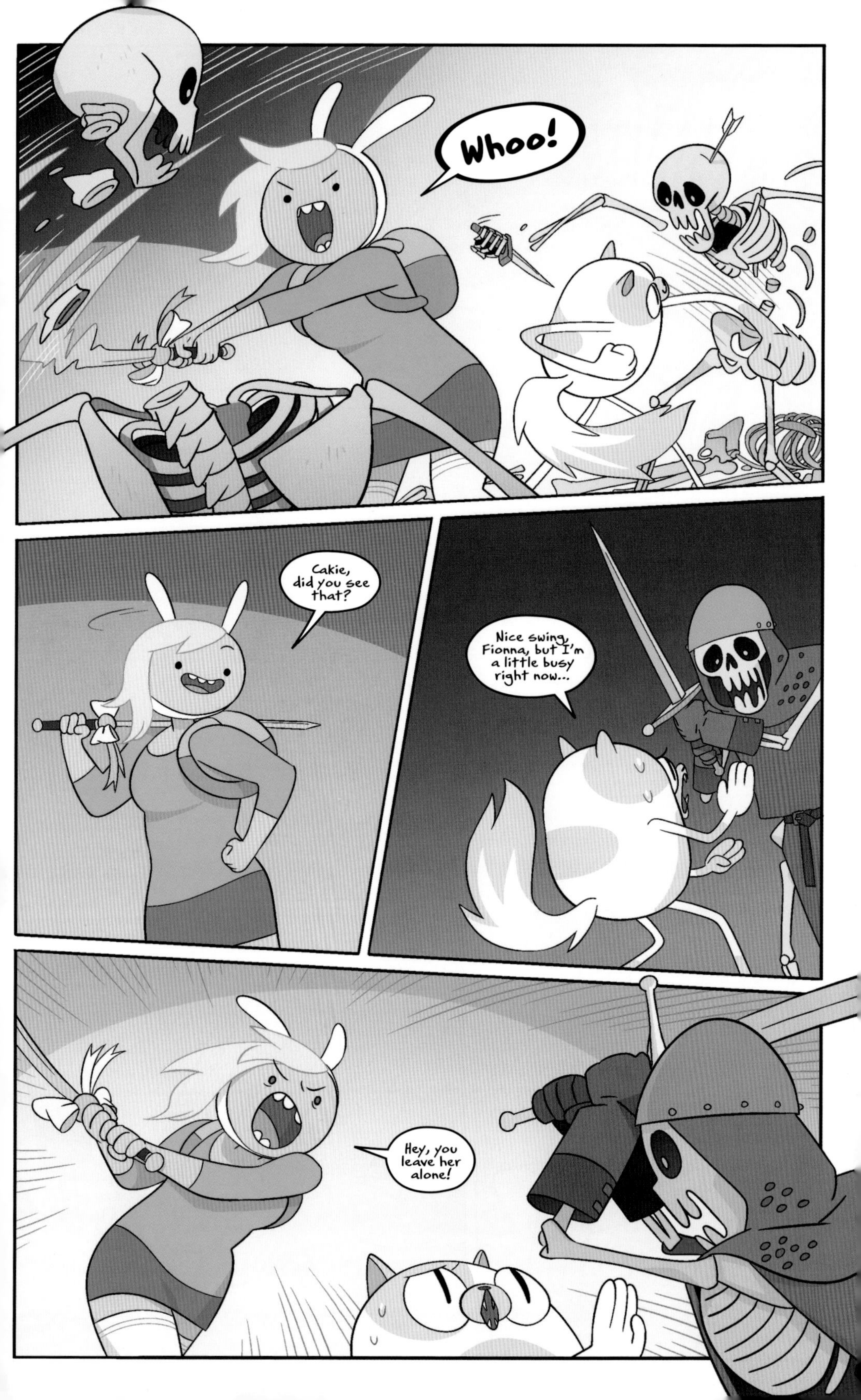
Whoo!
Cakie, did you see that?
Nice swing, Fiona, but I'm a little busy right now...
Hey, you leave her alone!

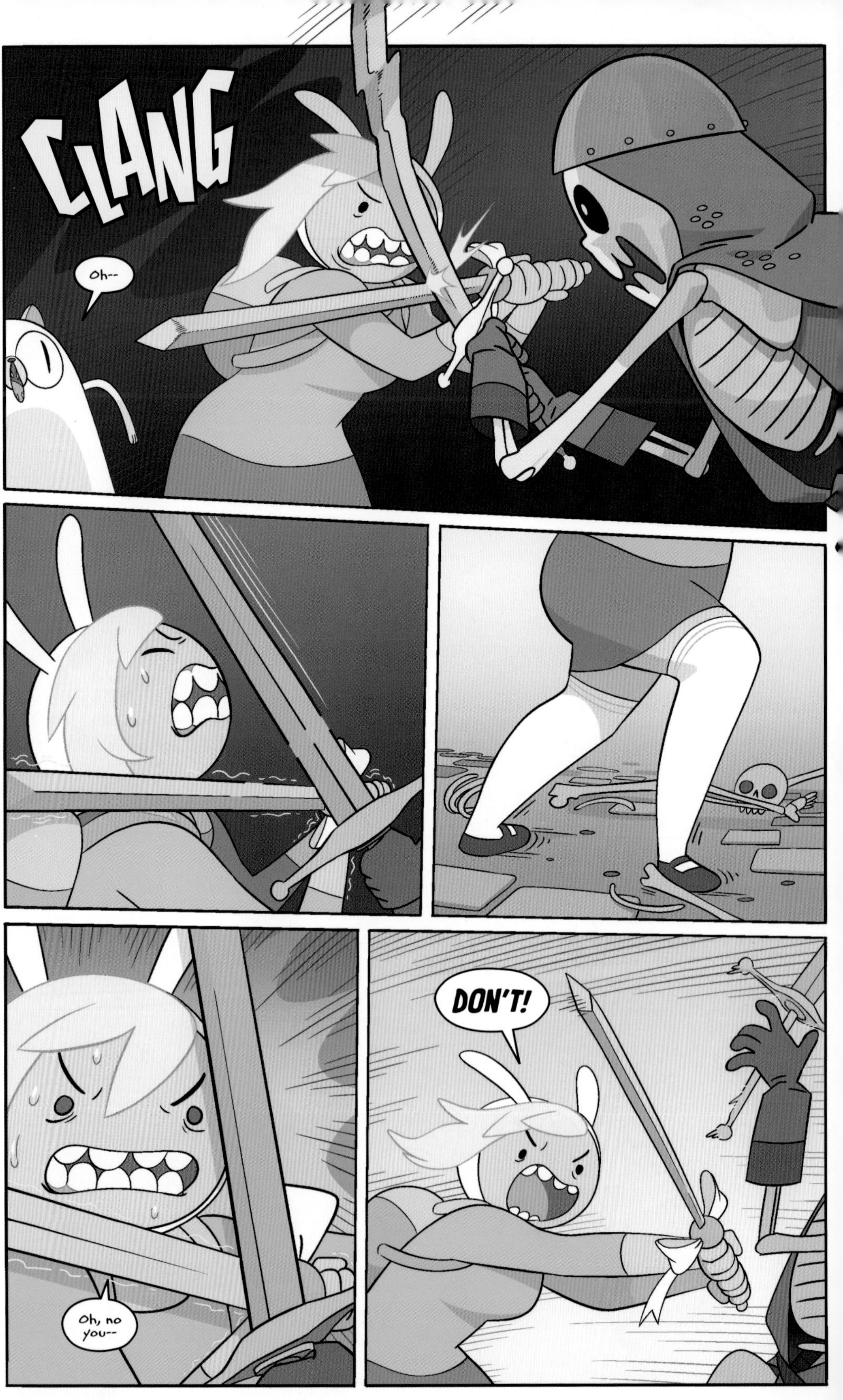
CLANG
Oh--
Oh, no you--
DON'T!

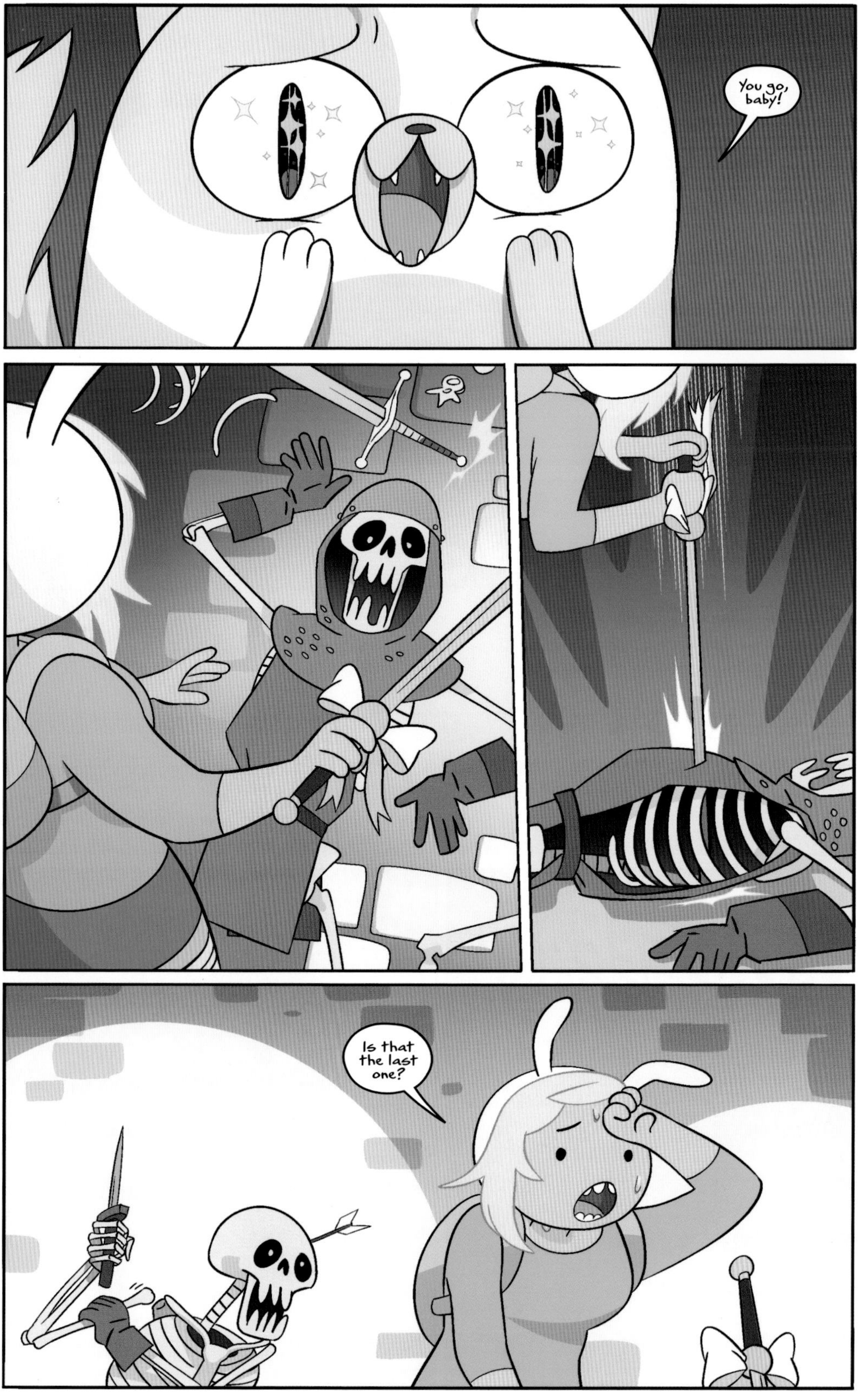
You go, baby!
Is that the last one?

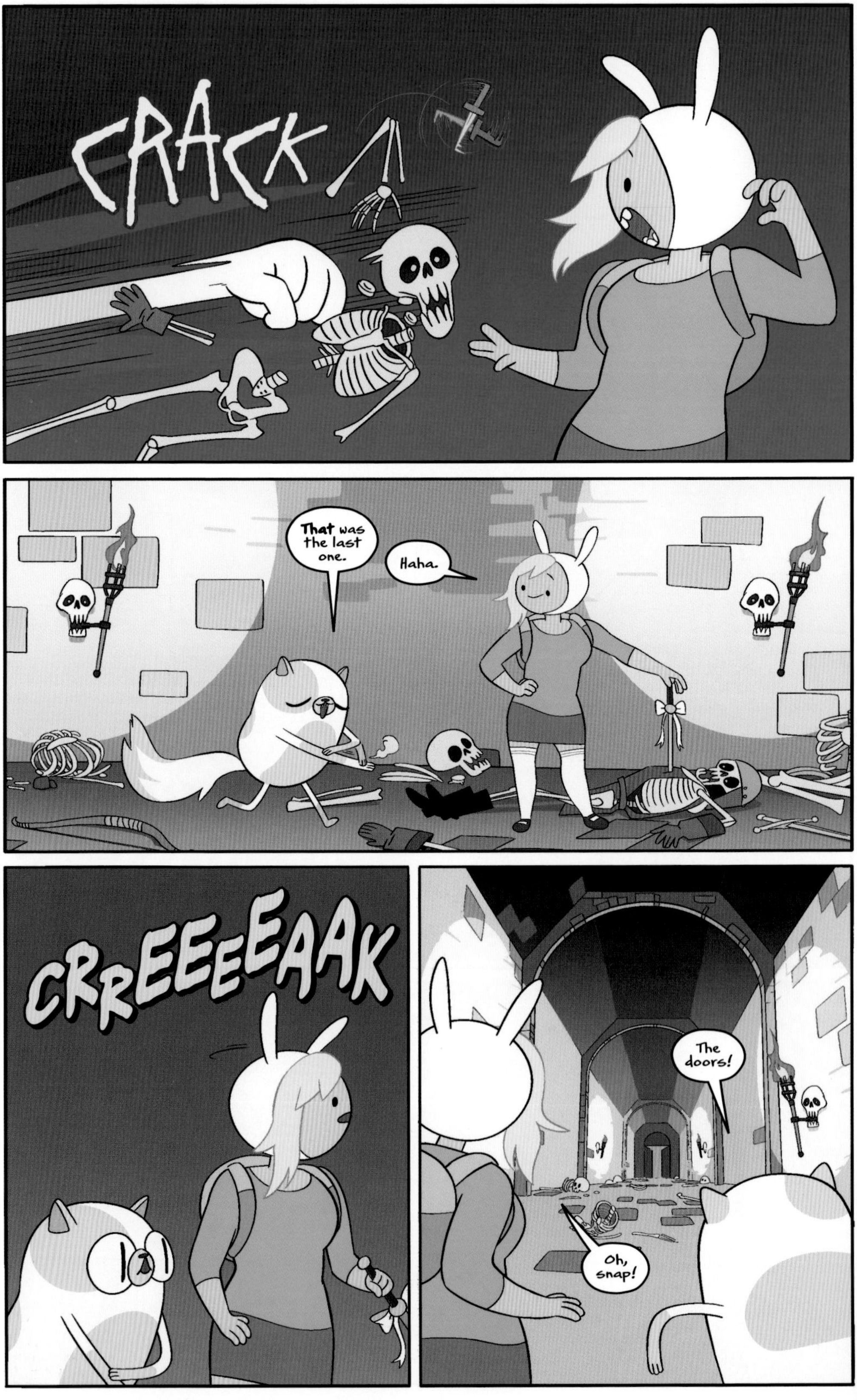
CRACK
That was the last one.
Haha.
CRREEEEAAK
The doors!
Oh, snap!

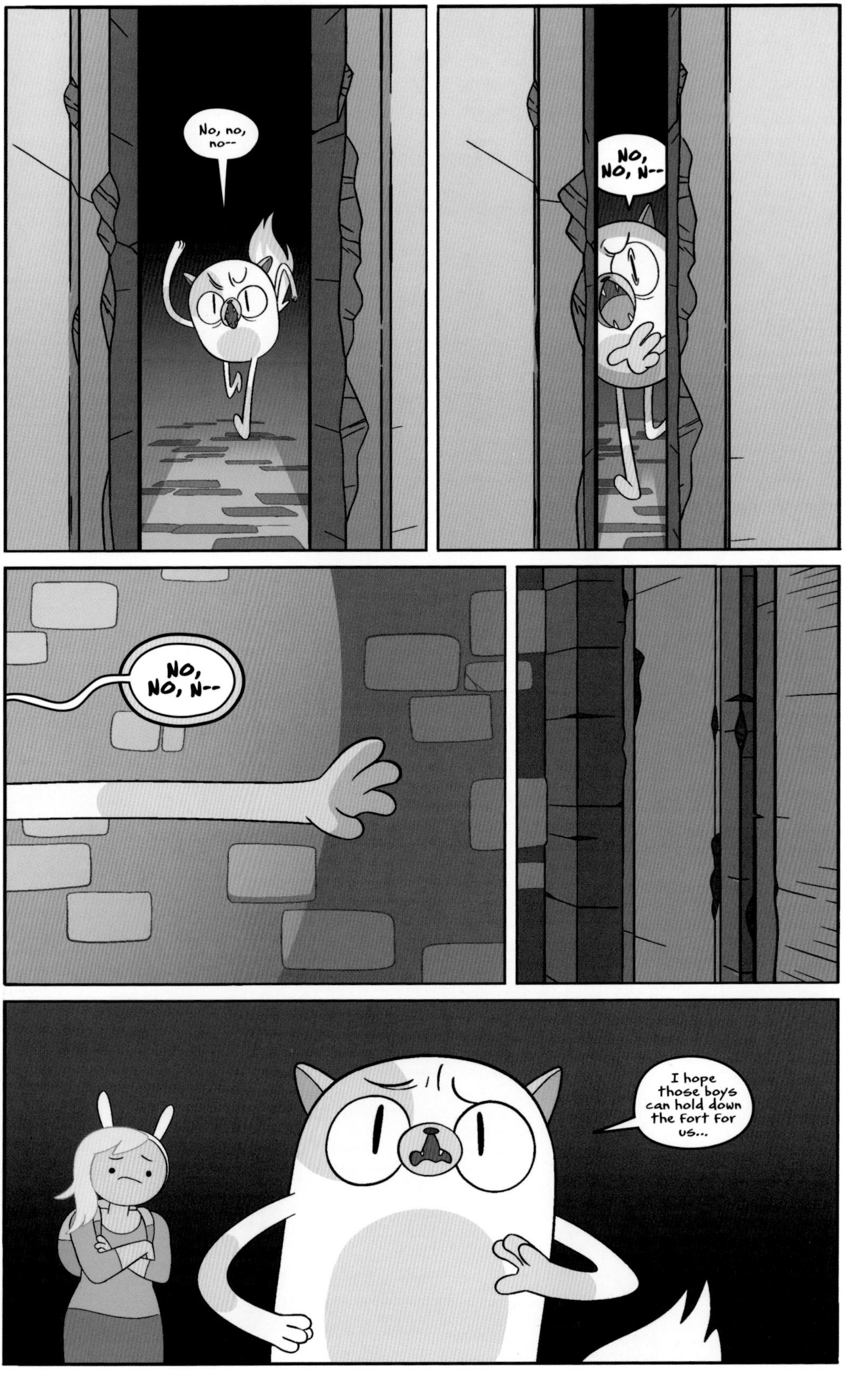
No, no, no--
NO, NO, N--
NO, NO, N--
I hope those boys can hold down the fort for us...

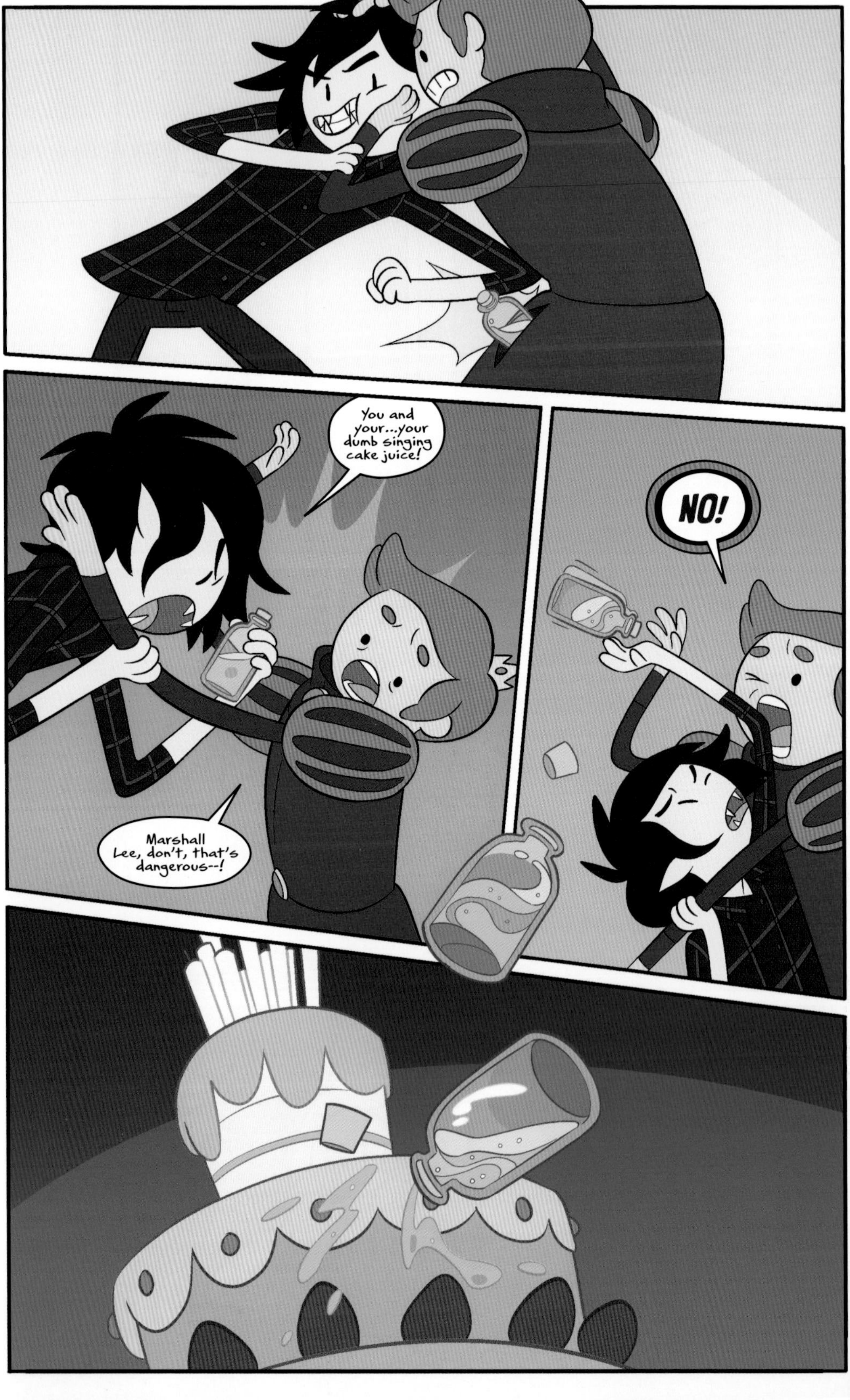
You and your...your dumb singing cake juice!
Marshall Lee, don't, that's dangerous--!
NO!

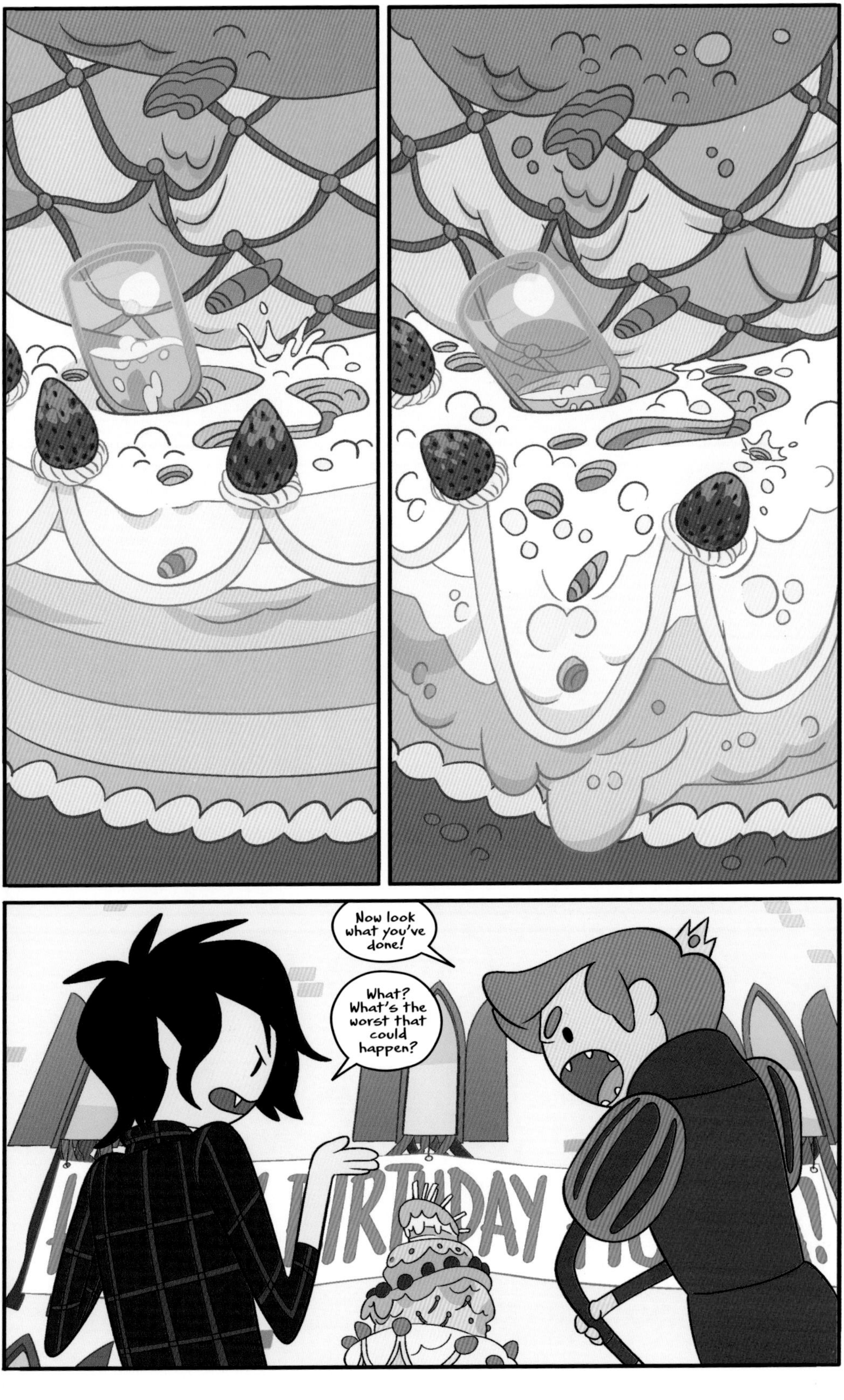
Now look what you've done!
What? What's the worst that could happen?
HAPPY BIRTHDAY

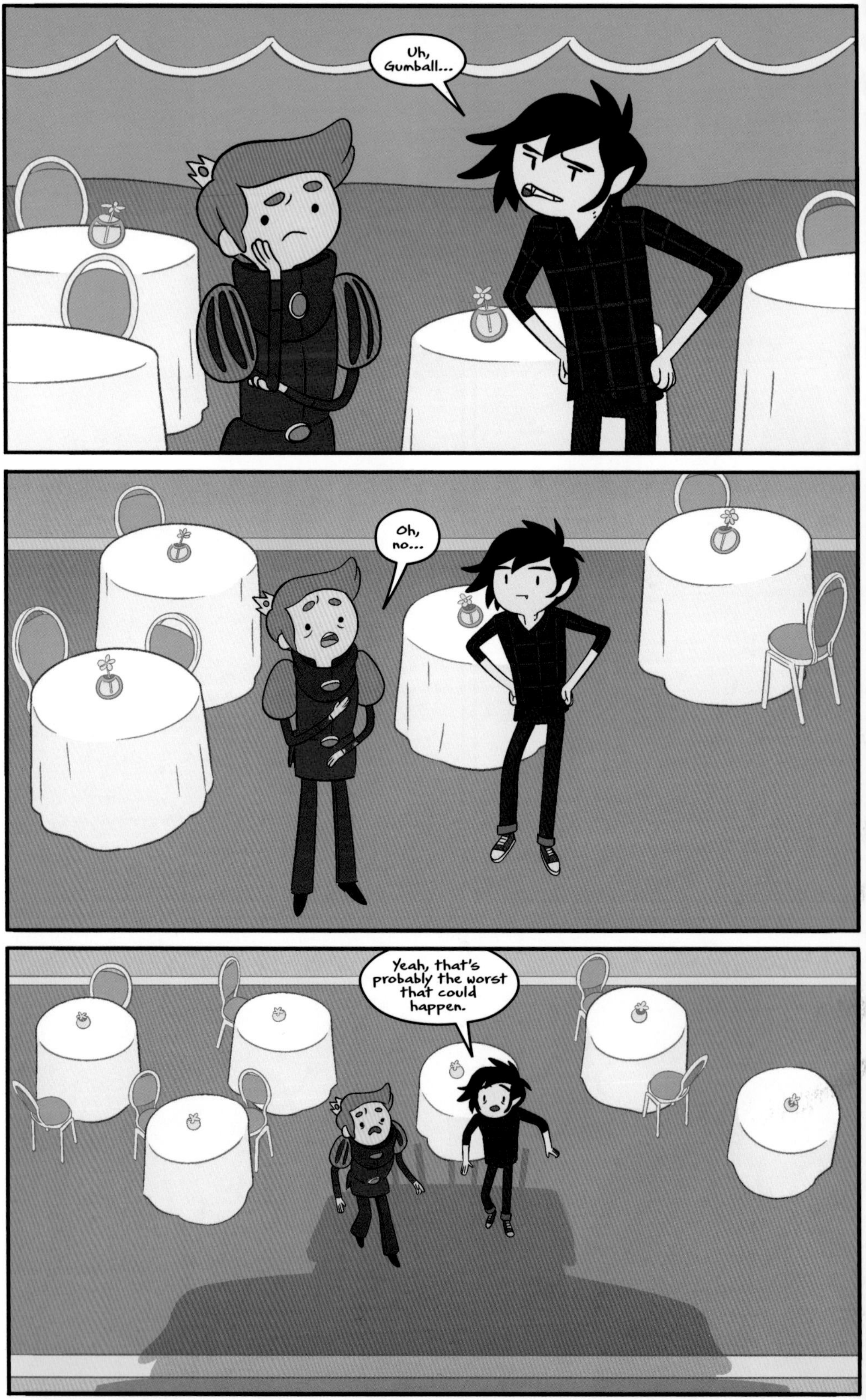
Uh, Gumball...
Oh, no...
Yeah, that's probably the worst that could happen.

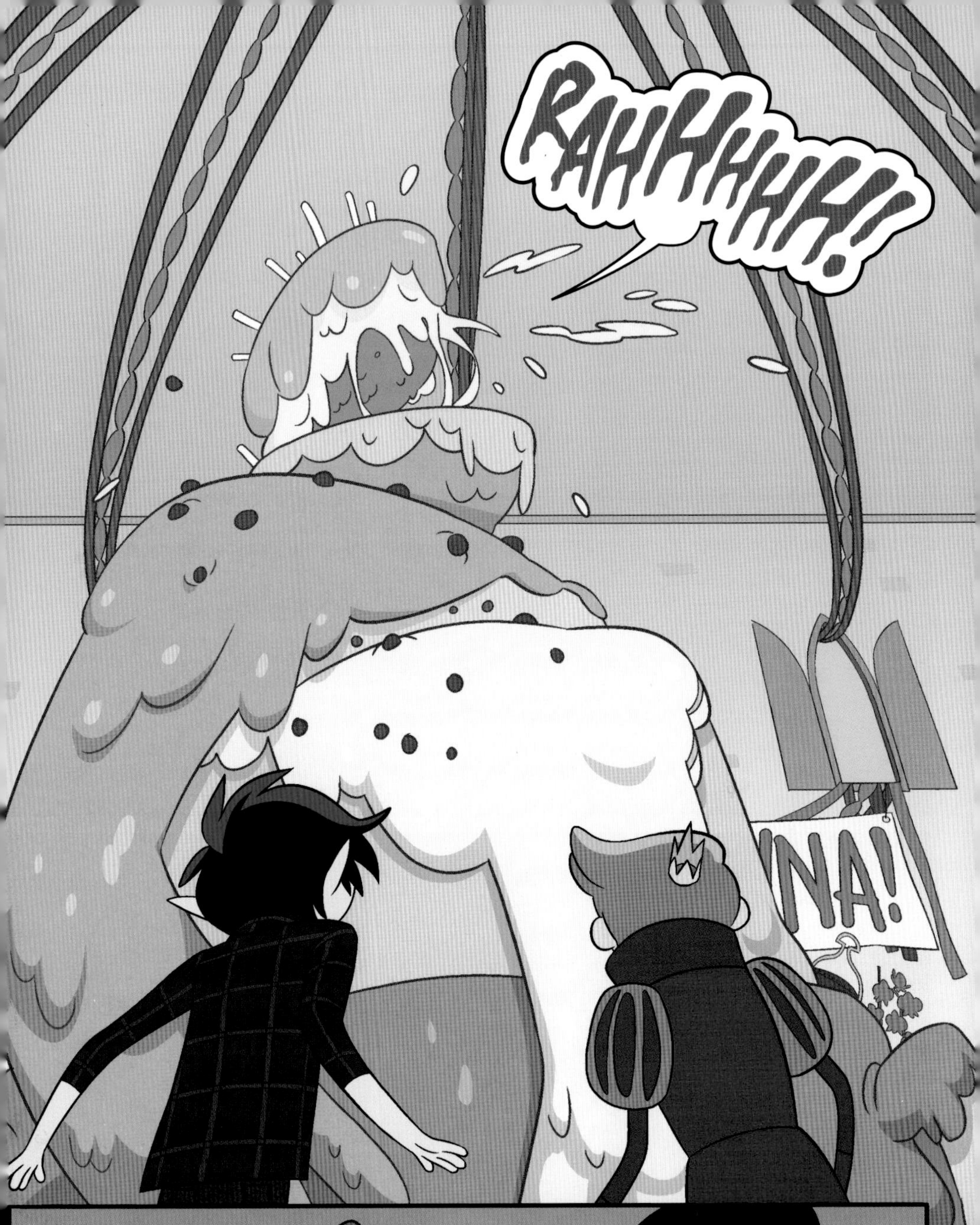
RAHHHHH!!
NA!
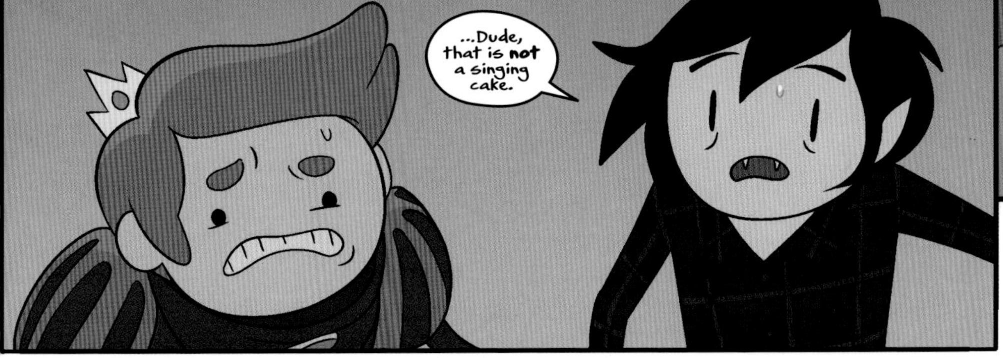
...Dude, that is **not** a singing cake.

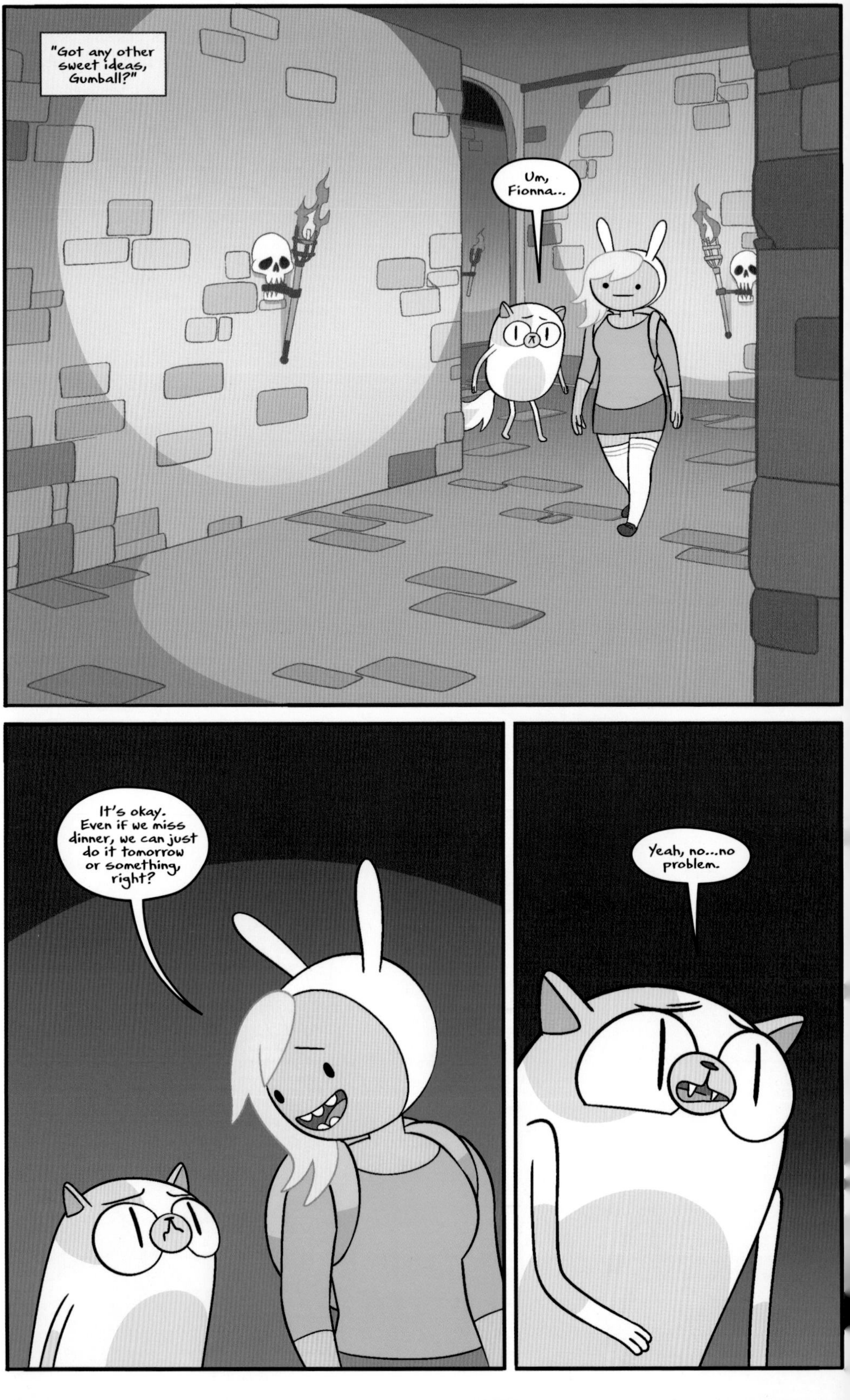
"Got any other sweet ideas, Gumball?"
Um, Fionna...
It's okay. Even if we miss dinner, we can just do it tomorrow or something, right?
Yeah, no...no problem.

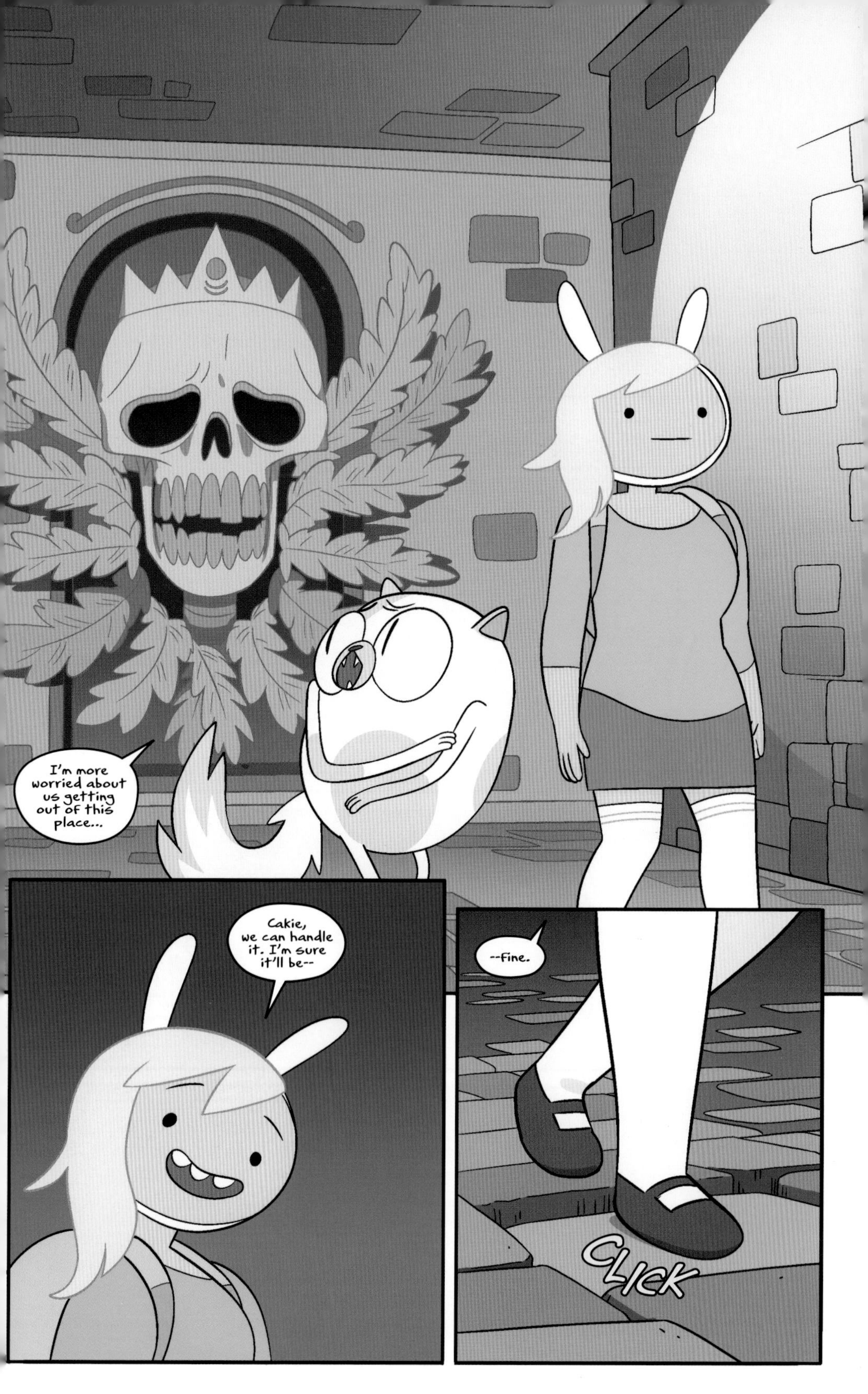
I'm more worried about us getting out of this place...
Cakie, we can handle it. I'm sure it'll be--
--Fine.
CLICK

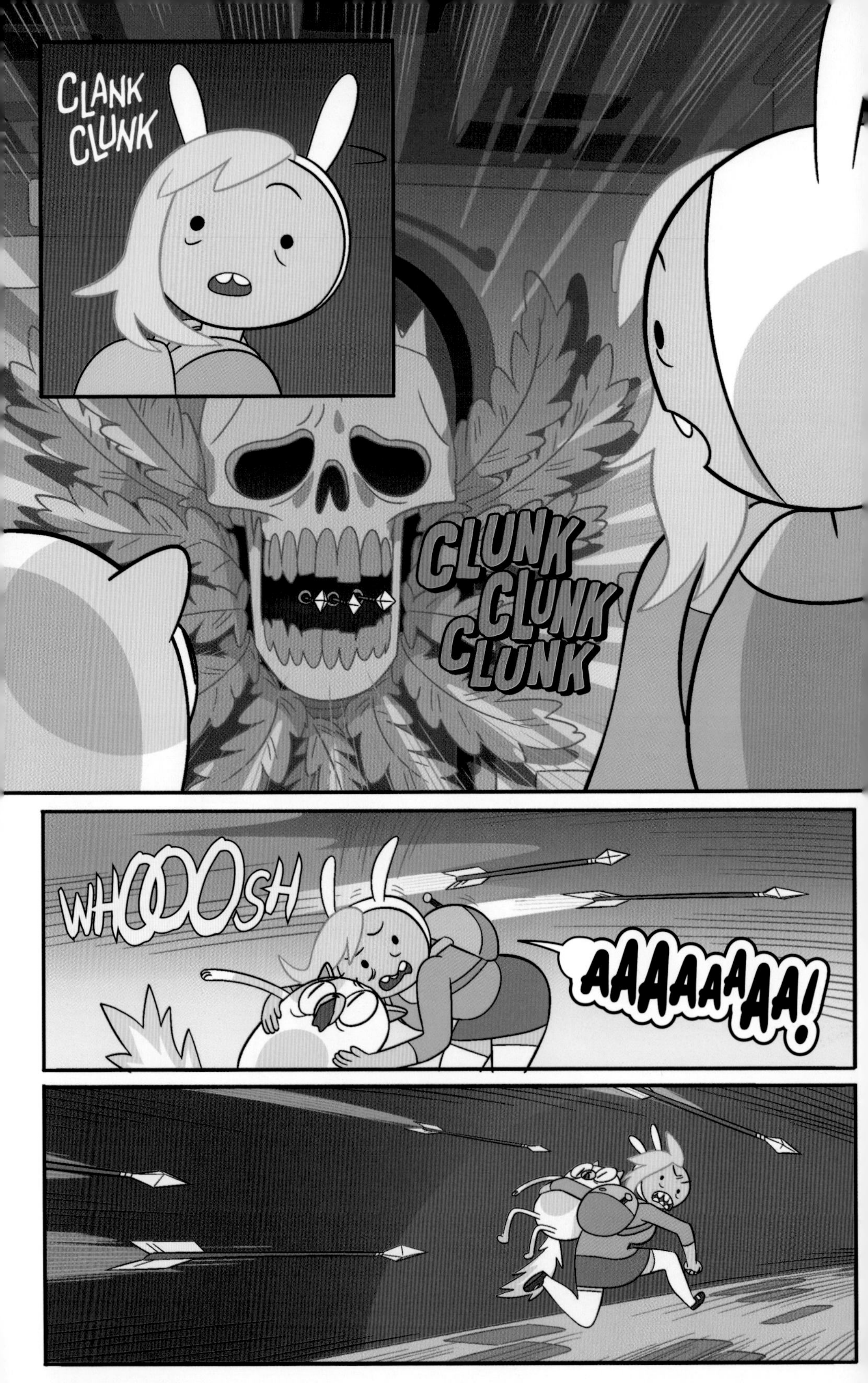
CLANK
CLUNK
CLUNK
CLUNK
CLUNK
WHOOOSH
AAAAAAAAA!

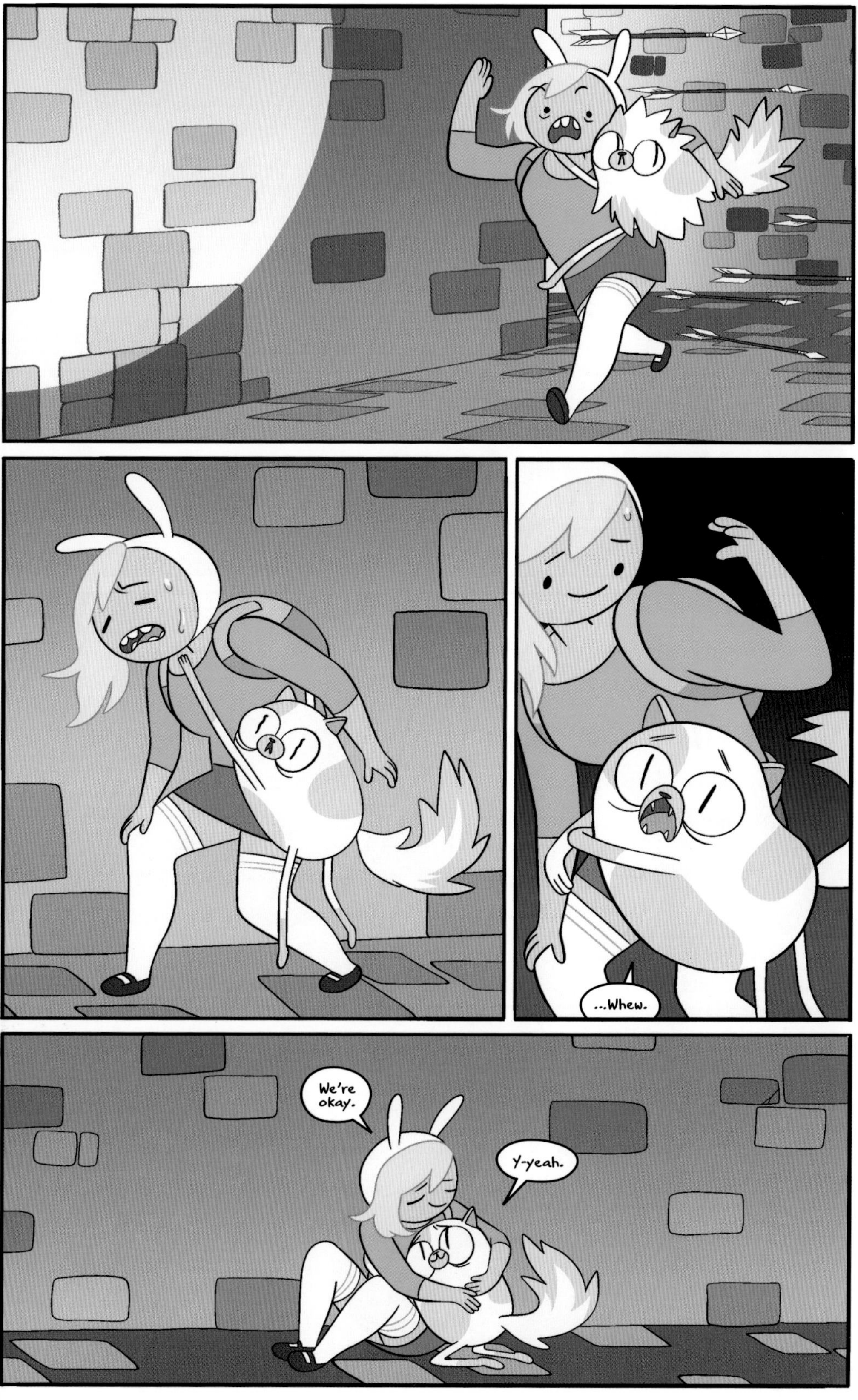
...Whew.
We're okay.
Y-yeah.

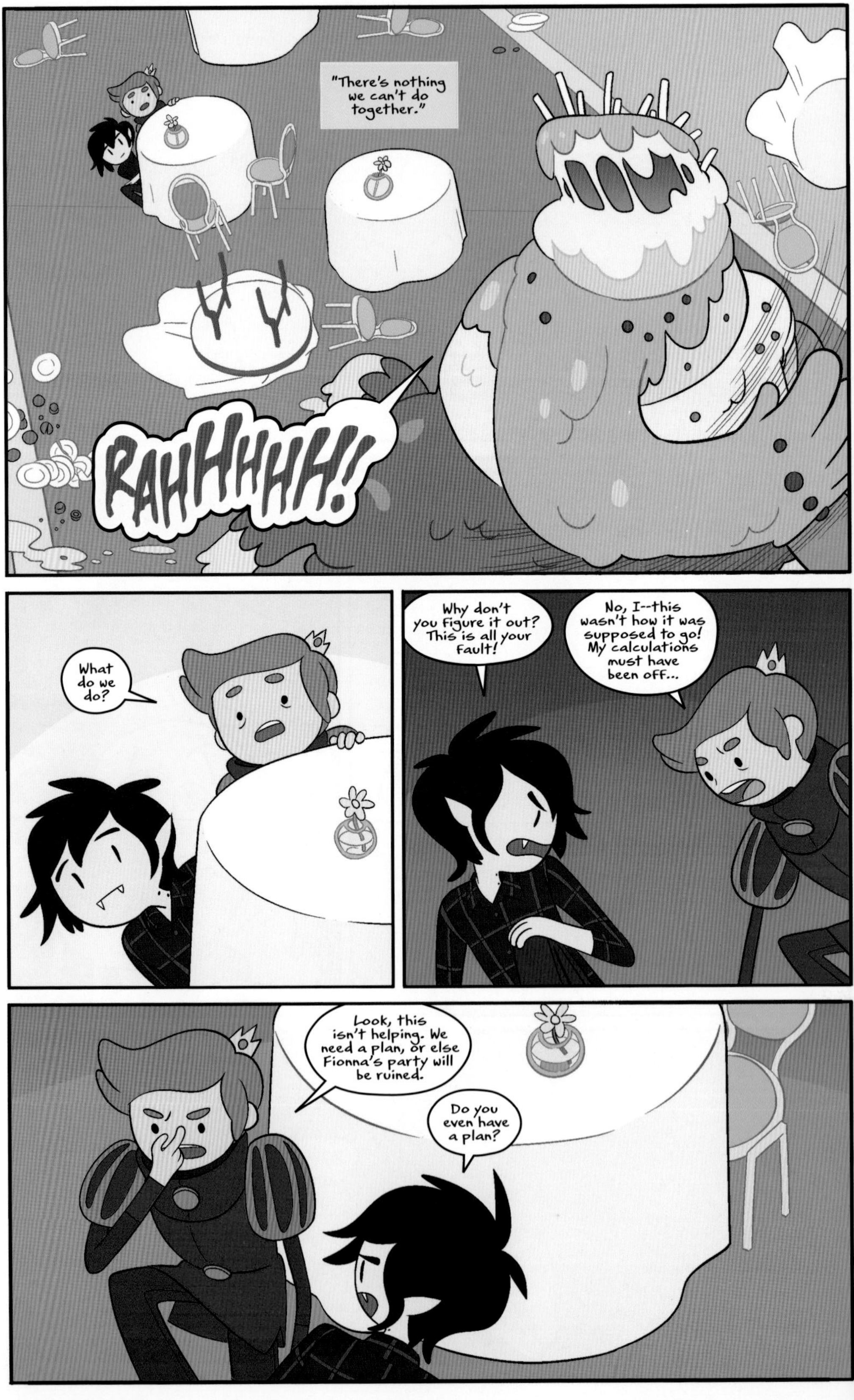
"There's nothing we can't do together."
RAHHHHH!
What do we do?
Why don't you figure it out? This is all your fault!
No, I--this wasn't how it was supposed to go! My calculations must have been off...
Look, this isn't helping. We need a plan, or else Fionna's party will be ruined.
Do you even have a plan?

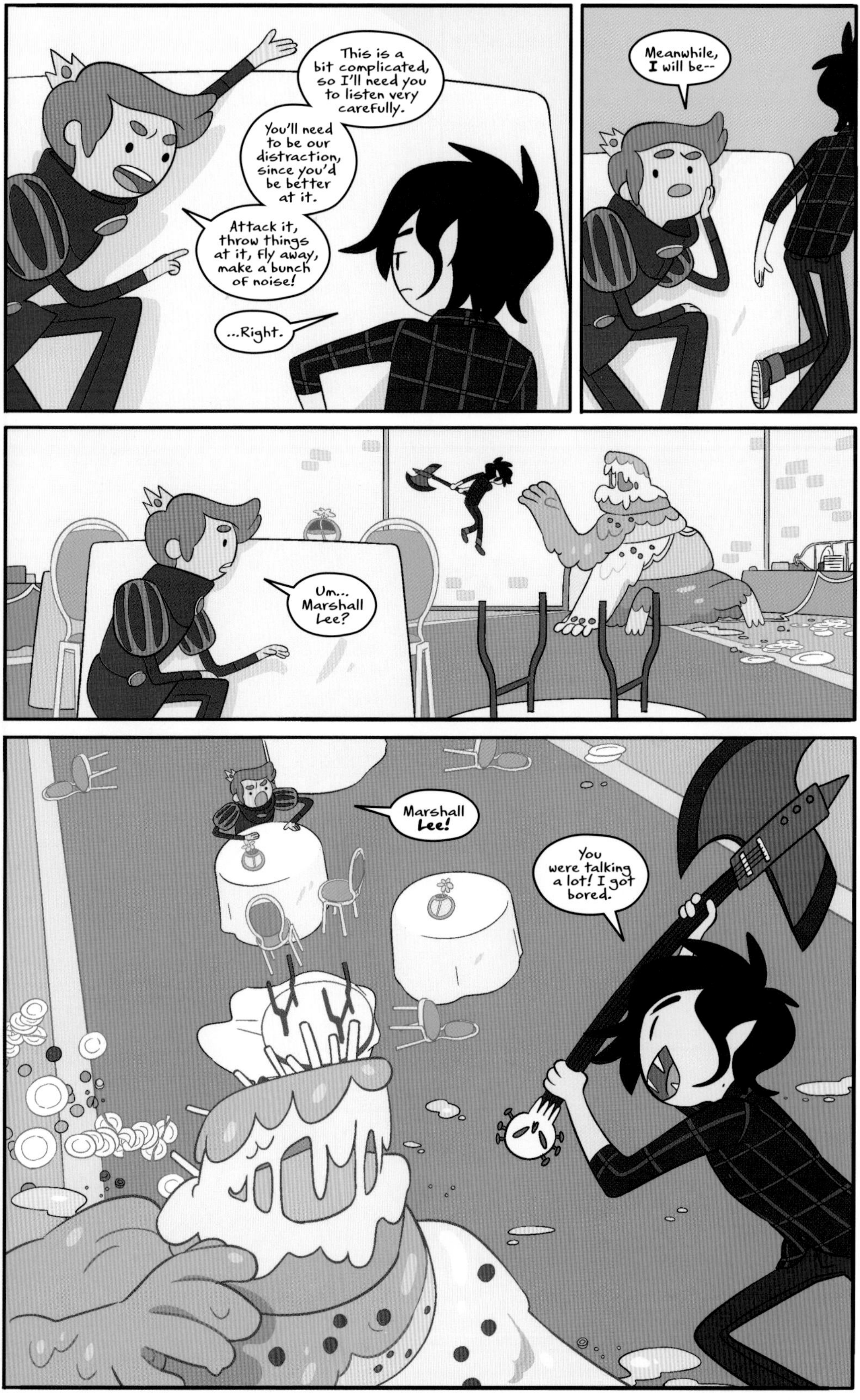
This is a bit complicated, so I'll need you to listen very carefully.
You'll need to be our distraction, since you'd be better at it.
Attack it, throw things at it, fly away, make a bunch of noise!
...Right.
Meanwhile, I will be--
Um... Marshall Lee?
Marshall Lee!
You were talking a lot! I got bored.

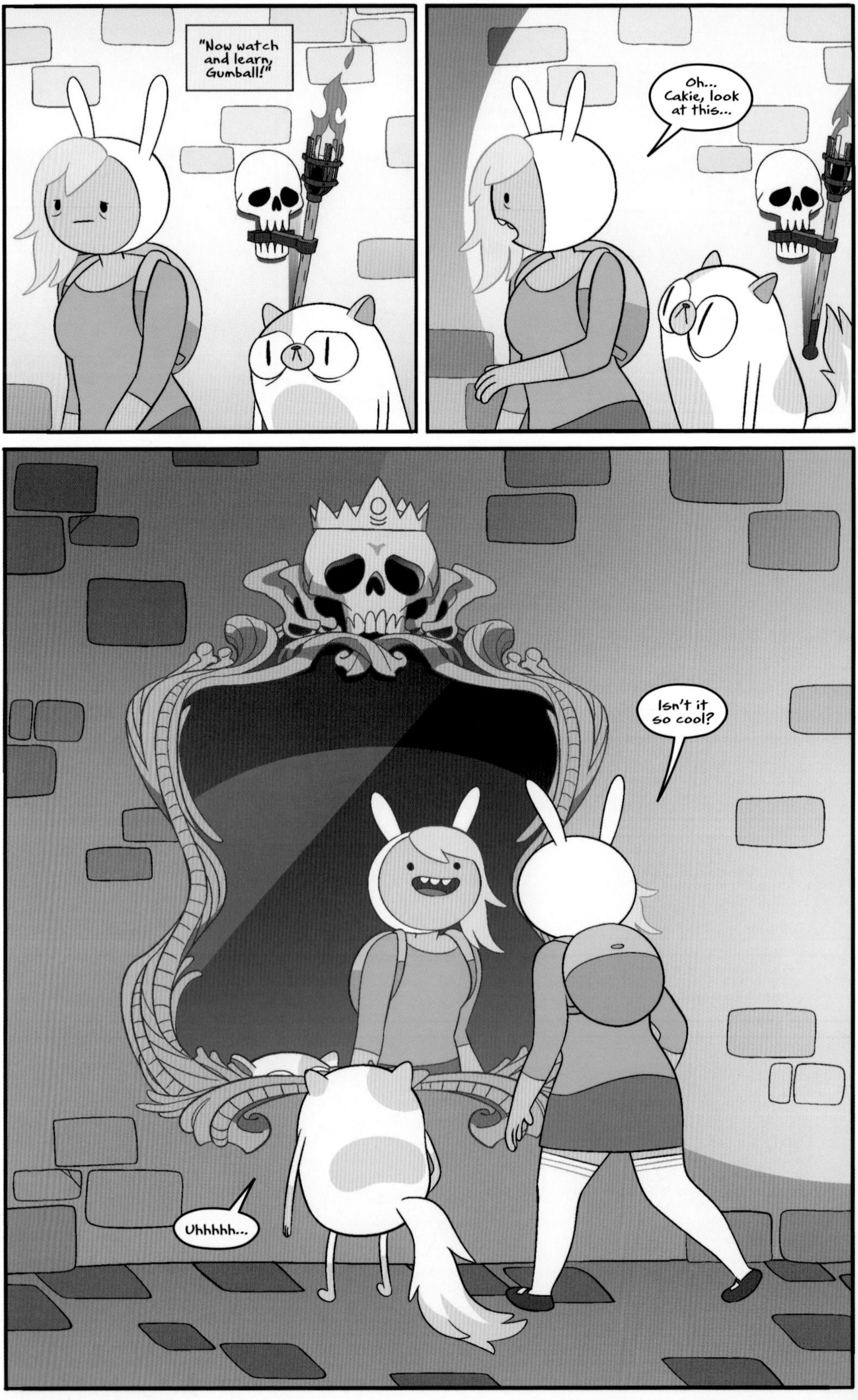
"Now watch and learn, Gumball!"
Oh... Cakie, look at this...
Isn't it so cool?
Uhhhhh...

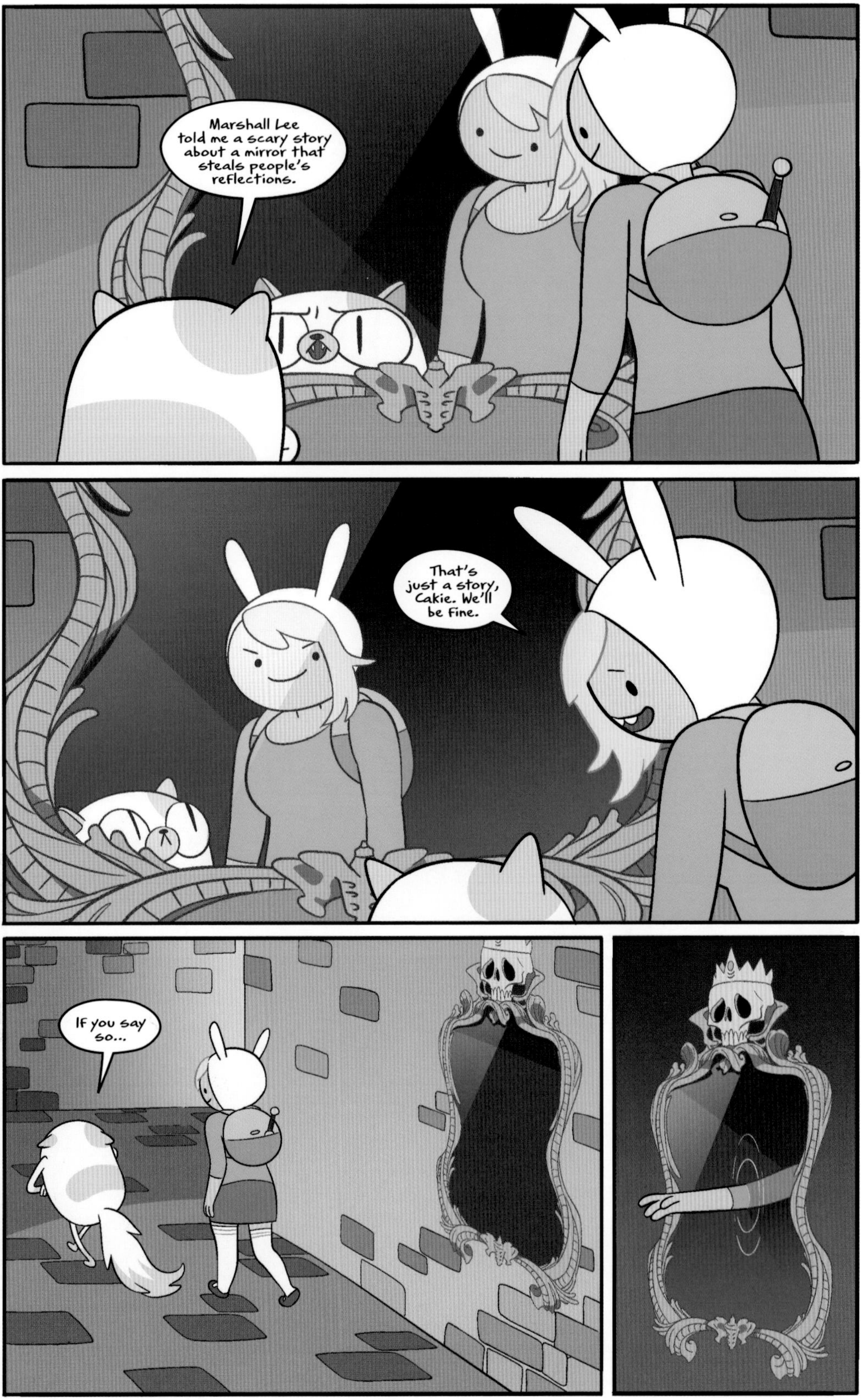
Marshall Lee told me a scary story about a mirror that steals people's reflections.
That's just a story, Cakie. We'll be fine.
If you say so...

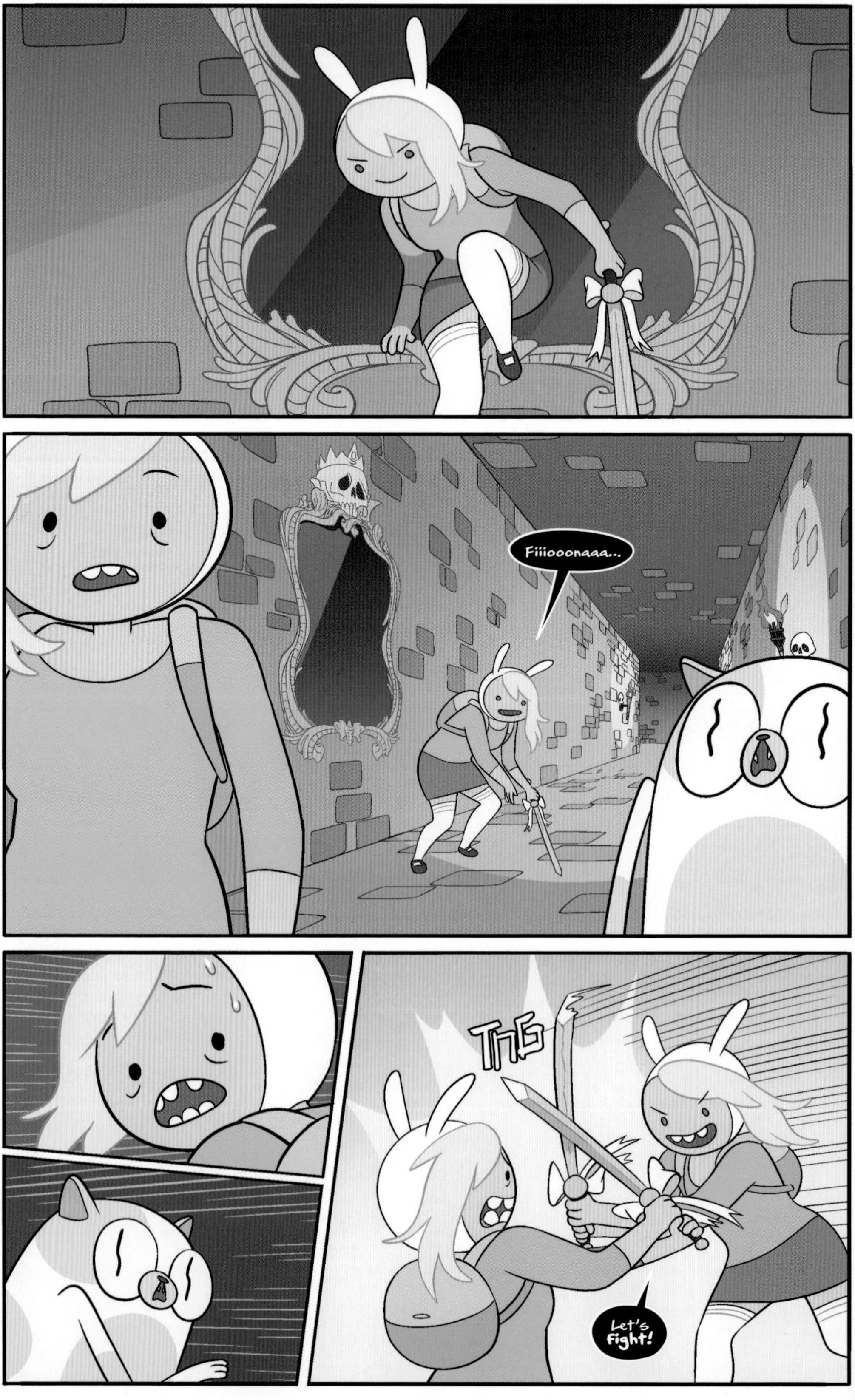
Fiiiooonaaa...
TING
Let's Fight!

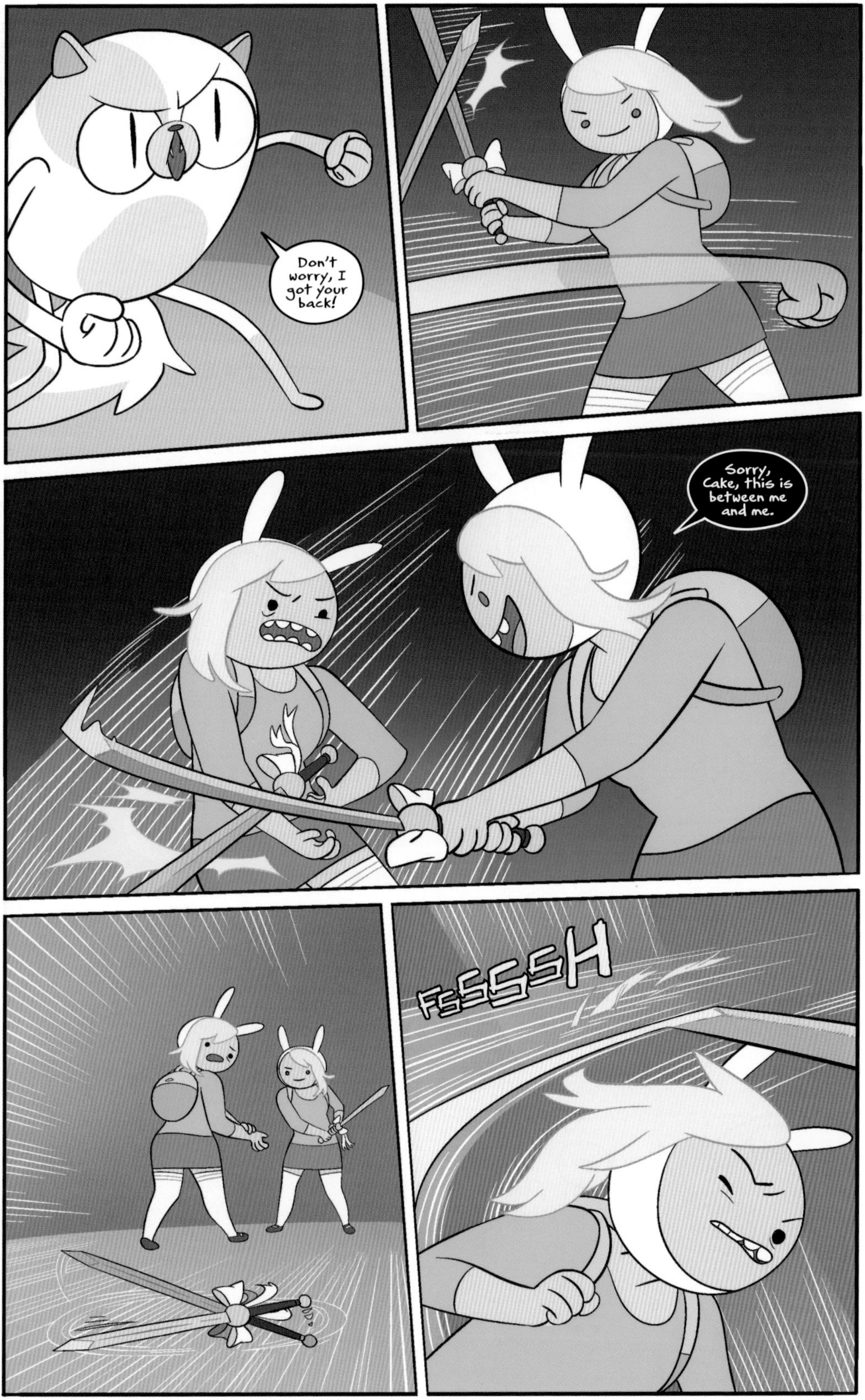
Don't worry, I got your back!
Sorry, Cake, this is between me and me.
FSSSSSH

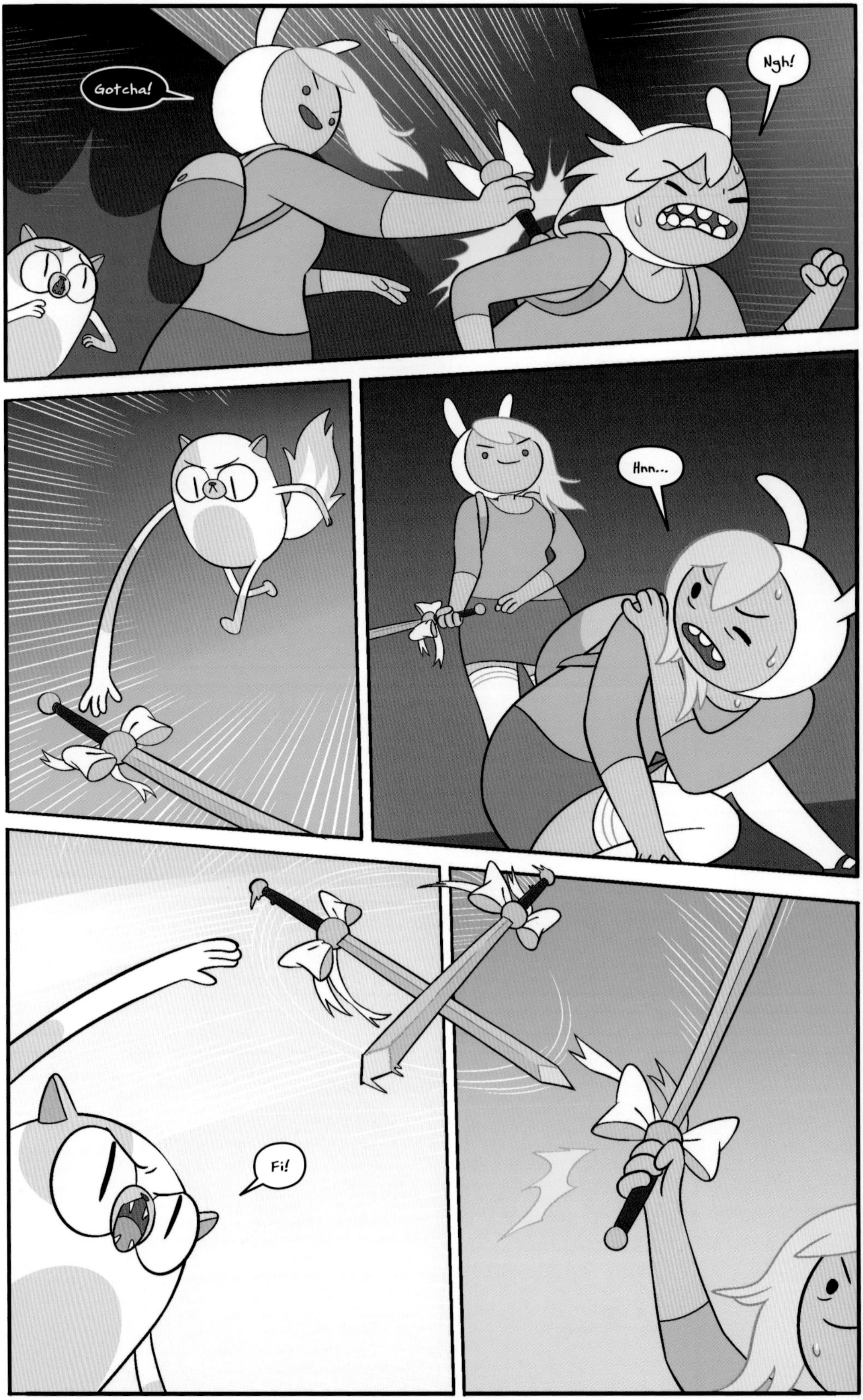
Gotcha!
Ngh!
Hnn...
Fi!

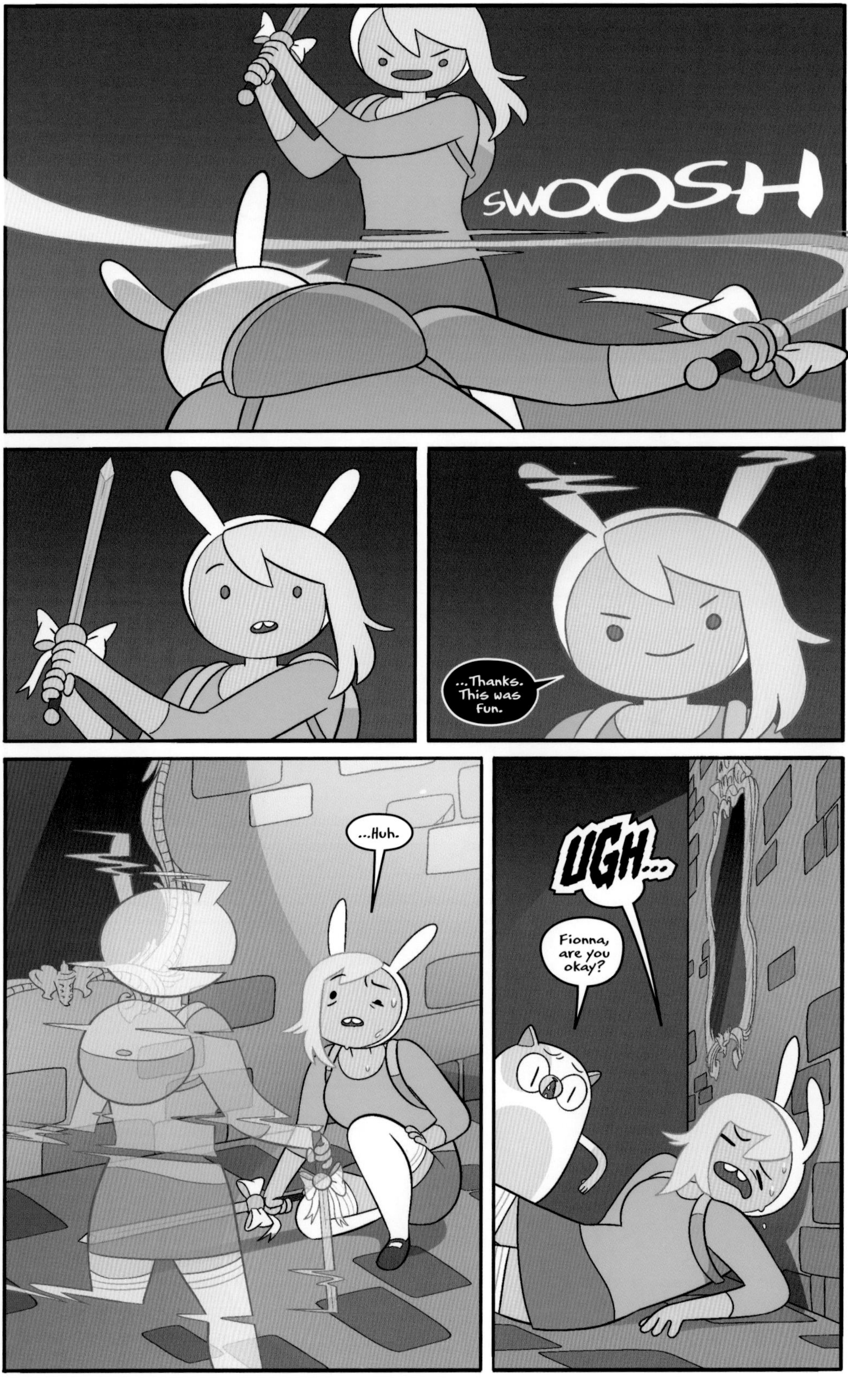
SWOOSH
...Thanks. This was Fun.
...Huh.
UGH...
Fiona, are you okay?

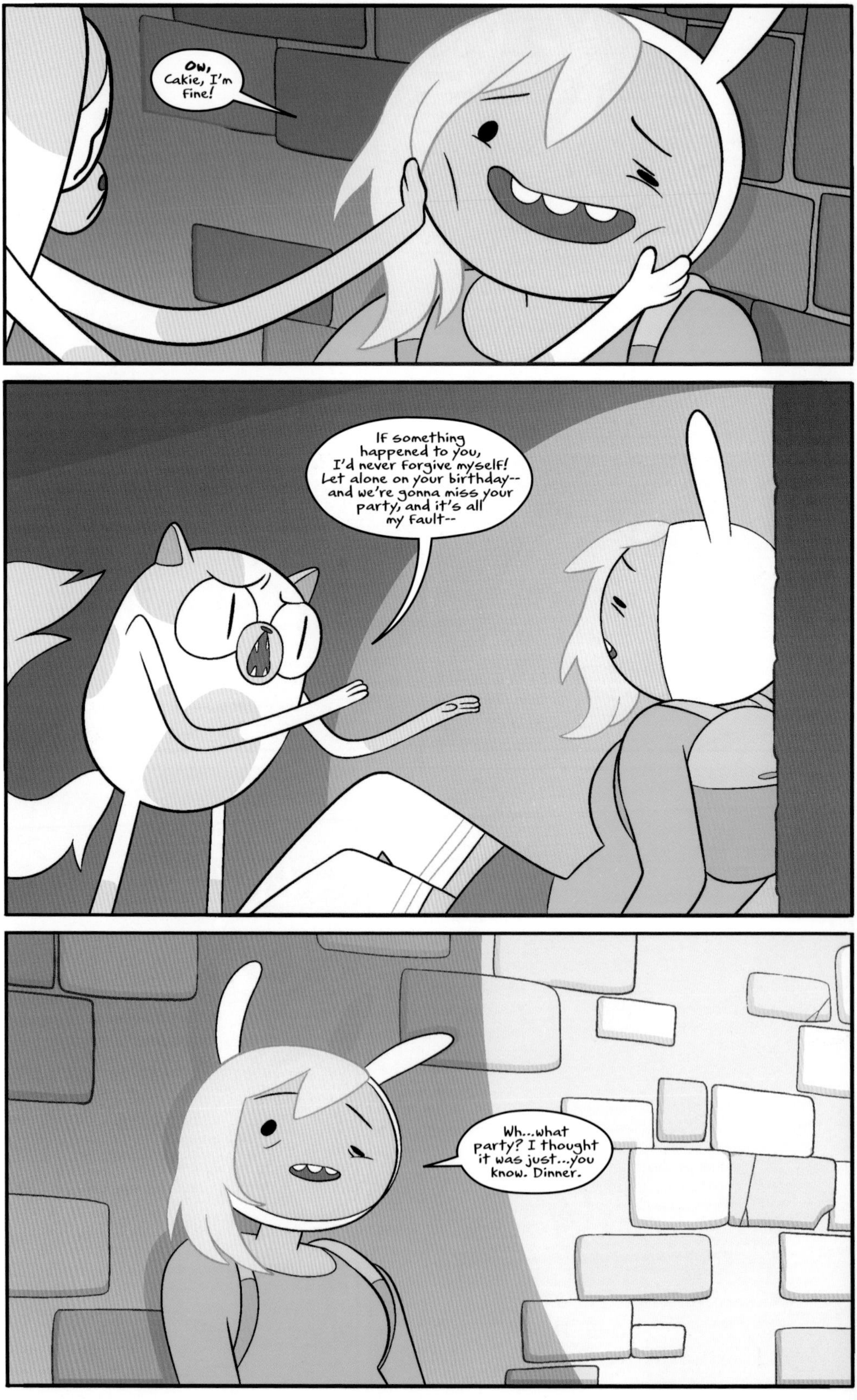

OW, Cakie, I'm fine!
If something happened to you, I'd never forgive myself! Let alone on your birthday-- and we're gonna miss your party, and it's all my fault--
Wh...what party? I thought it was just...you know. Dinner.

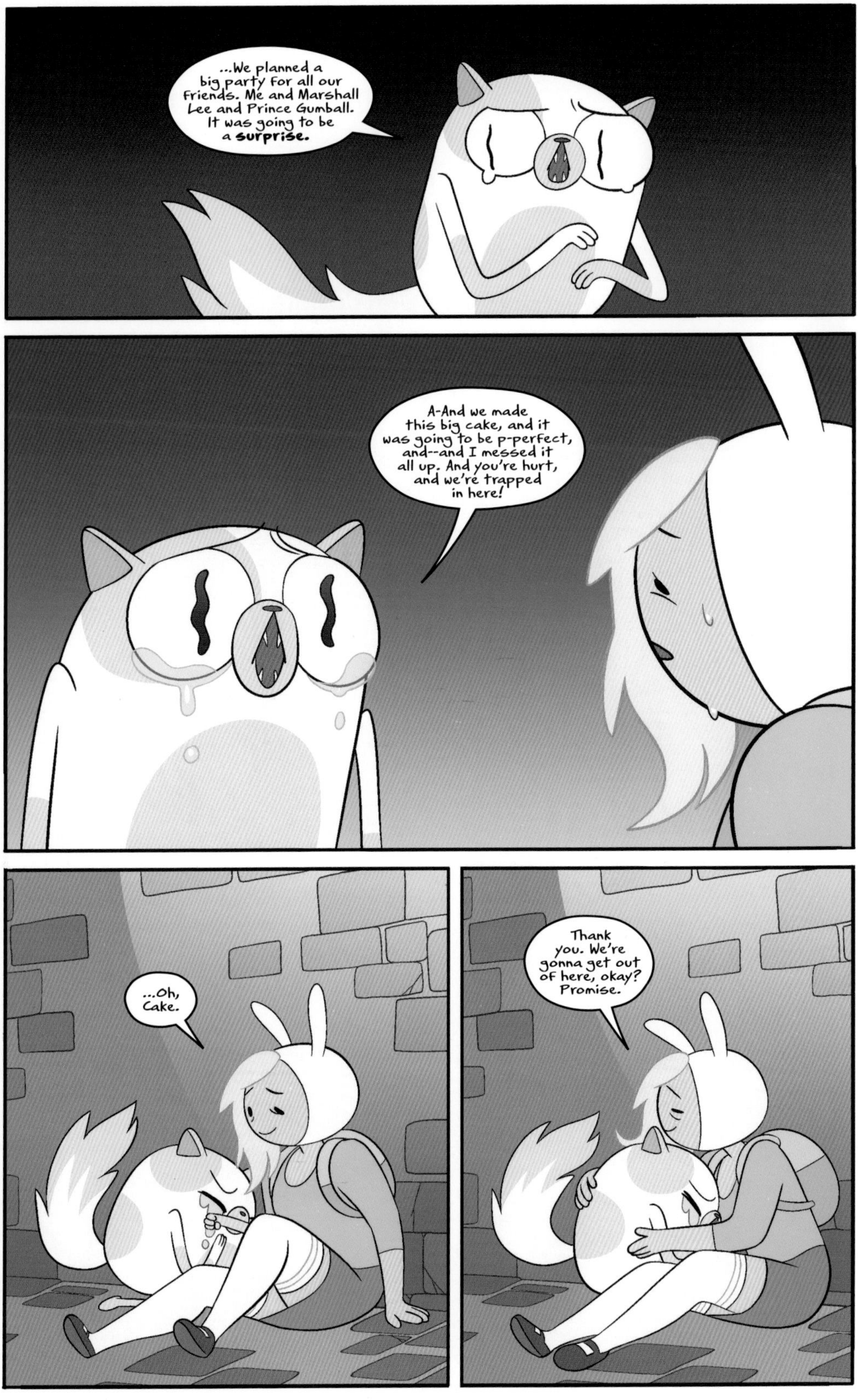
...We planned a big party for all our friends. Me and Marshall Lee and Prince Gumball. It was going to be a **surprise.**
A-And we made this big cake, and it was going to be p-perfect, and--and I messed it all up. And you're hurt, and we're trapped in here!
...Oh, Cake.
Thank you. We're gonna get out of here, okay? Promise.

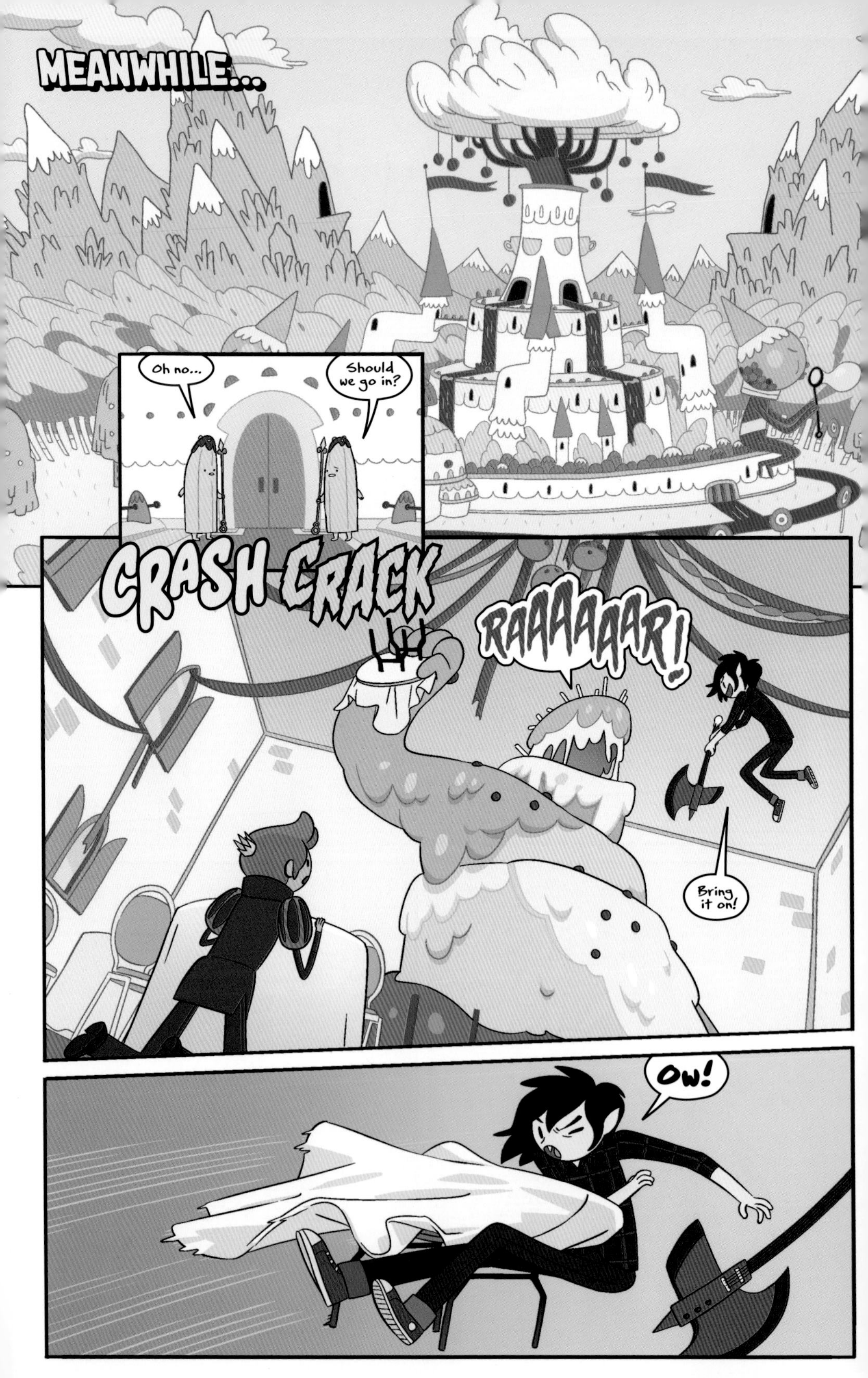
MEANWHILE...
Oh no...
Should we go in?
CRASH CRACK
RAAAAAAR!
Bring it on!
OW!

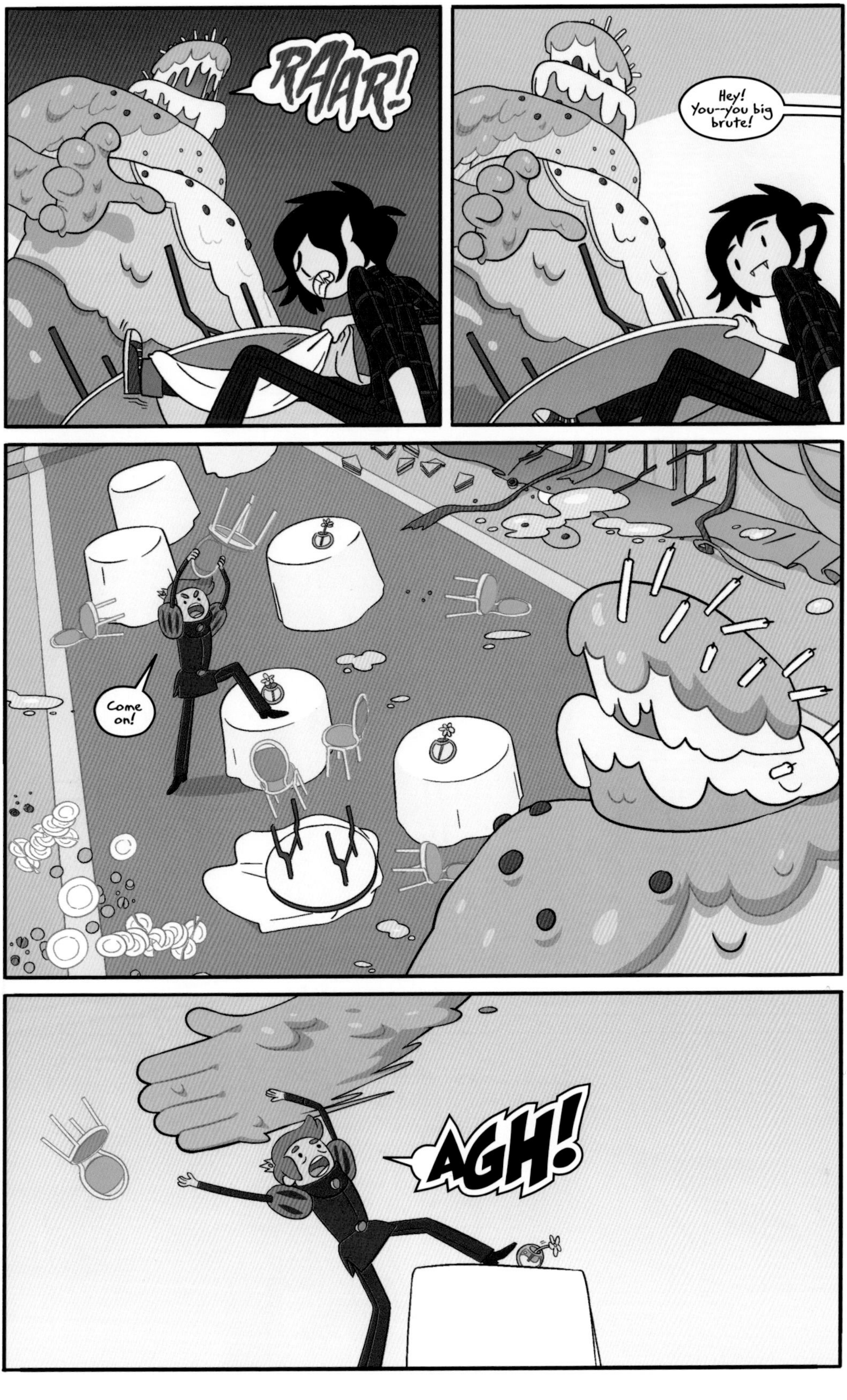
RAAR!
Hey! You--you big brute!
Come on!
AGH!

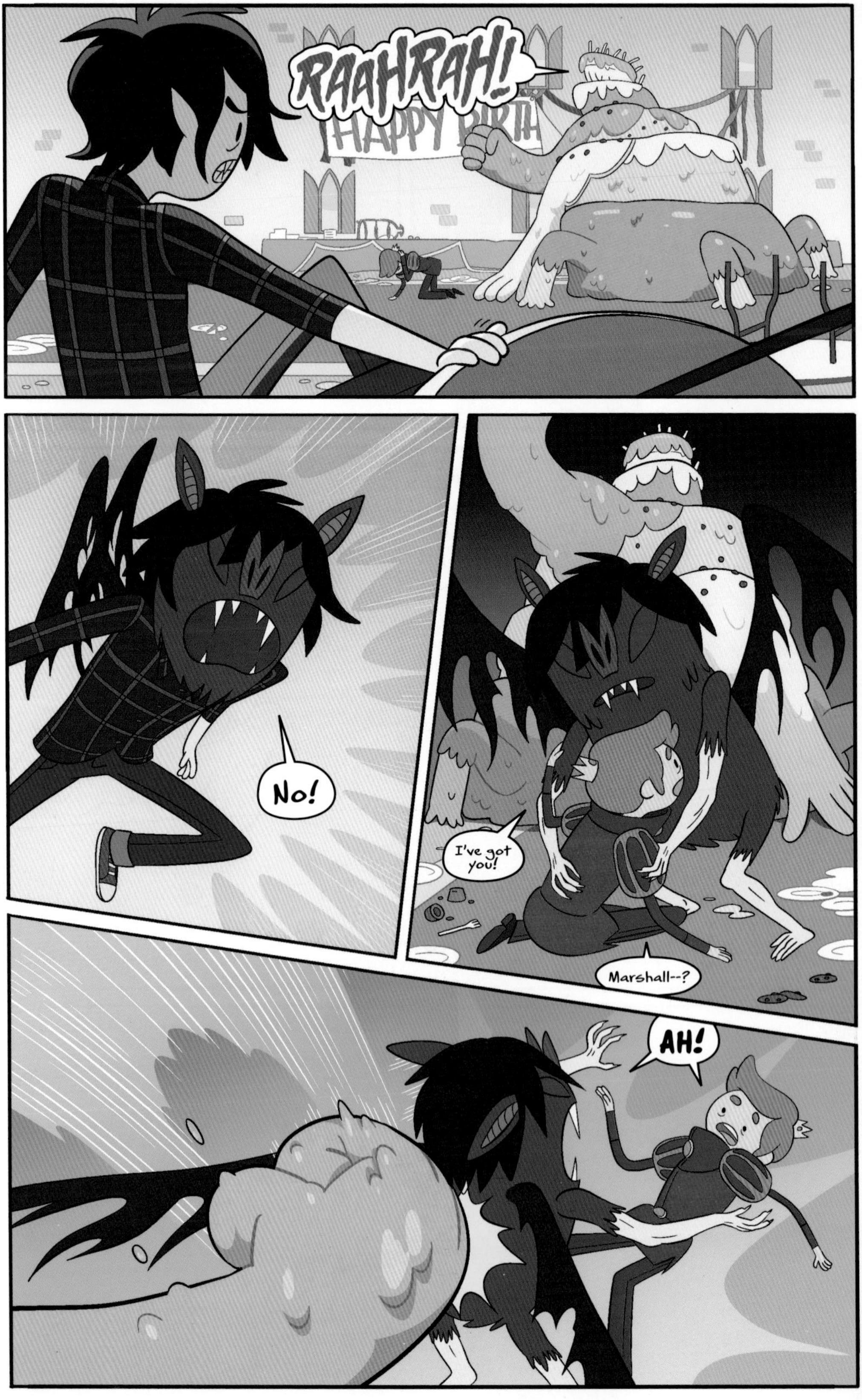

RAAHRAH!
HAPPY BIRTH
No!
I've got you!
Marshall--?
AH!

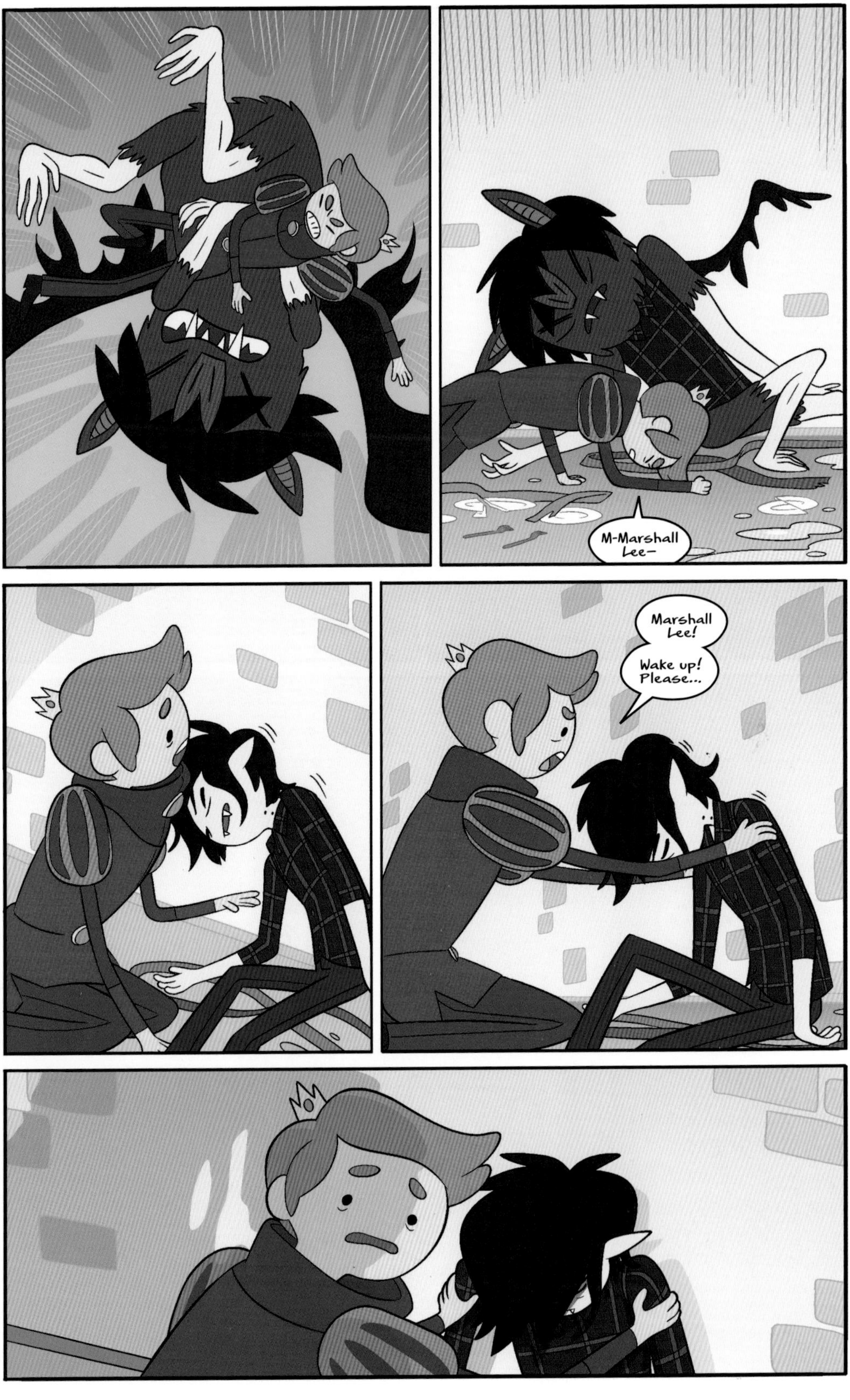
M-Marshall Lee-
Marshall Lee!
Wake up! Please...

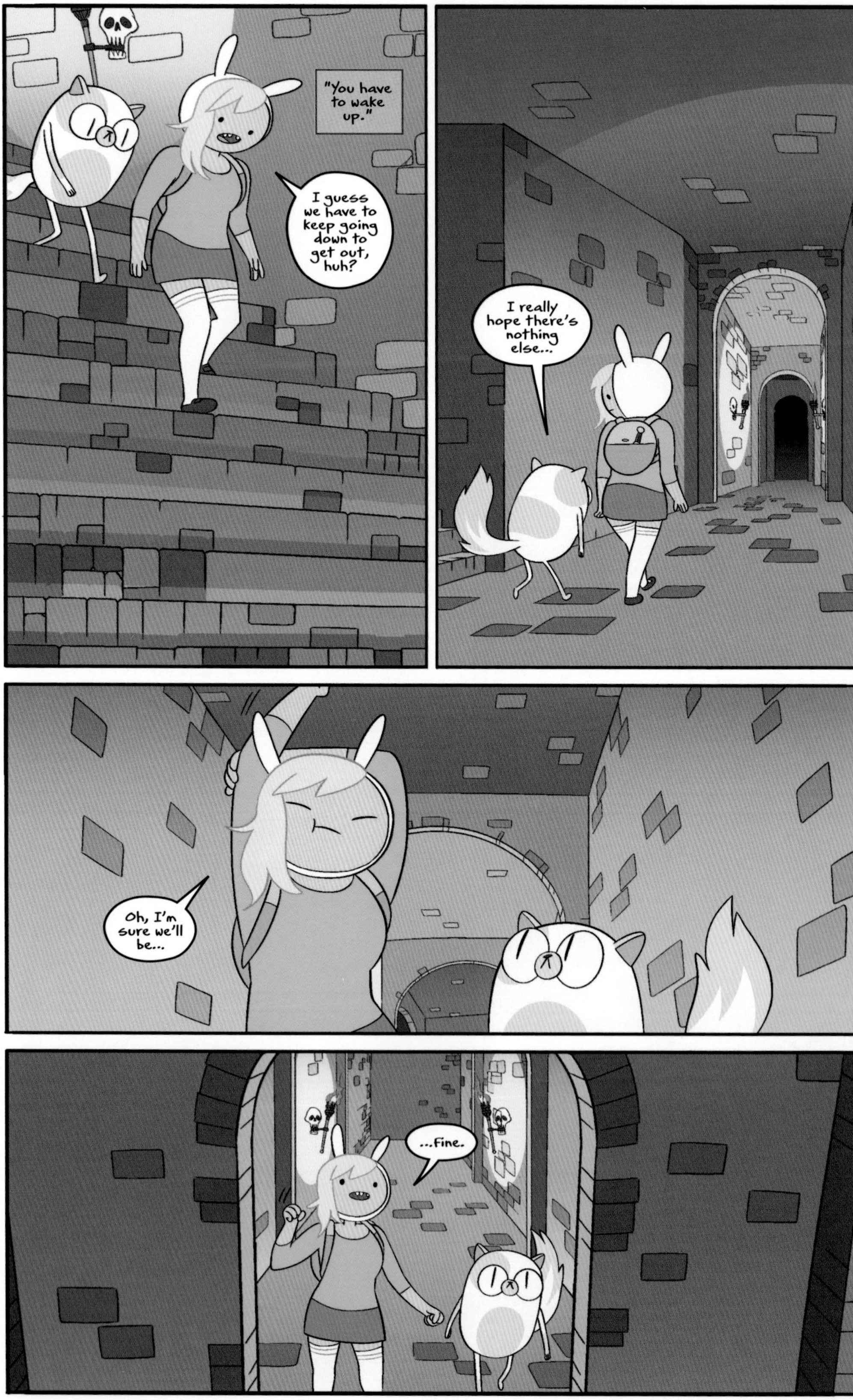
"You have to wake up."
I guess we have to keep going down to get out, huh?
I really hope there's nothing else...
Oh, I'm sure we'll be...
...Fine.

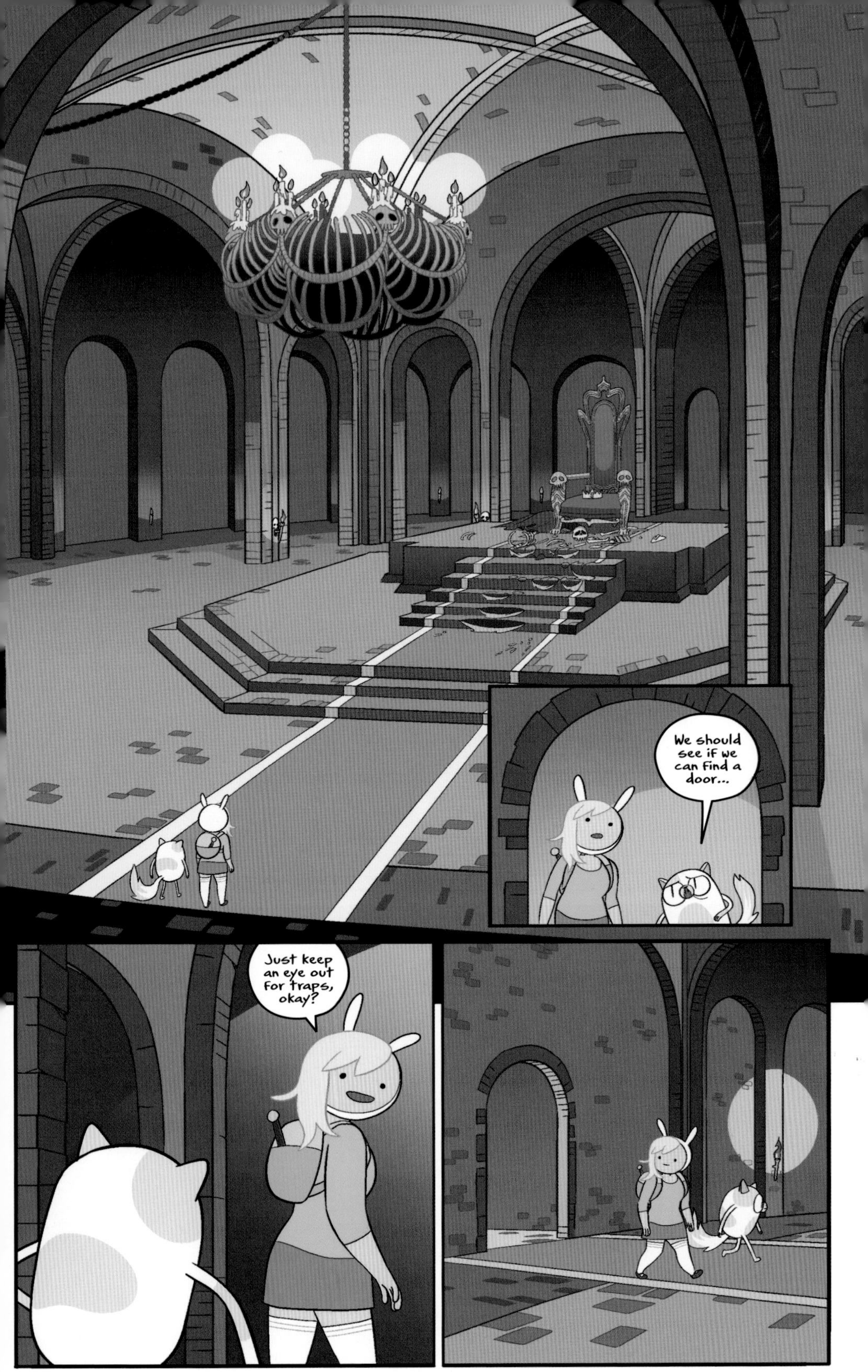
We should see if we can find a door...
Just keep an eye out for traps, okay?

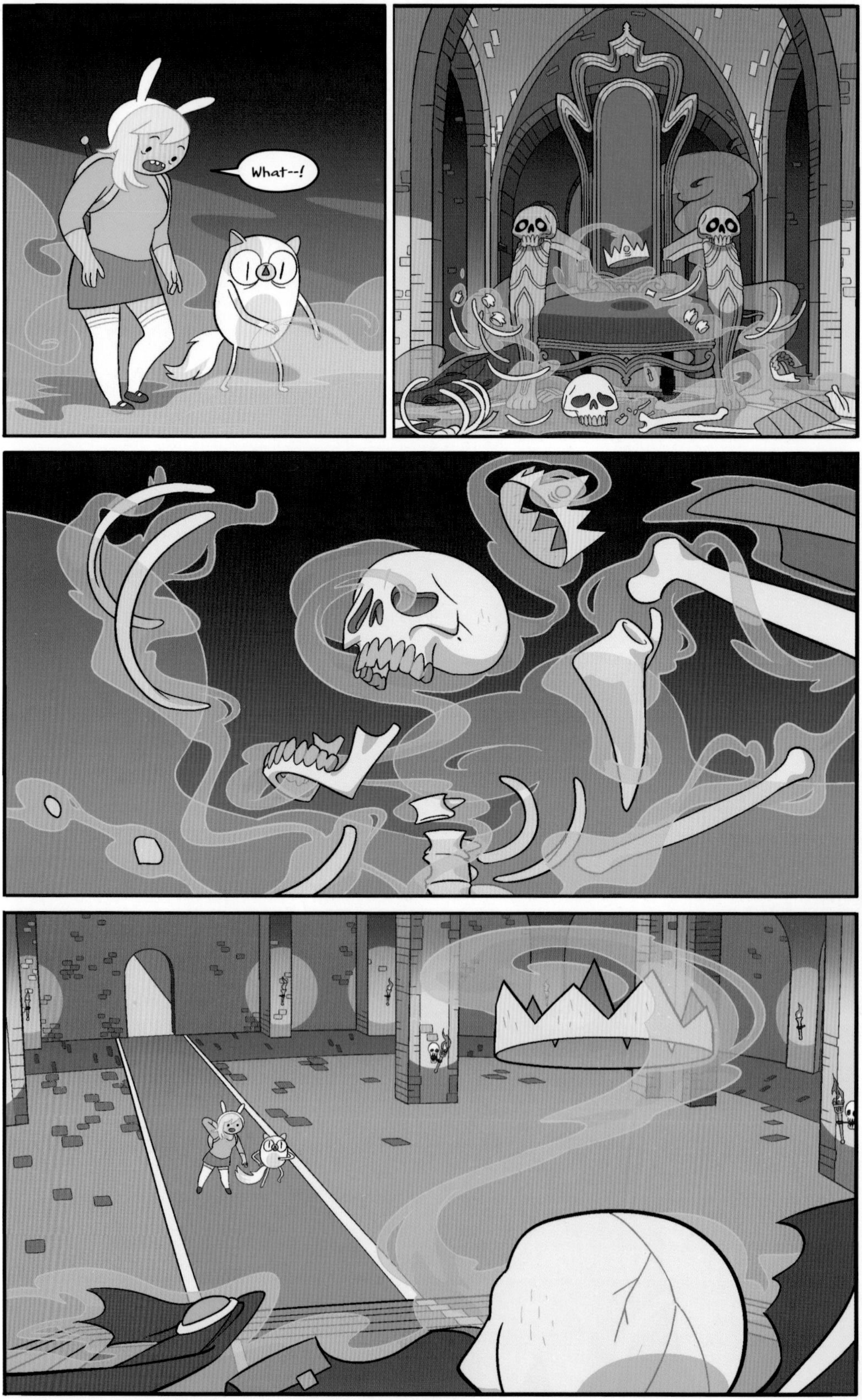
What--!

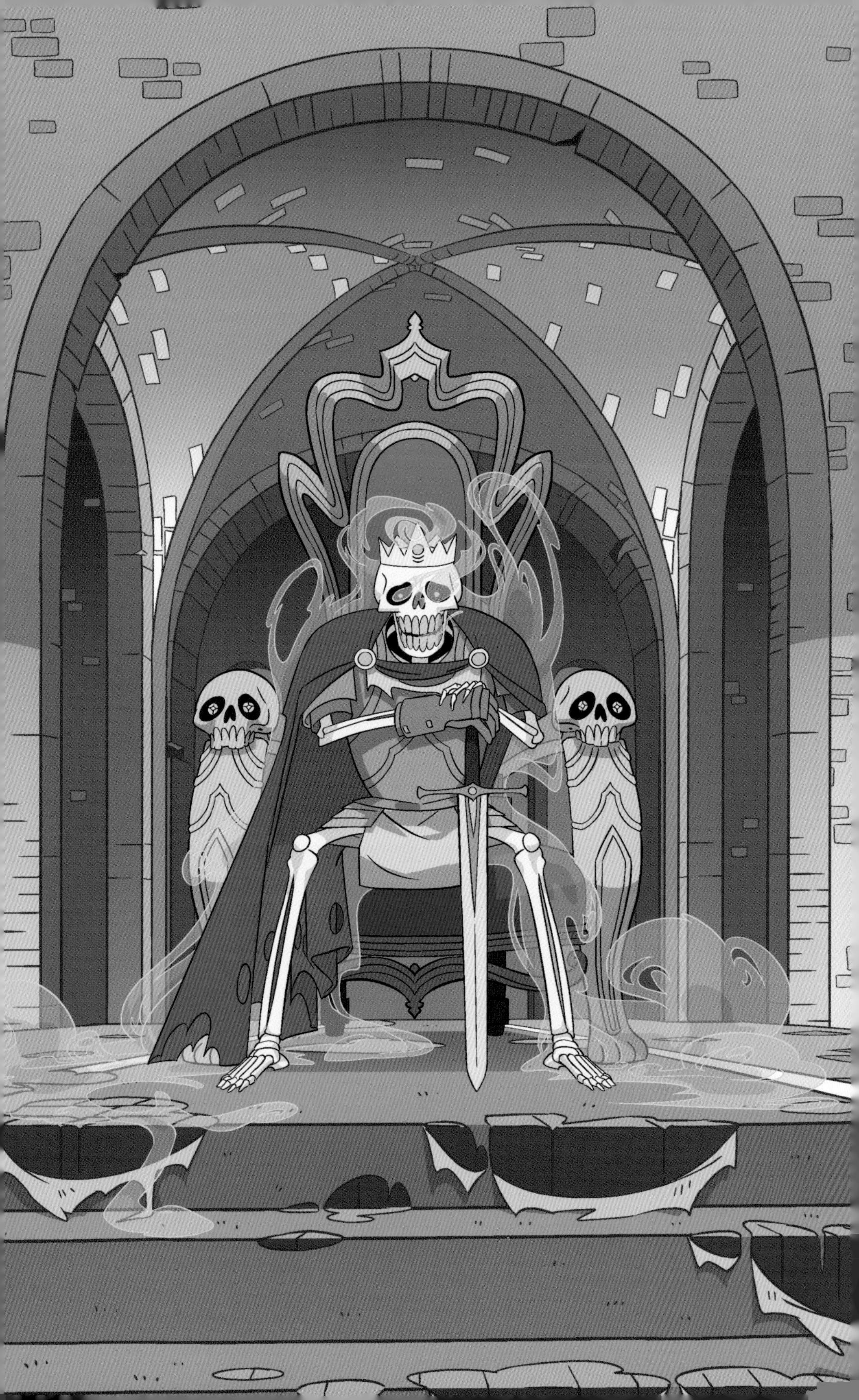

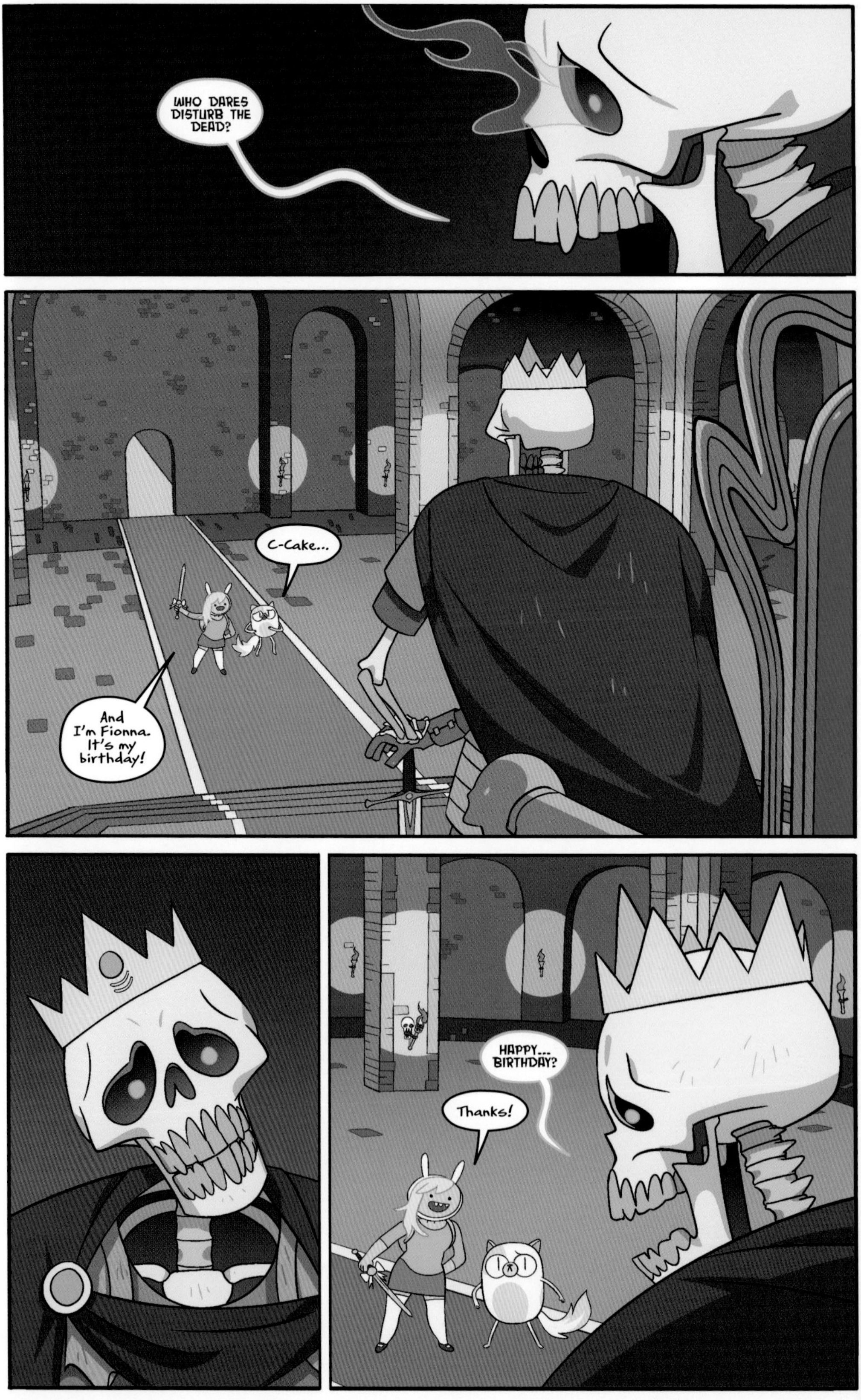
WHO DARES DISTURB THE DEAD?
C-Cake...
And I'm Fionna. It's my birthday!
HAPPY... BIRTHDAY?
Thanks!

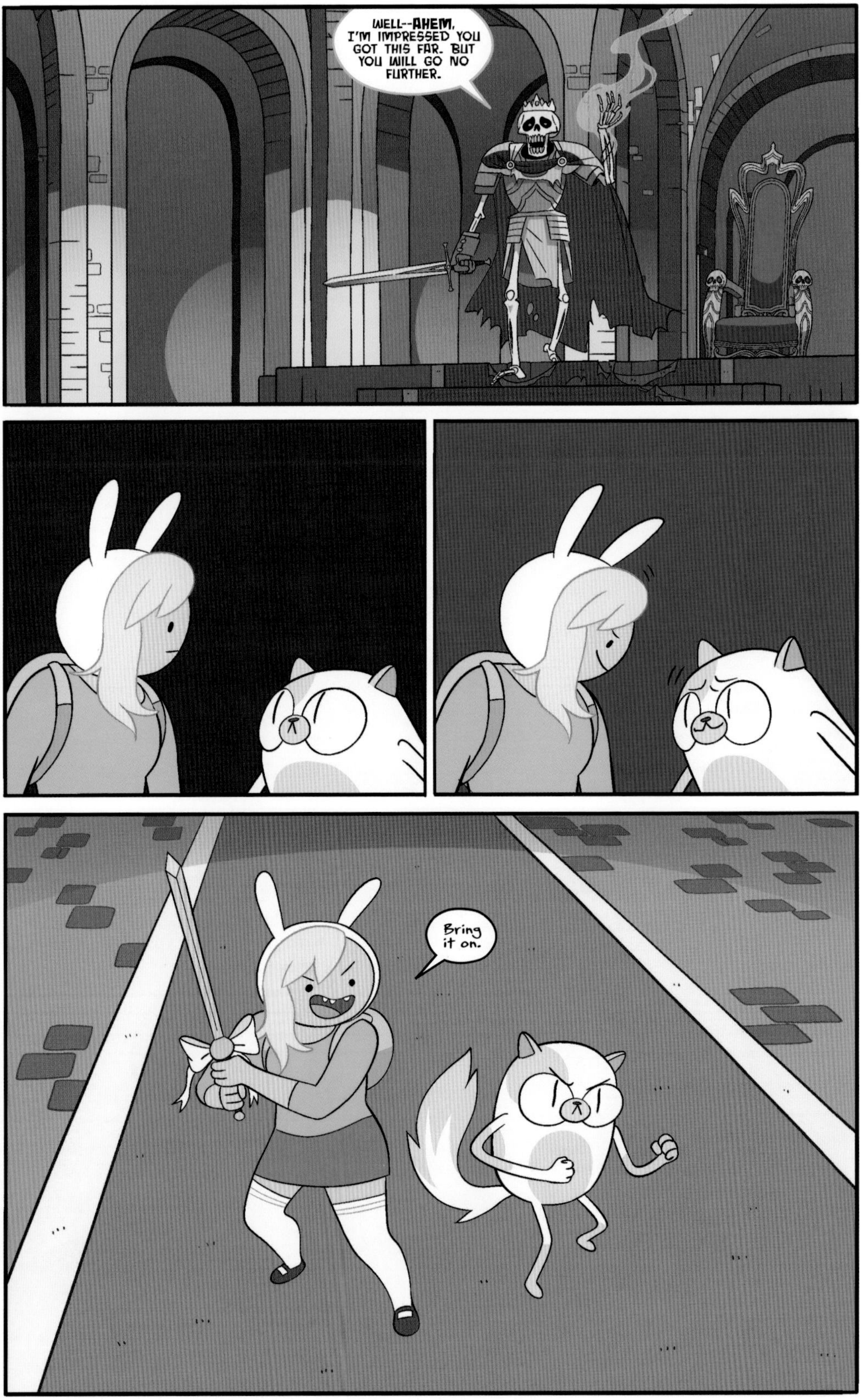
WELL--AHEM, I'M IMPRESSED YOU GOT THIS FAR. BUT YOU WILL GO NO FURTHER.
Bring it on.

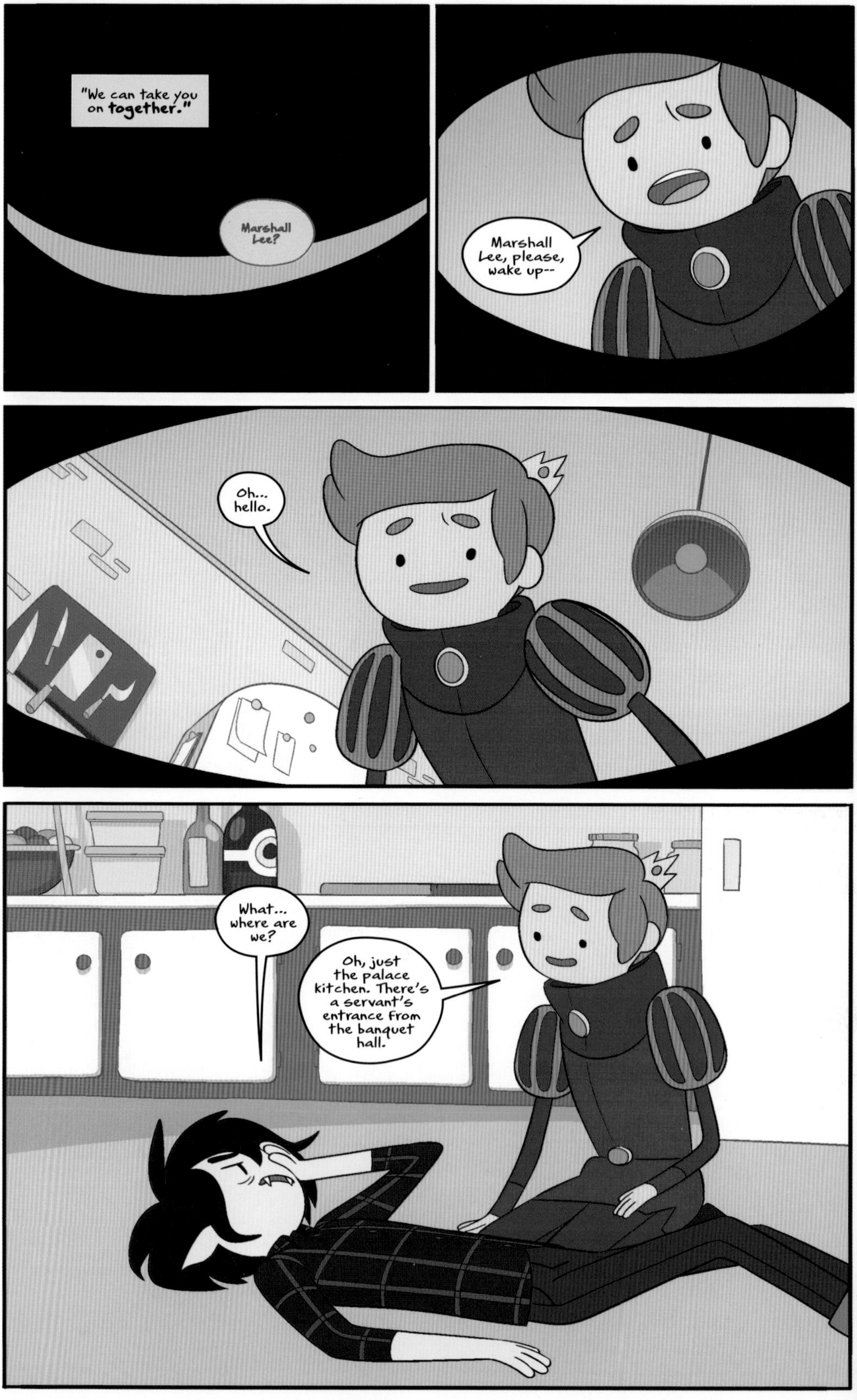
"We can take you on **together.**"
Marshall Lee?
Marshall Lee, please, wake up--
Oh... hello.
What... where are we?
Oh, just the palace kitchen. There's a servant's entrance from the banquet hall.

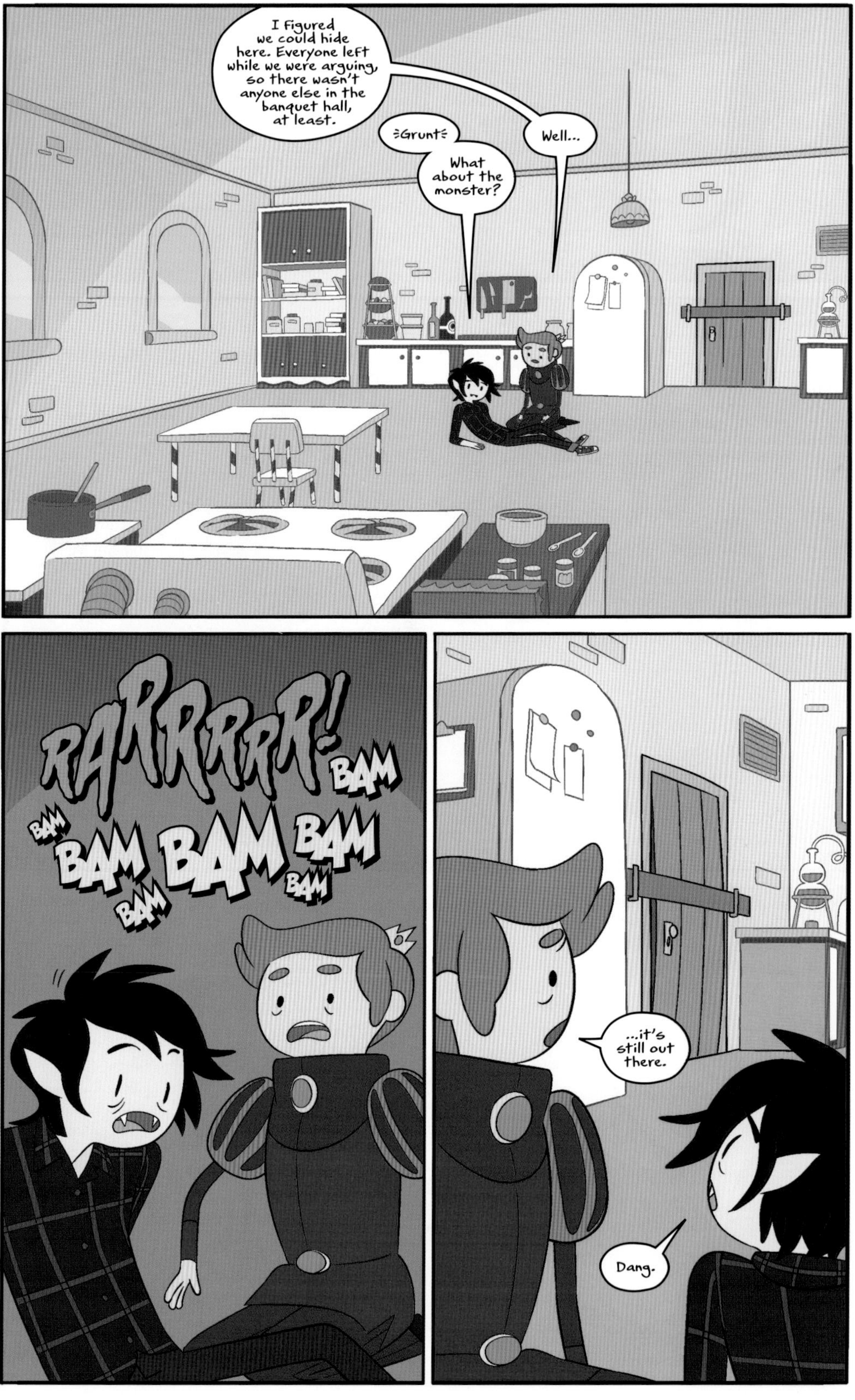
I figured we could hide here. Everyone left while we were arguing, so there wasn't anyone else in the banquet hall, at least.
Grunt
What about the monster?
Well...
RARRRRR!
BAM
BAM
BAM
BAM
BAM
BAM
BAM
BAM
...it's still out there.
Dang.

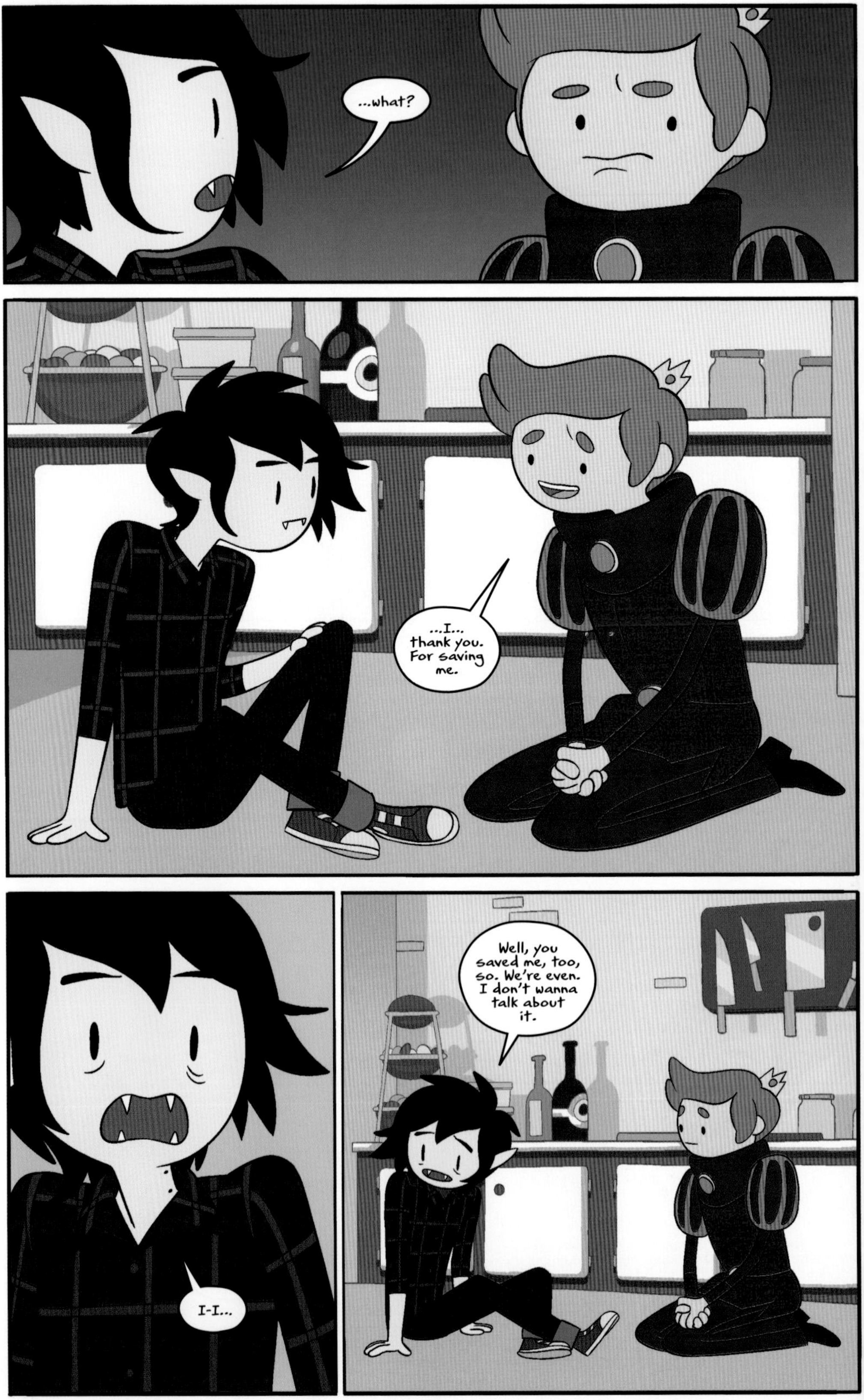
...what?
...I... thank you. For saving me.
I-I...
Well, you saved me, too, so. We're even. I don't wanna talk about it.

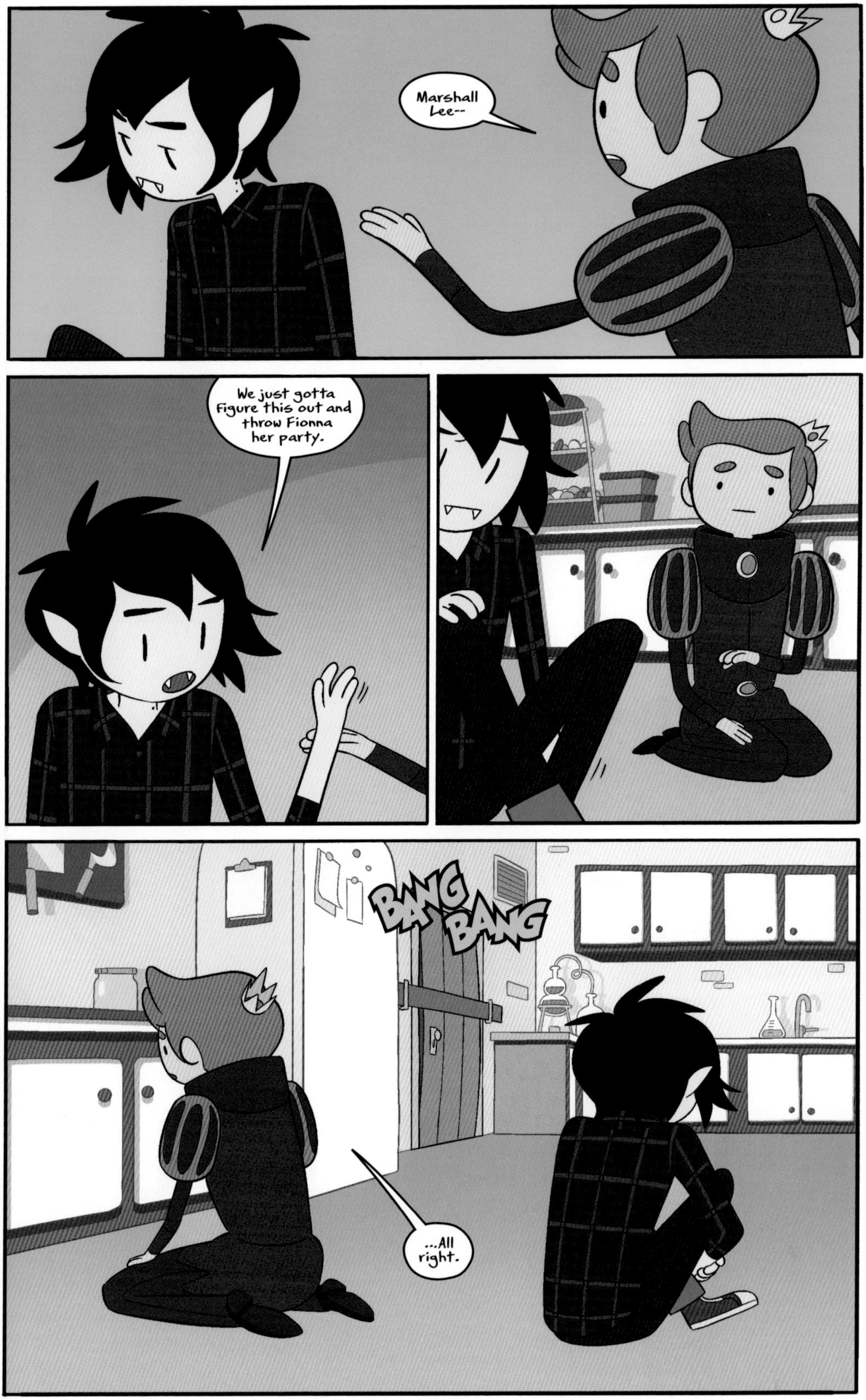
Marshall Lee--
We just gotta figure this out and throw Fionna her party.
BANG BANG
...All right.

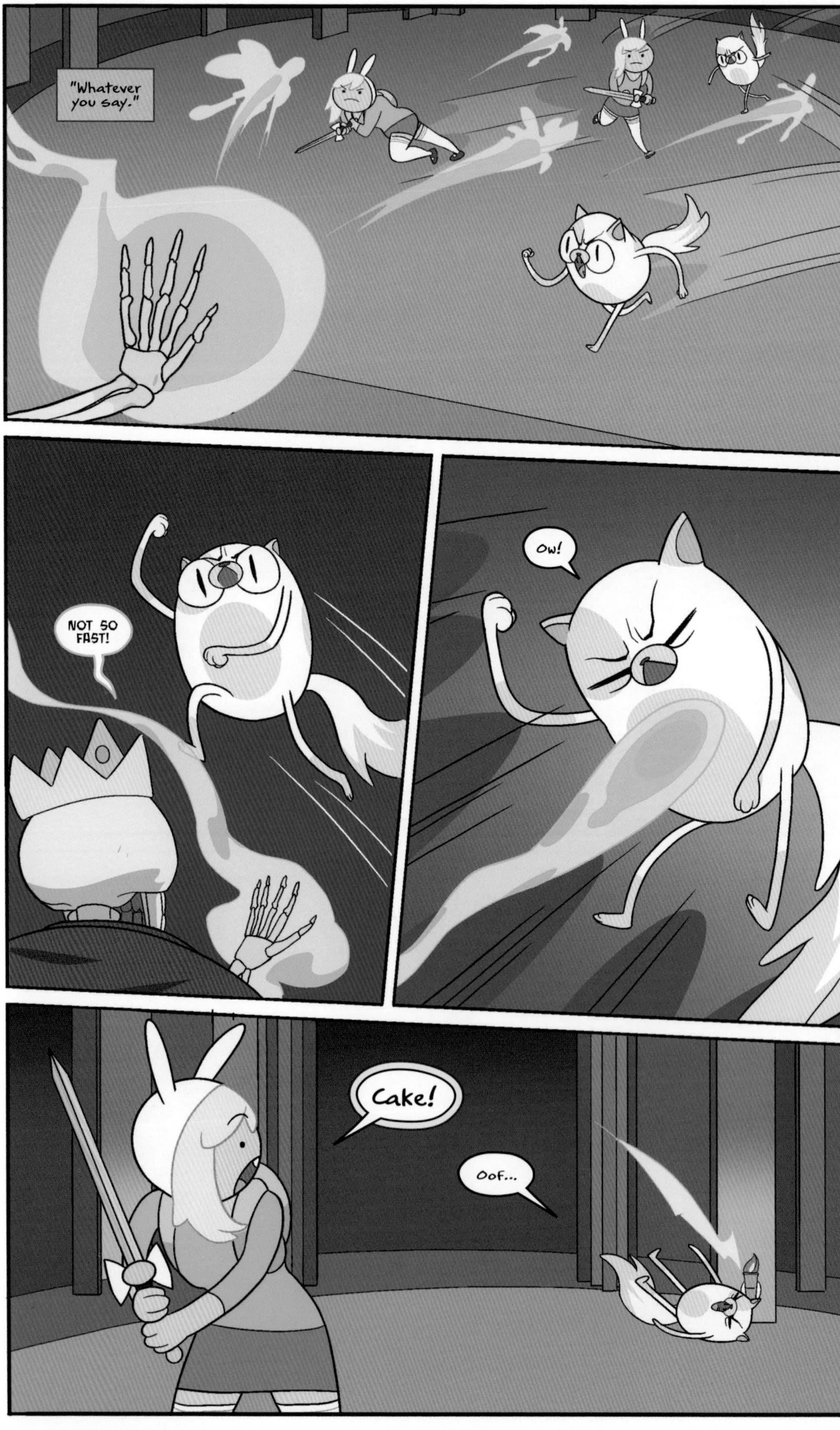
"Whatever you say."
NOT SO FAST!
Ow!
Cake!
Oof...

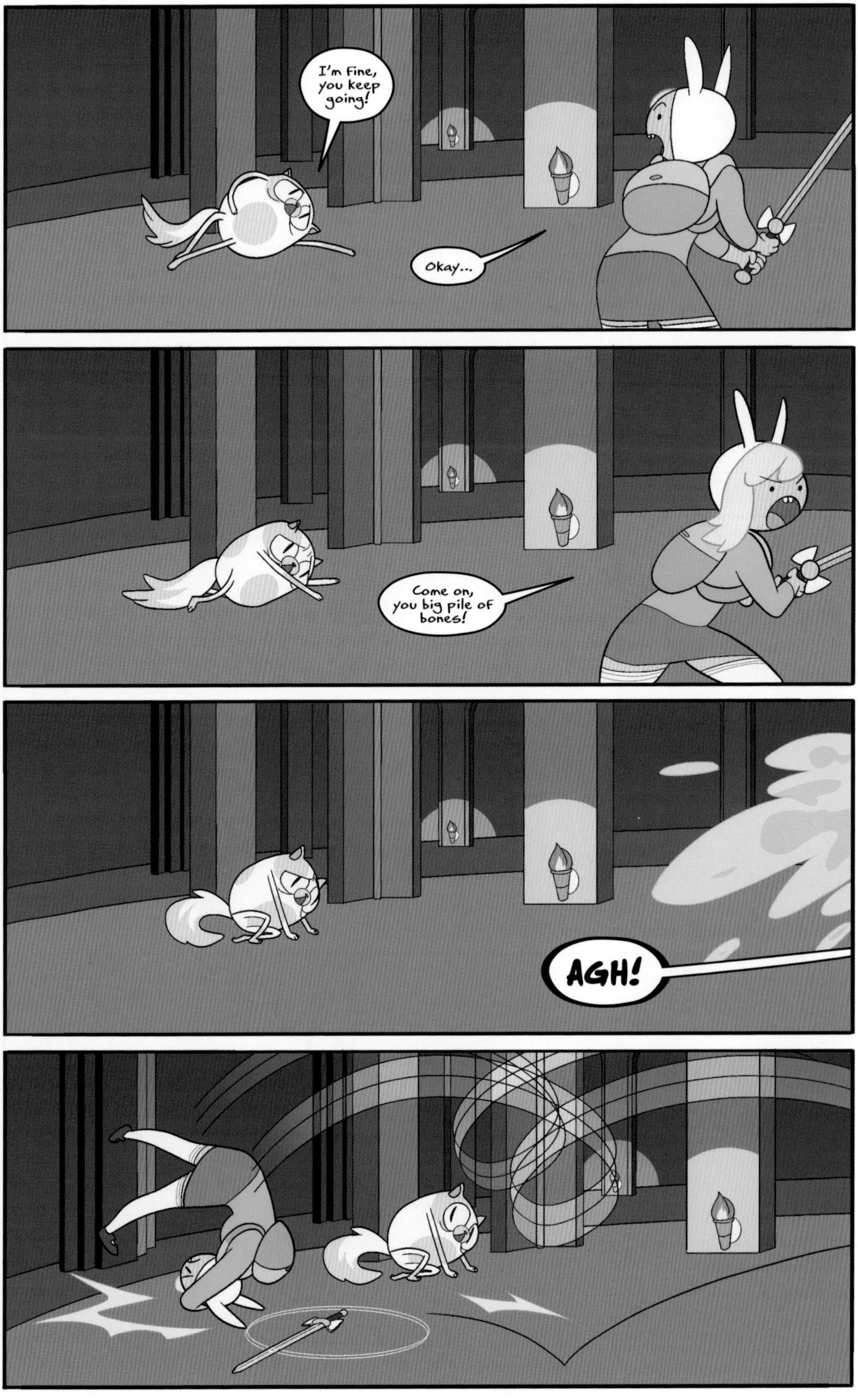
I'm fine, you keep going!
Okay...
Come on, you big pile of bones!
AGH!

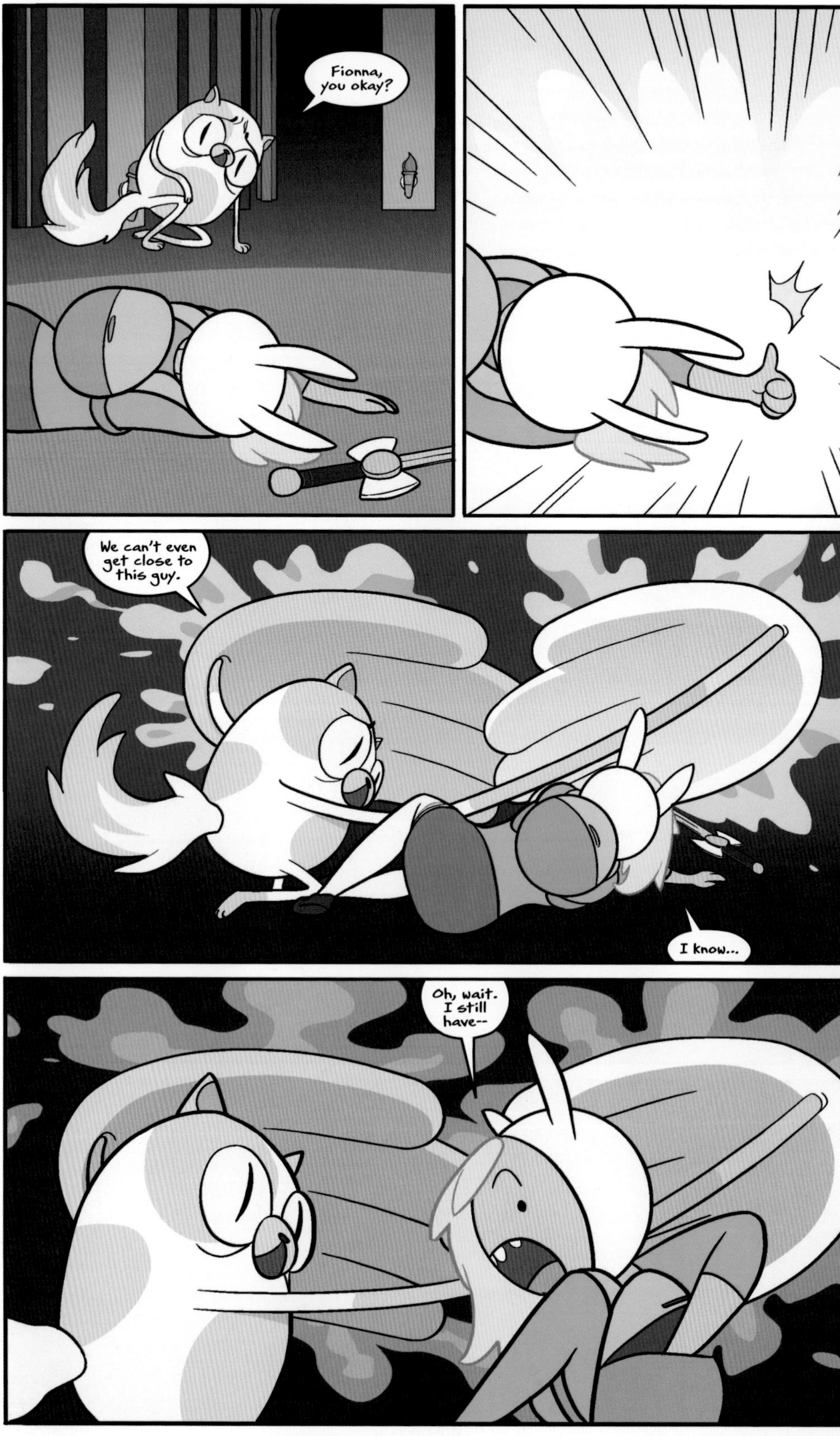
Fionna, you okay?
We can't even get close to this guy.
I know...
Oh, wait. I still have--

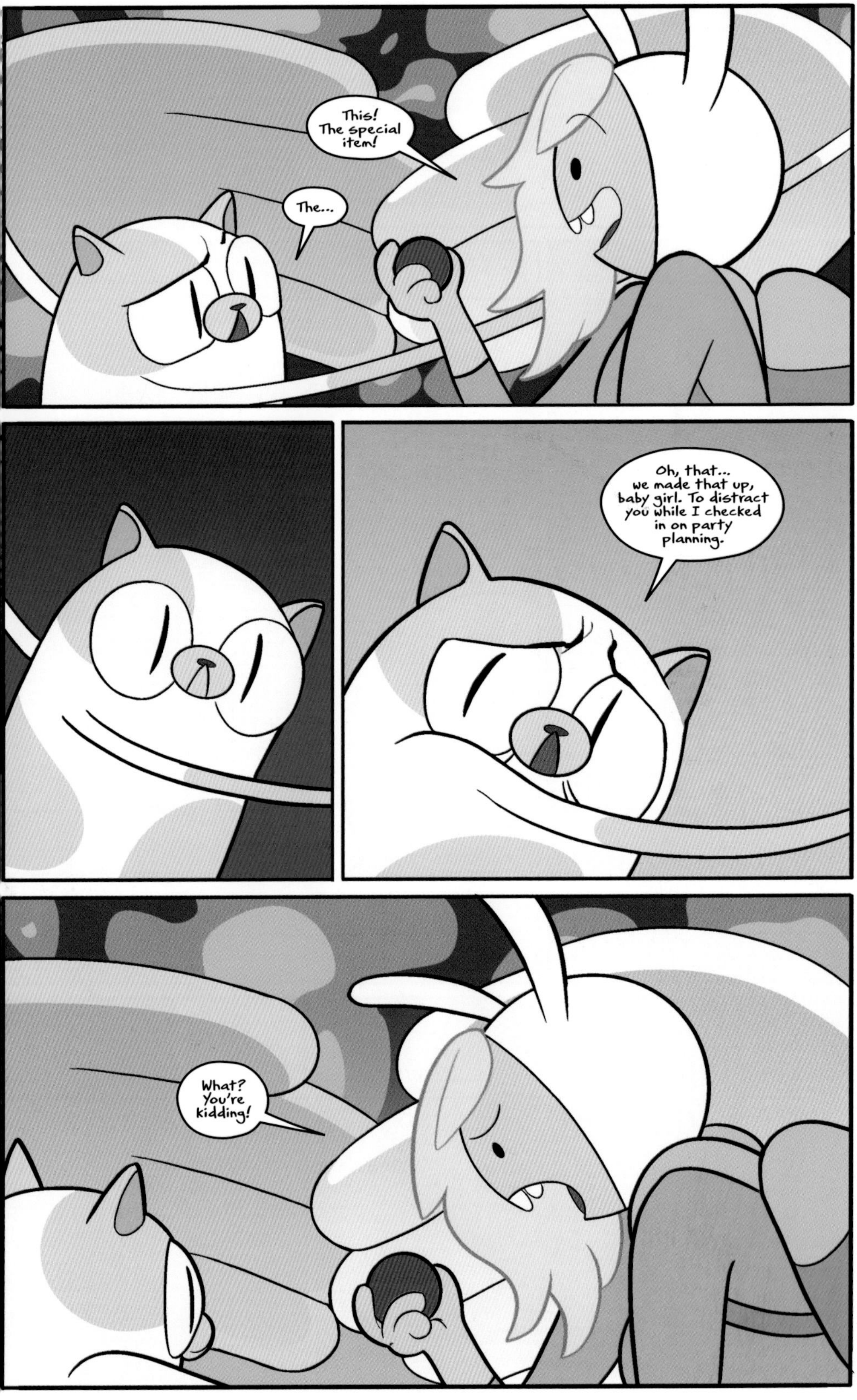
This! The special item!
The...
Oh, that... we made that up, baby girl. To distract you while I checked in on party planning.
What? You're kidding!

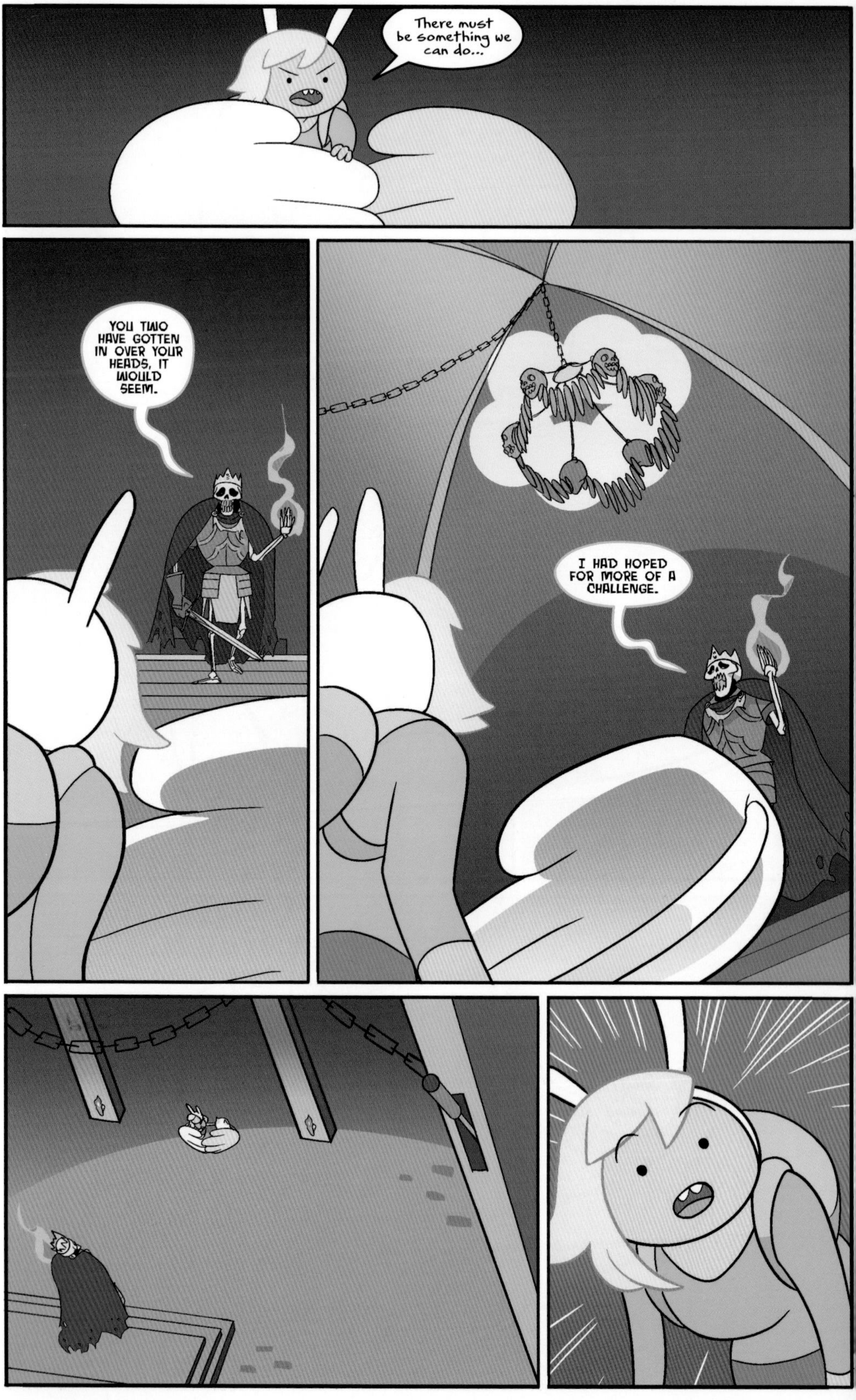
There must be something we can do...
YOU TWO HAVE GOTTEN IN OVER YOUR HEADS, IT WOULD SEEM.
I HAD HOPED FOR MORE OF A CHALLENGE.

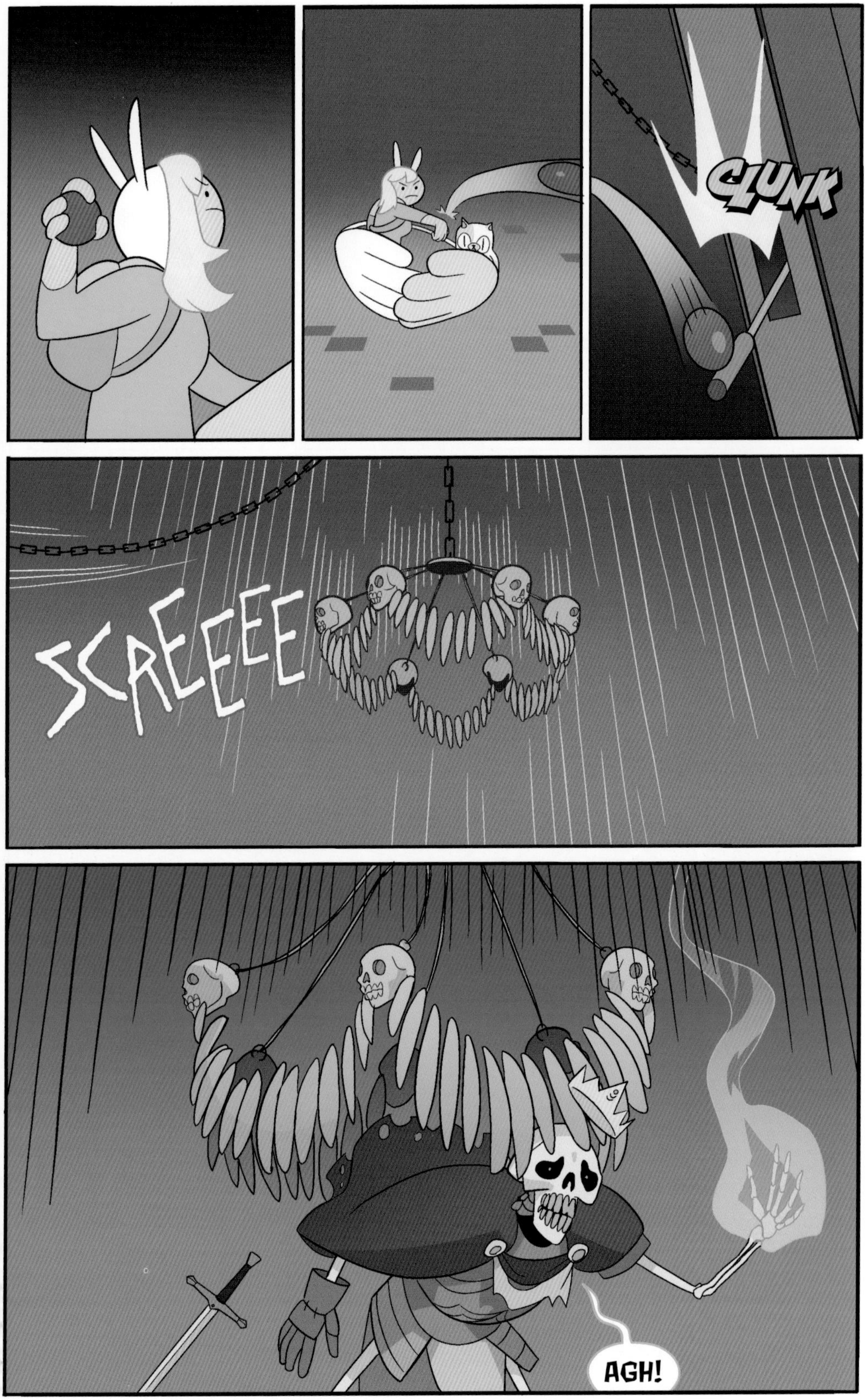
CLUNK
SCREEEE
AGH!

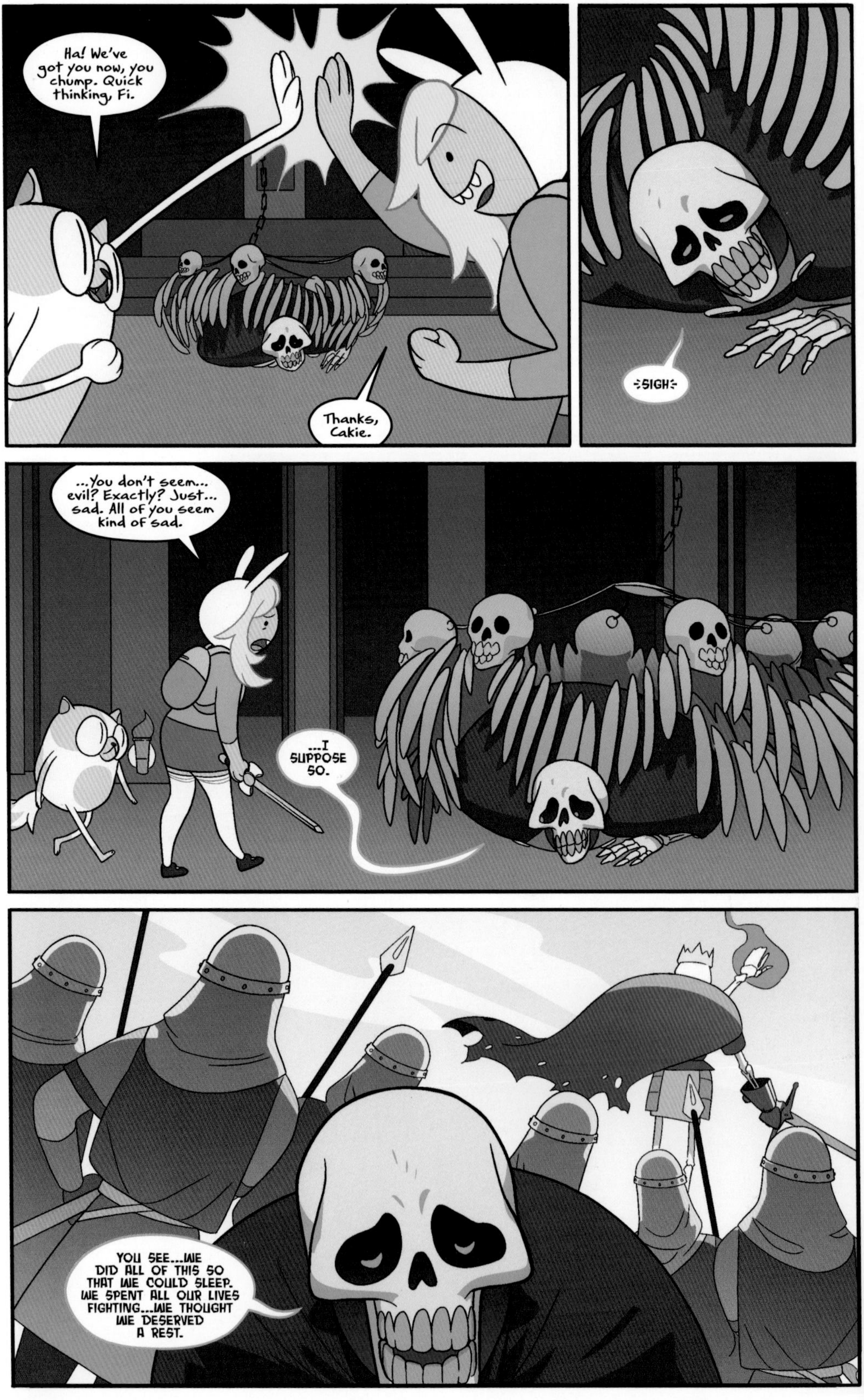
Ha! We've got you now, you chump. Quick thinking, Fi.
Thanks, Cakie.
SIGH
...You don't seem... evil? Exactly? Just... sad. All of you seem kind of sad.
...I SUPPOSE SO.
YOU SEE...WE DID ALL OF THIS SO THAT WE COULD SLEEP. WE SPENT ALL OUR LIVES FIGHTING...WE THOUGHT WE DESERVED A REST.

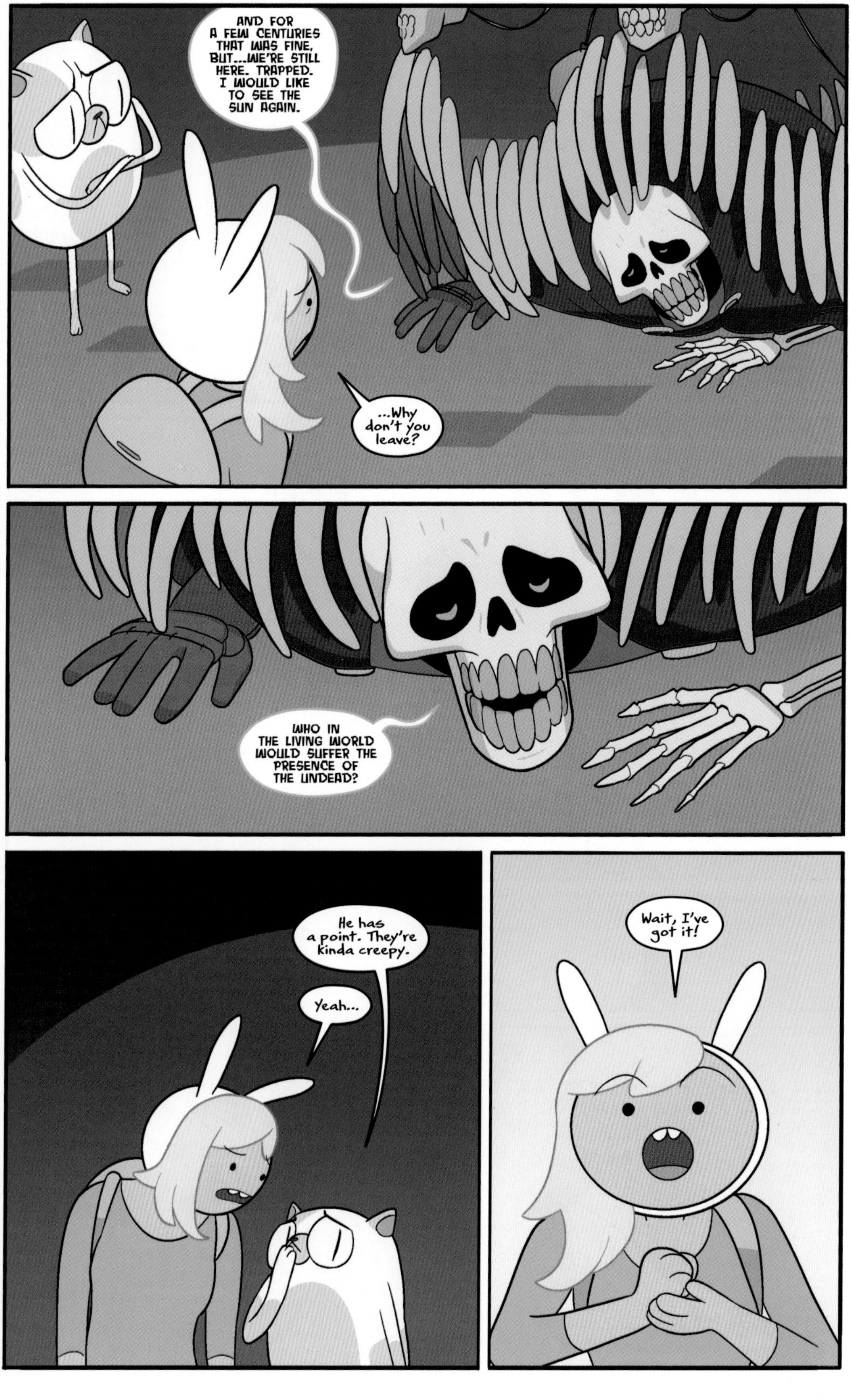
AND FOR A FEW CENTURIES THAT WAS FINE, BUT...WE'RE STILL HERE. TRAPPED. I WOULD LIKE TO SEE THE SUN AGAIN.
...Why don't you leave?
WHO IN THE LIVING WORLD WOULD SUFFER THE PRESENCE OF THE UNDEAD?
He has a point. They're kinda creepy.
Yeah...
Wait, I've got it!

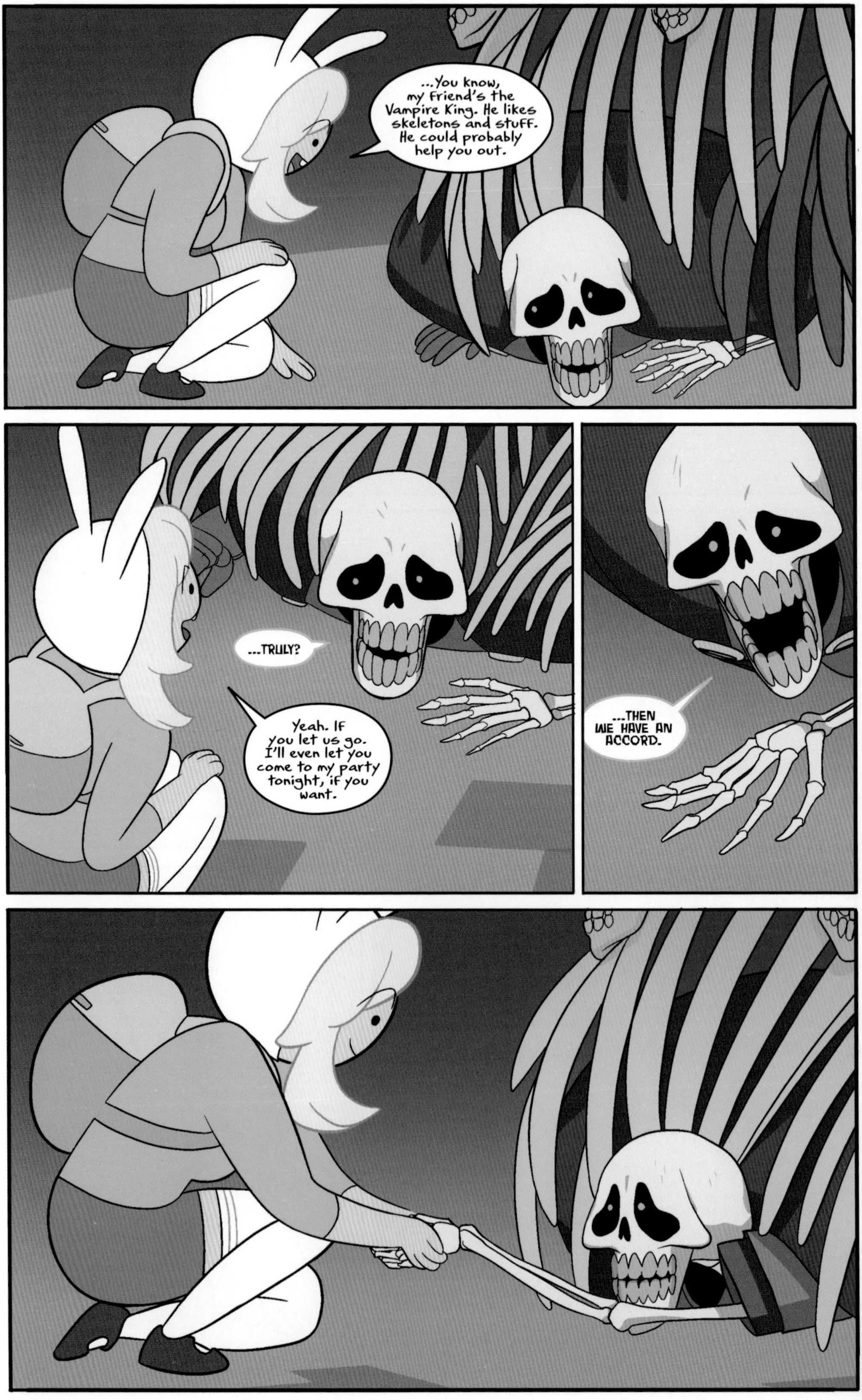
...You know, my friend's the Vampire King. He likes skeletons and stuff. He could probably help you out.
...TRULY?
Yeah. If you let us go. I'll even let you come to my party tonight, if you want.
...THEN WE HAVE AN ACCORD.

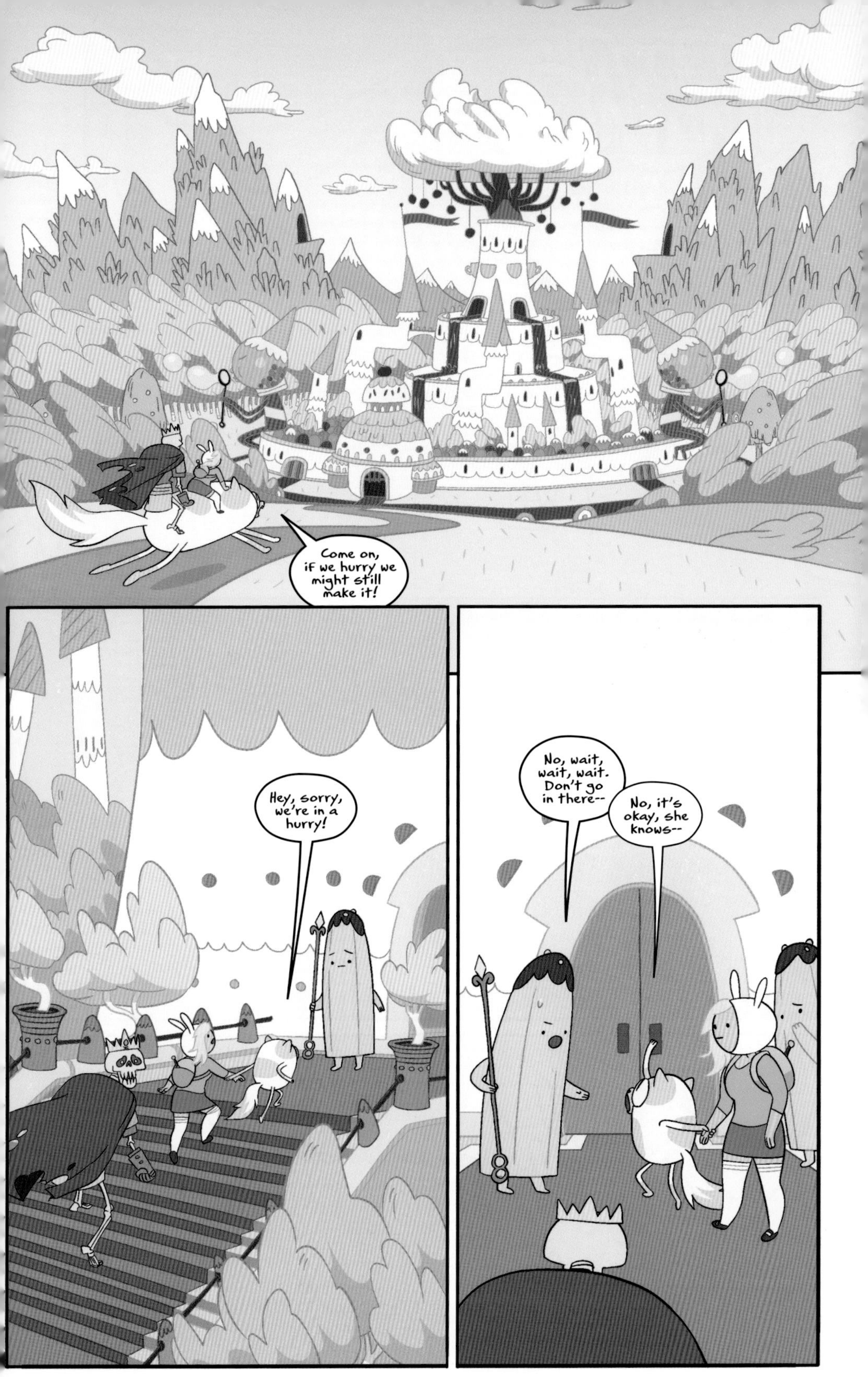
Come on, if we hurry we might still make it!
Hey, sorry, we're in a hurry!
No, wait, wait, wait. Don't go in there--
No, it's okay, she knows--

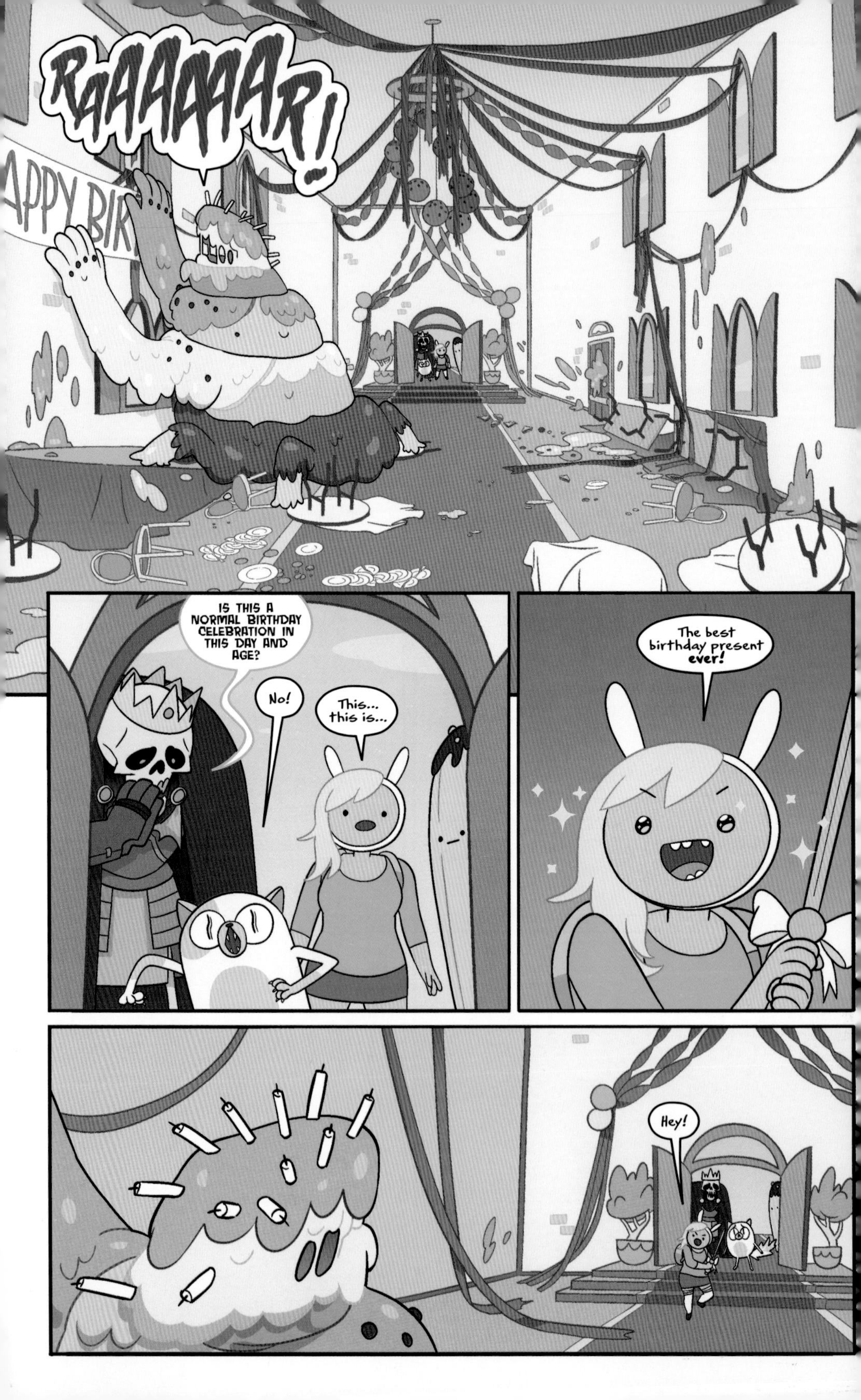
RAAAAAR!
APPY BIR
IS THIS A NORMAL BIRTHDAY CELEBRATION IN THIS DAY AND AGE?
No!
This... this is...
The best birthday present ever!
Hey!

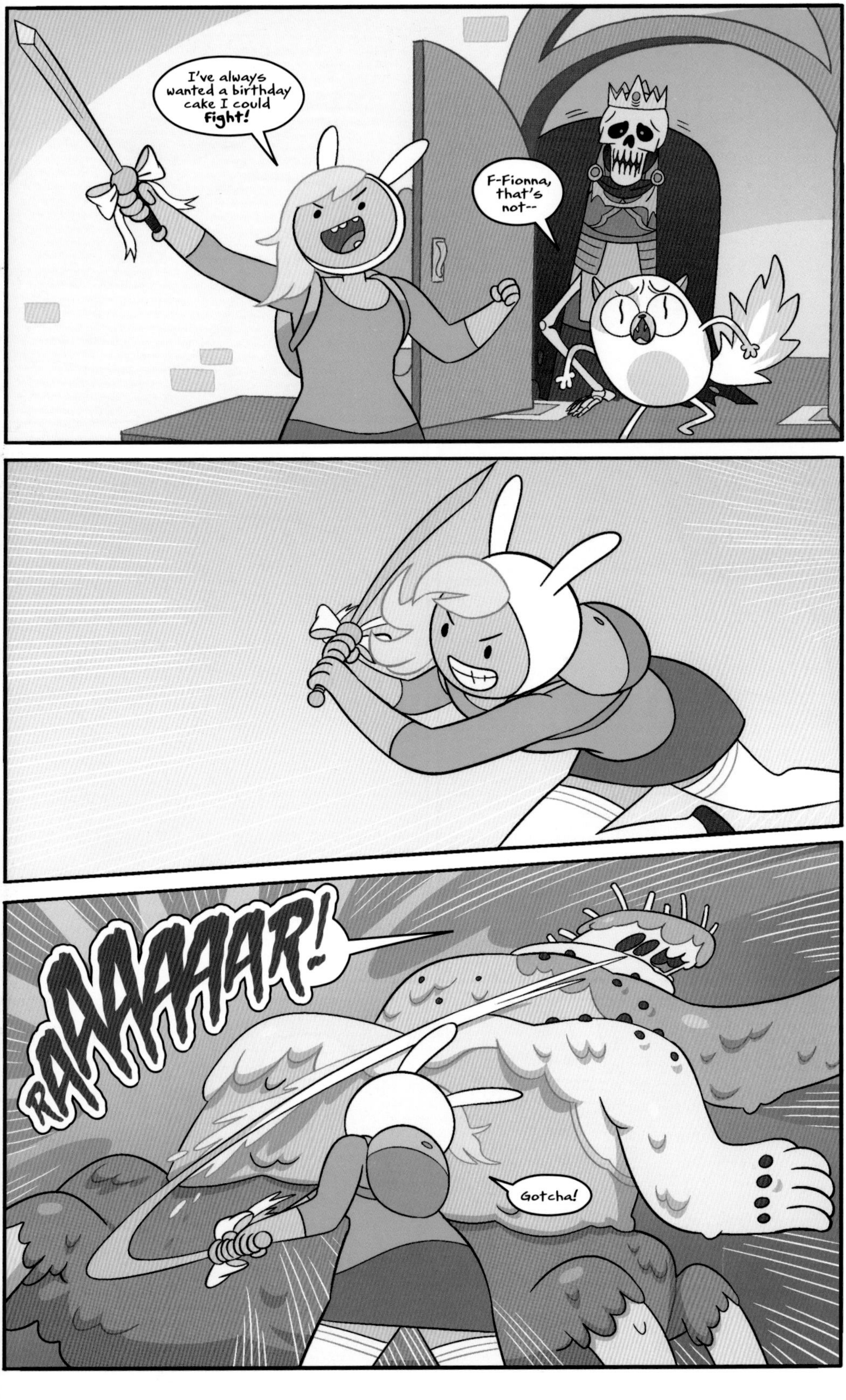
I've always wanted a birthday cake I could **fight!**
F-Fionna, that's not--
rAAAAAAR!
Gotcha!

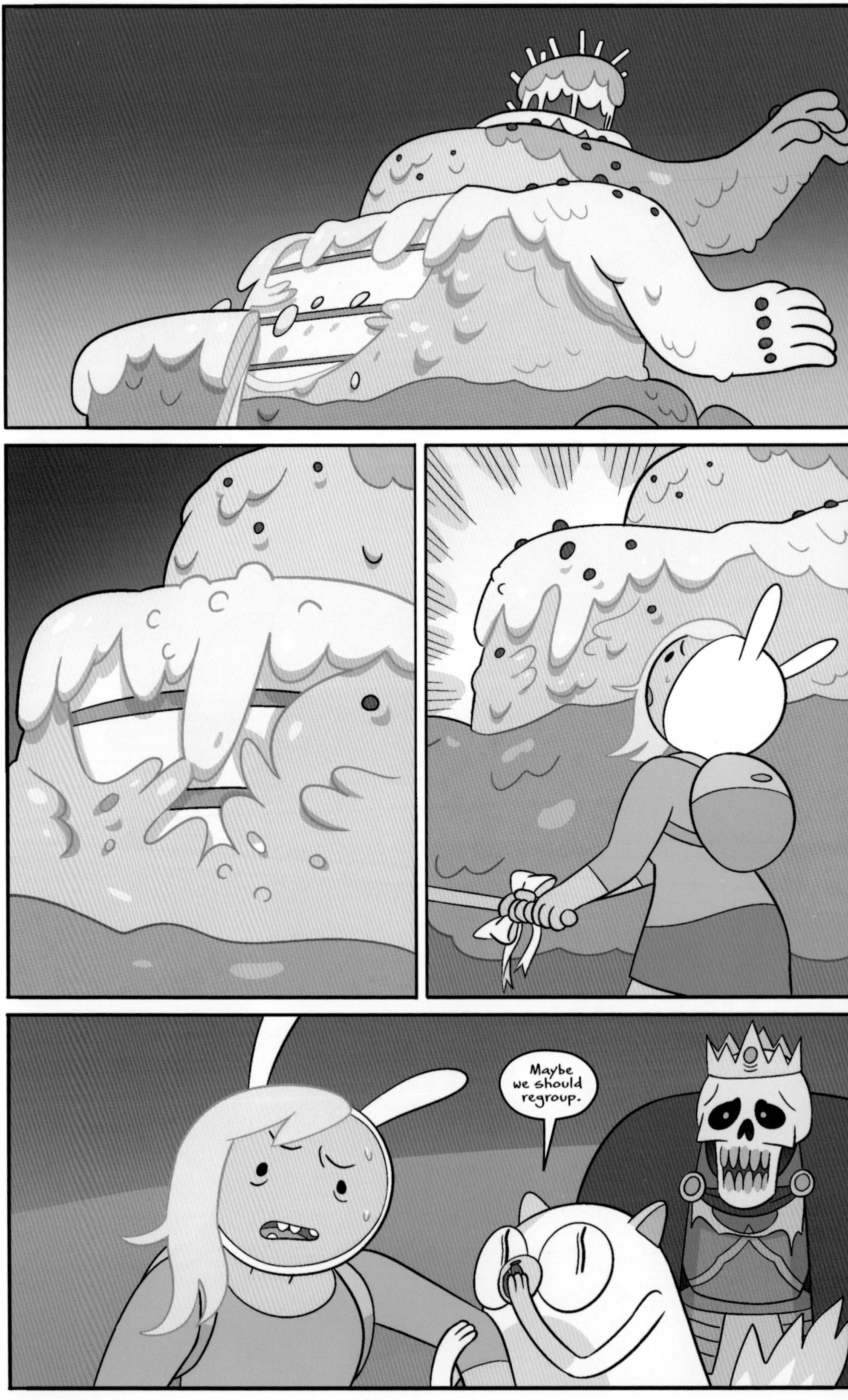
Maybe we should regroup.

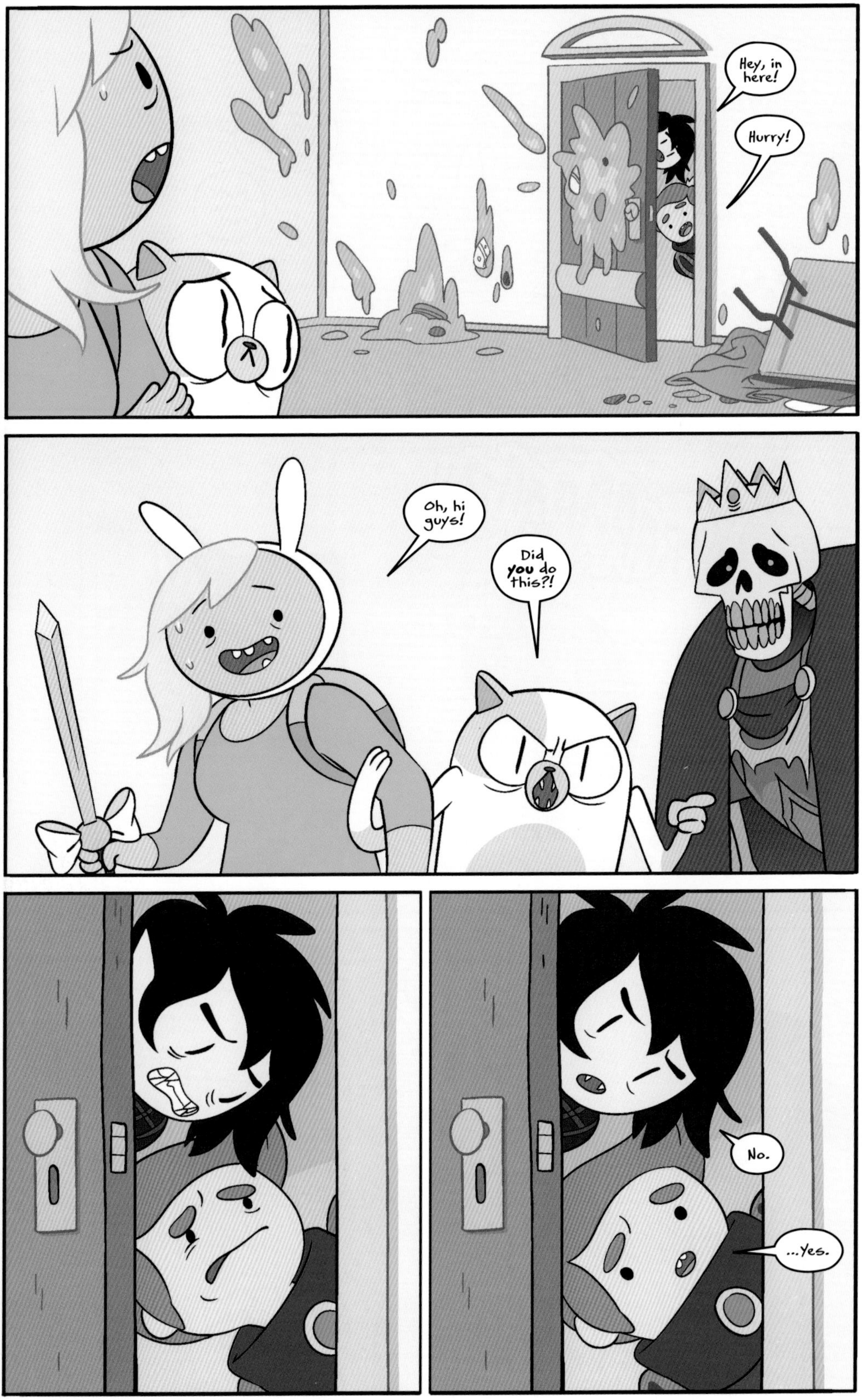
Hey, in here!
Hurry!
Oh, hi guys!
Did **you** do this?!
No.
...Yes.

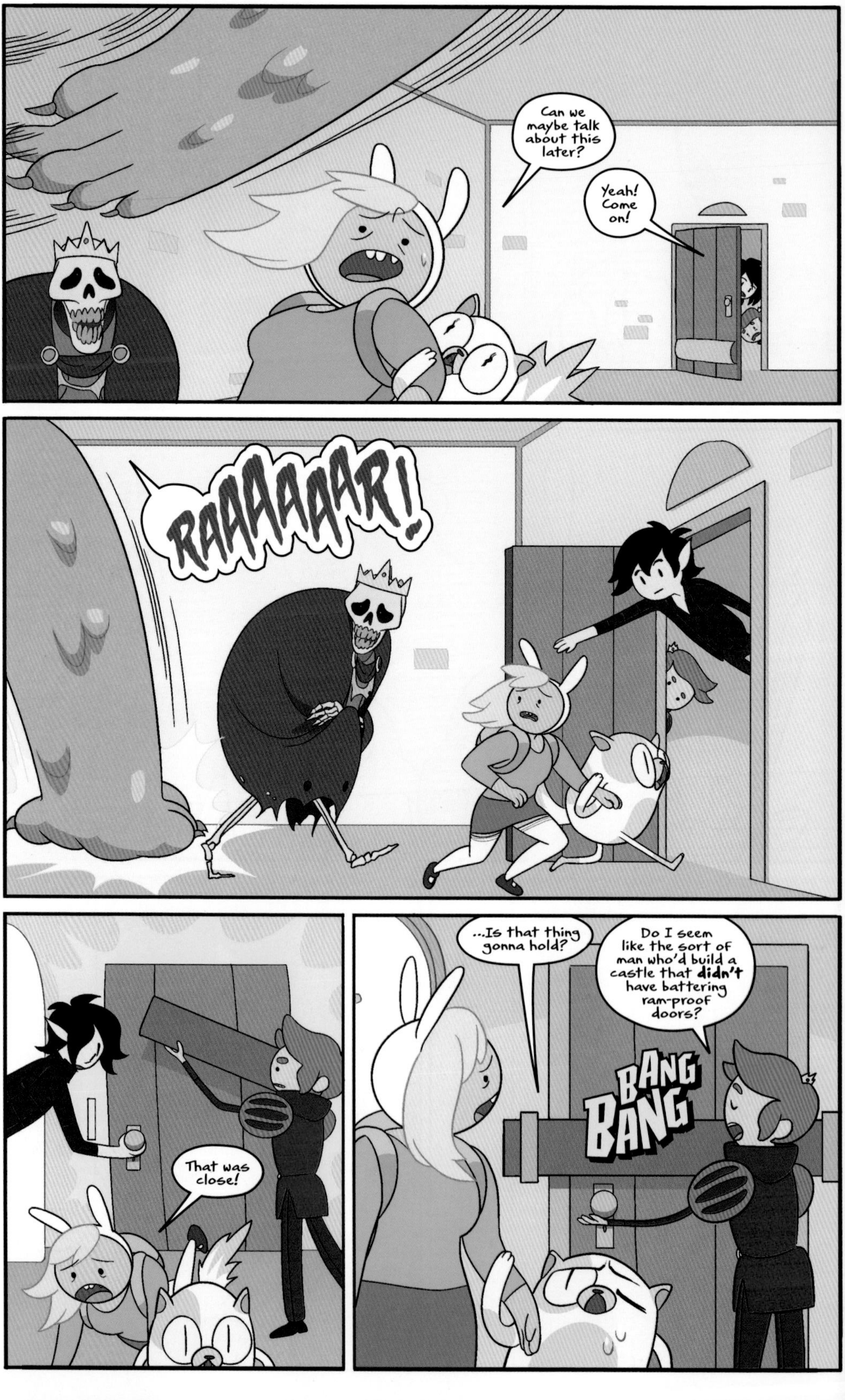

Can we maybe talk about this later?
Yeah! Come on!
RAAAAAAR!
That was close!
...Is that thing gonna hold?
Do I seem like the sort of man who'd build a castle that **didn't** have battering ram-proof doors?
BANG BANG

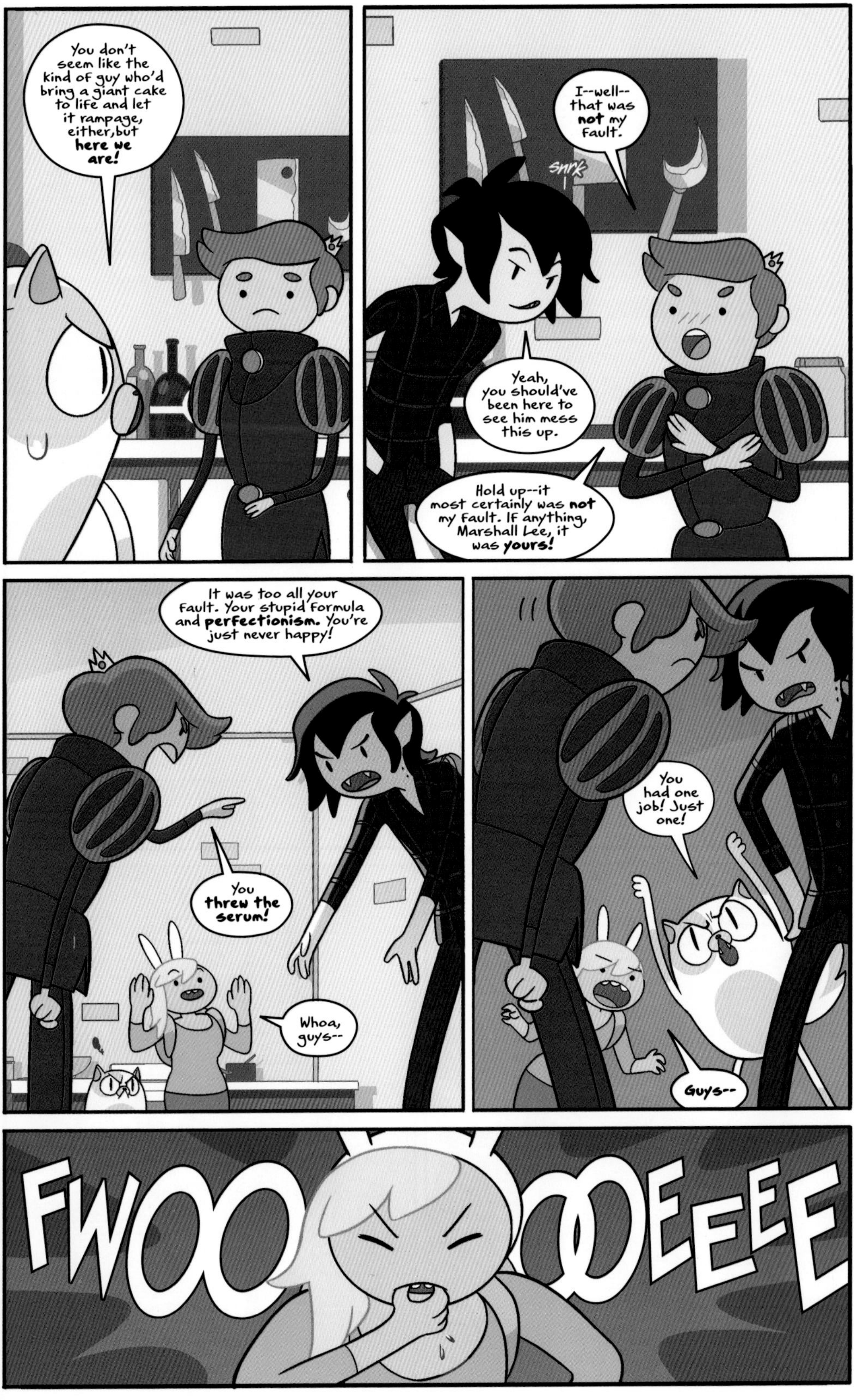
You don't seem like the kind of guy who'd bring a giant cake to life and let it rampage, either, but **here we are!**
I--well-- that was **not** my fault.
SNRK
Yeah, you should've been here to see him mess this up.
Hold up--it most certainly was **not** my fault. If anything, Marshall Lee, it was **yours!**
It was too all your fault. Your stupid formula and **perfectionism.** You're just never happy!
You **threw the serum!**
Whoa, guys--
You had one job! Just one!
Guys--
FWOOOOEEEE

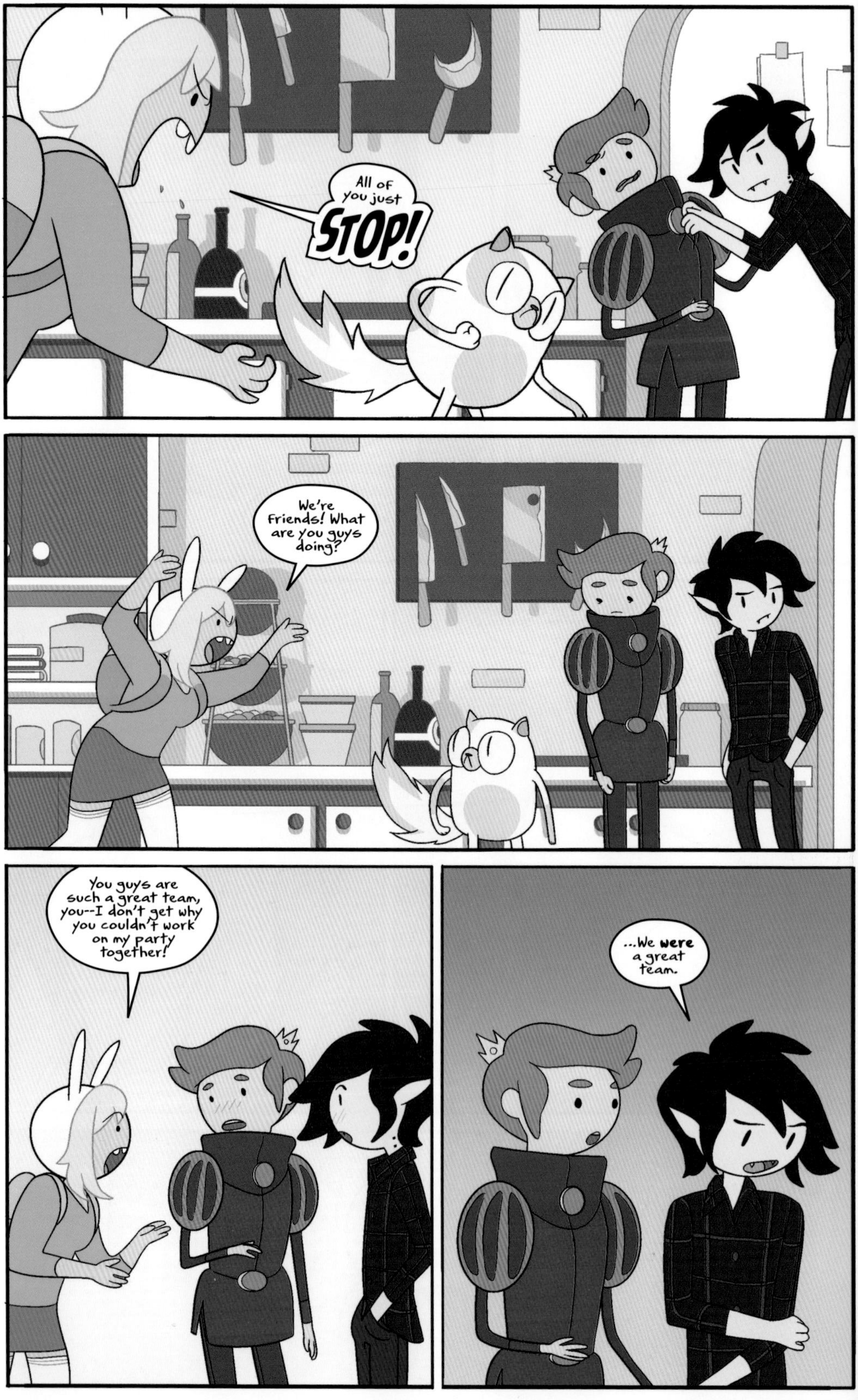
All of you just STOP!
We're Friends! What are you guys doing?
You guys are such a great team, you--I don't get why you couldn't work on my party together!
...We **were** a great team.

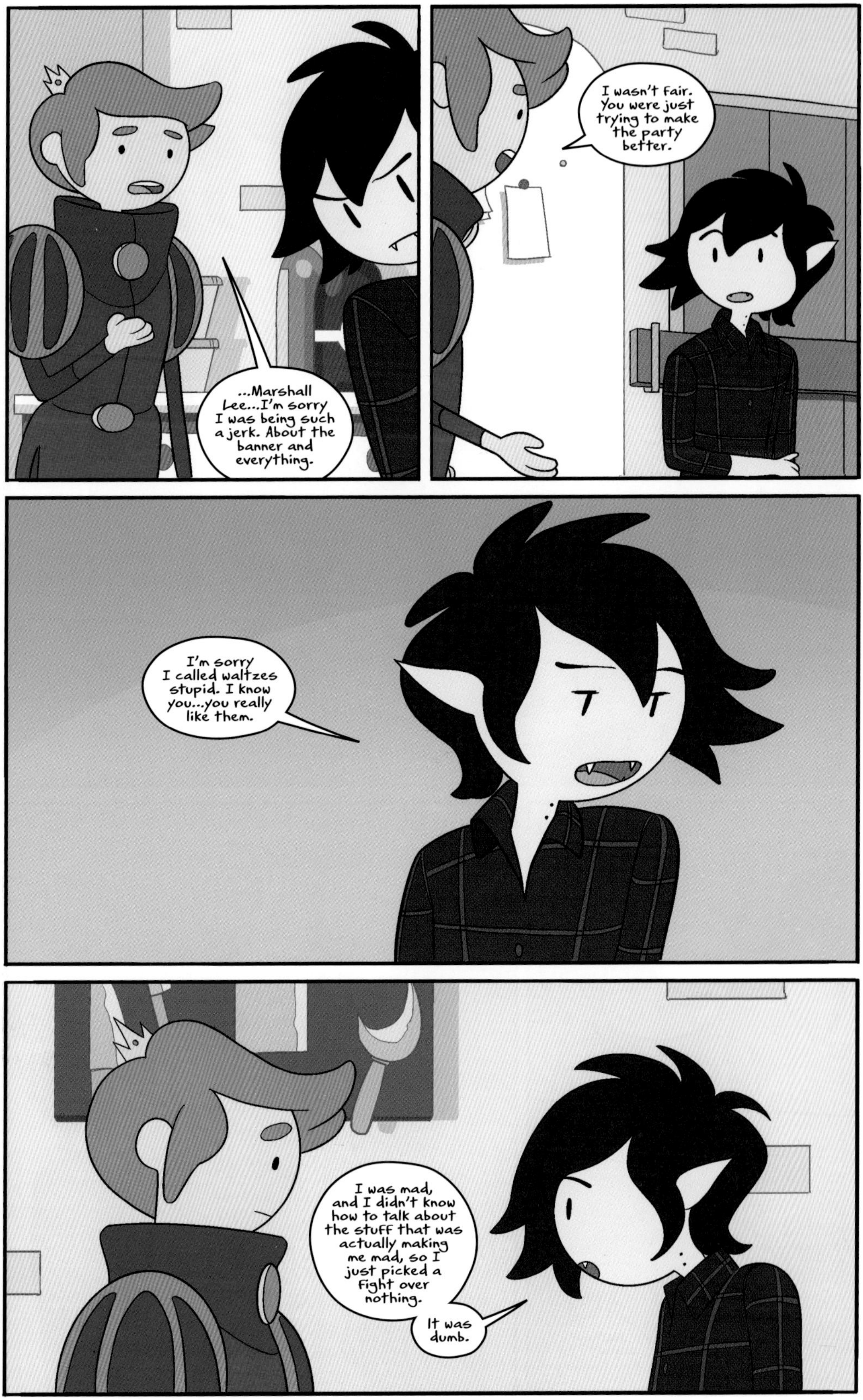
...Marshall Lee...I'm sorry I was being such a jerk. About the banner and everything.
I wasn't fair. You were just trying to make the party better.
I'm sorry I called waltzes stupid. I know you...you really like them.
I was mad, and I didn't know how to talk about the stuff that was actually making me mad, so I just picked a fight over nothing.
It was dumb.

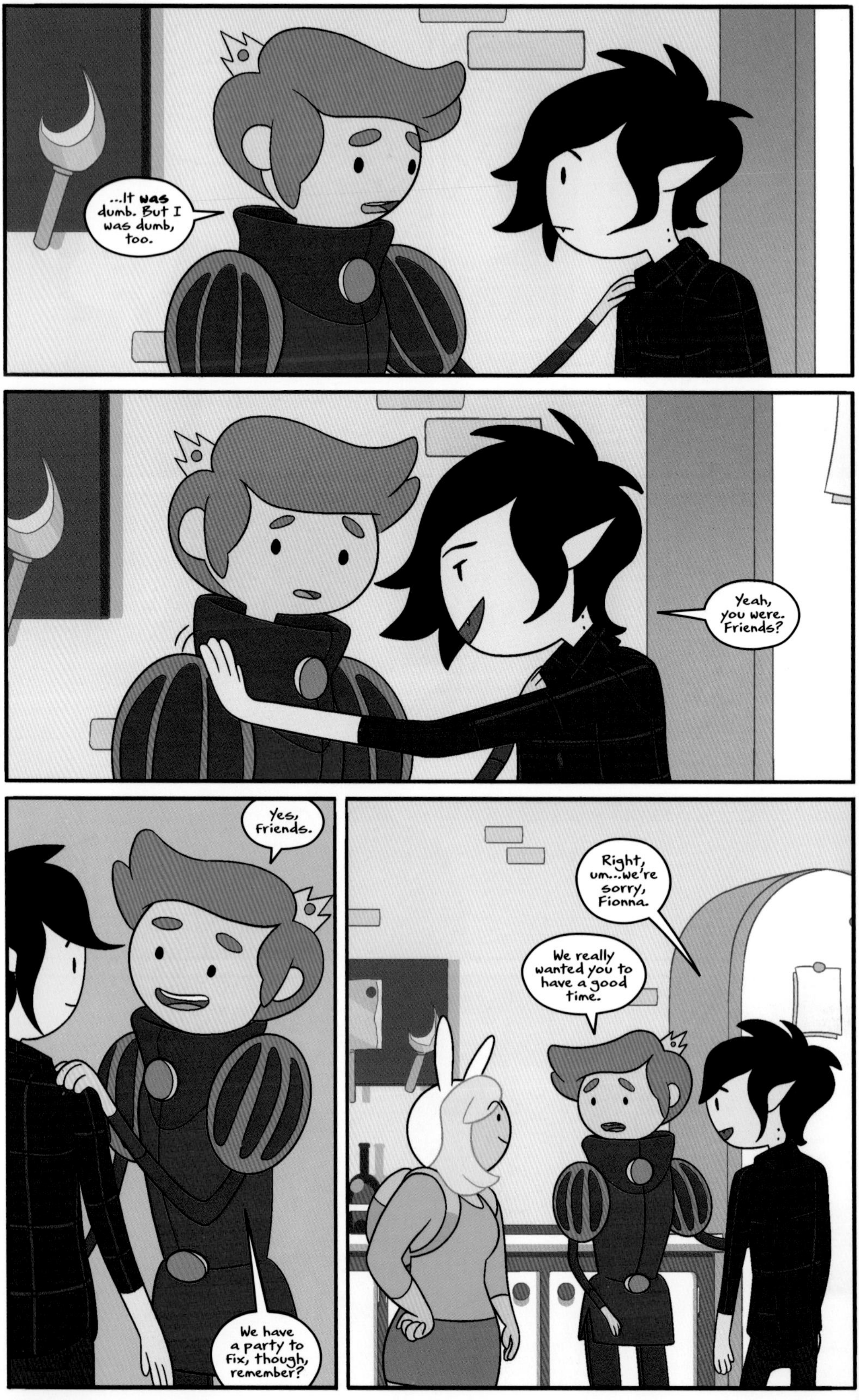
...It **was** dumb. But I was dumb, too.
Yeah, you were. Friends?
Yes, Friends.
We have a party to fix, though, remember?
Right, um...we're sorry, Fionna.
We really wanted you to have a good time.

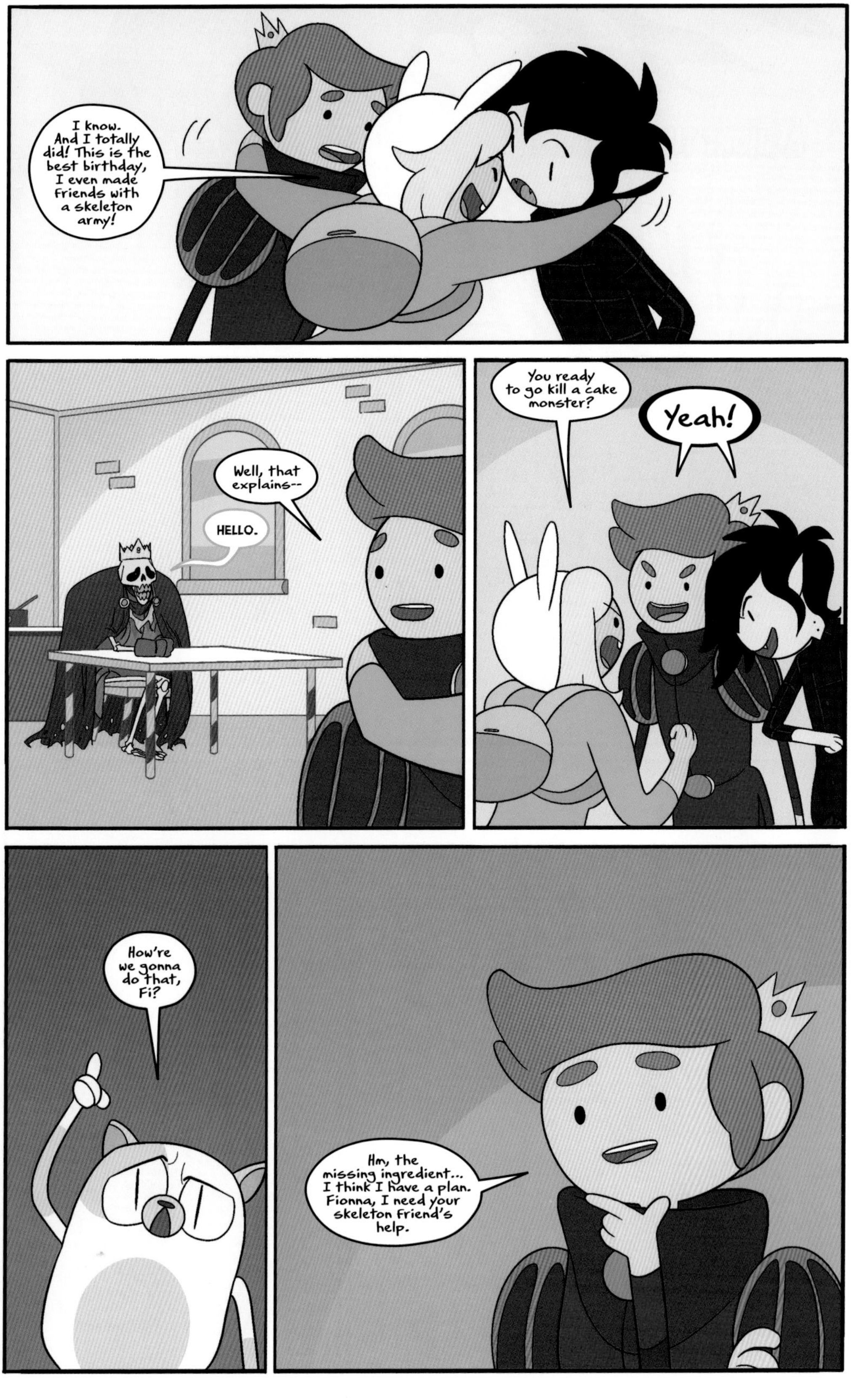
I know. And I totally did! This is the best birthday, I even made friends with a skeleton army!
Well, that explains--
HELLO.
You ready to go kill a cake monster?
Yeah!
How're we gonna do that, Fi?
Hm, the missing ingredient... I think I have a plan. Fionna, I need your skeleton friend's help.

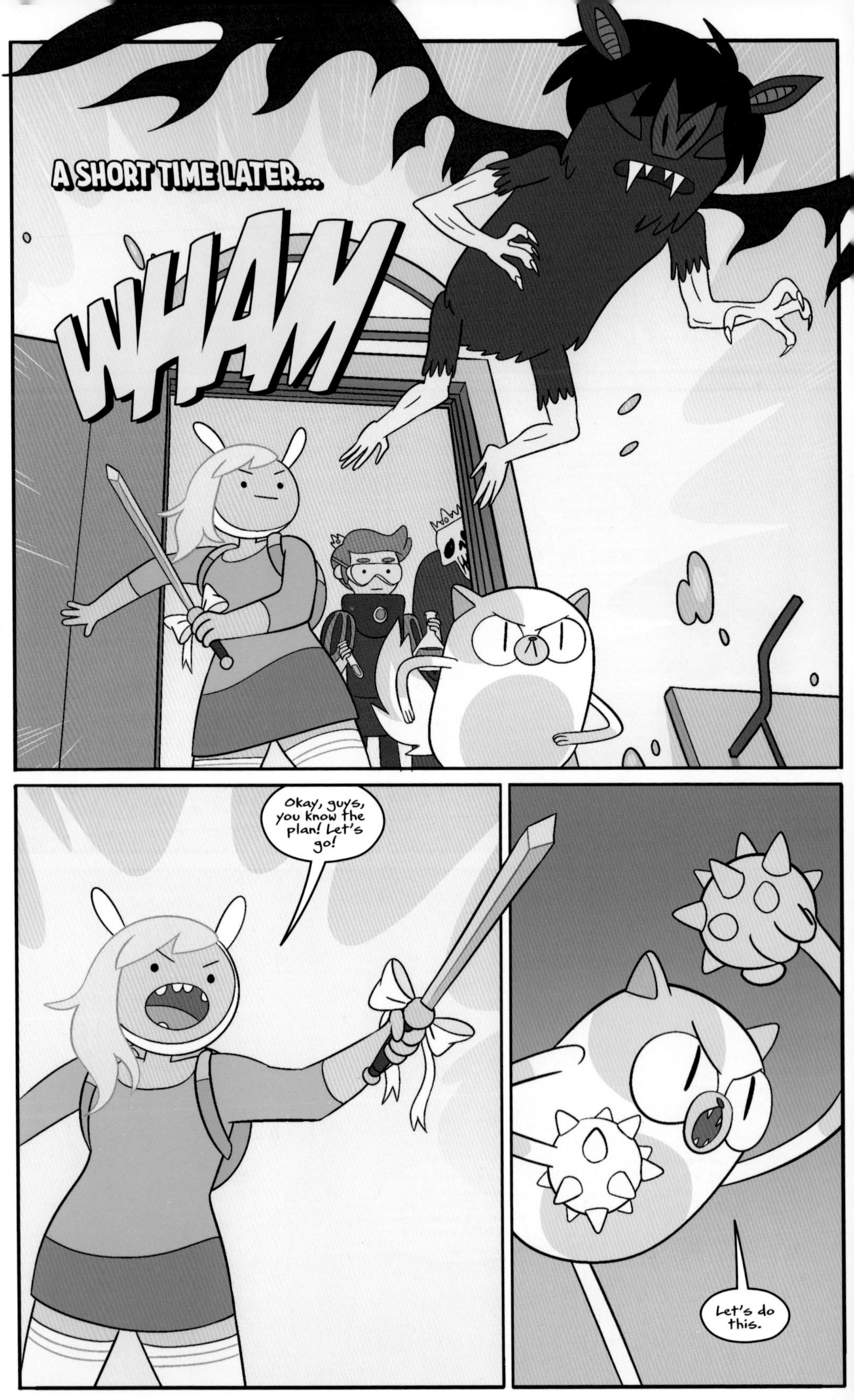
A SHORT TIME LATER...
WHAM
Okay, guys, you know the plan! Let's go!
Let's do this.

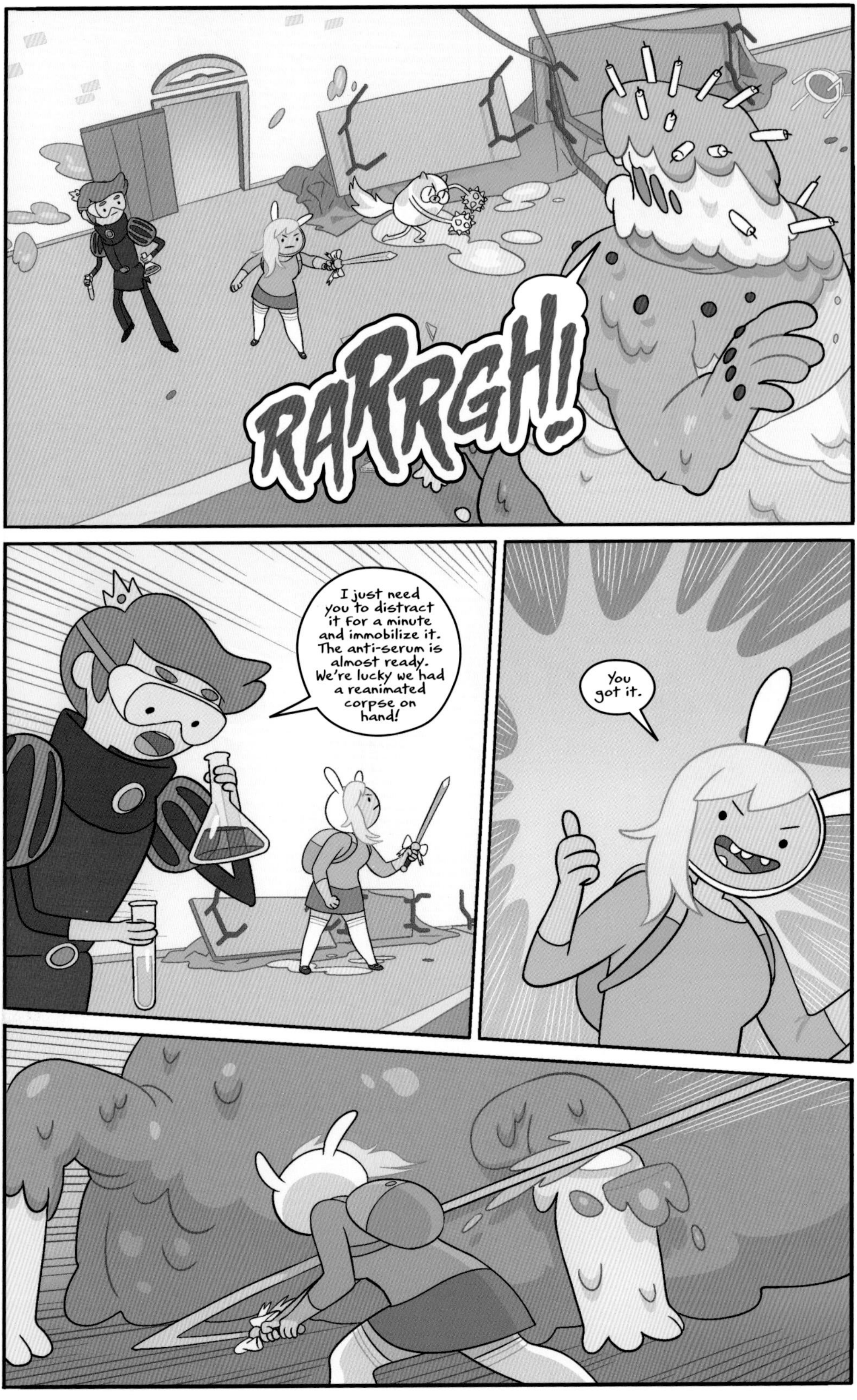
RARRGH!
I just need you to distract it for a minute and immobilize it. The anti-serum is almost ready. We're lucky we had a reanimated corpse on hand!
You got it.

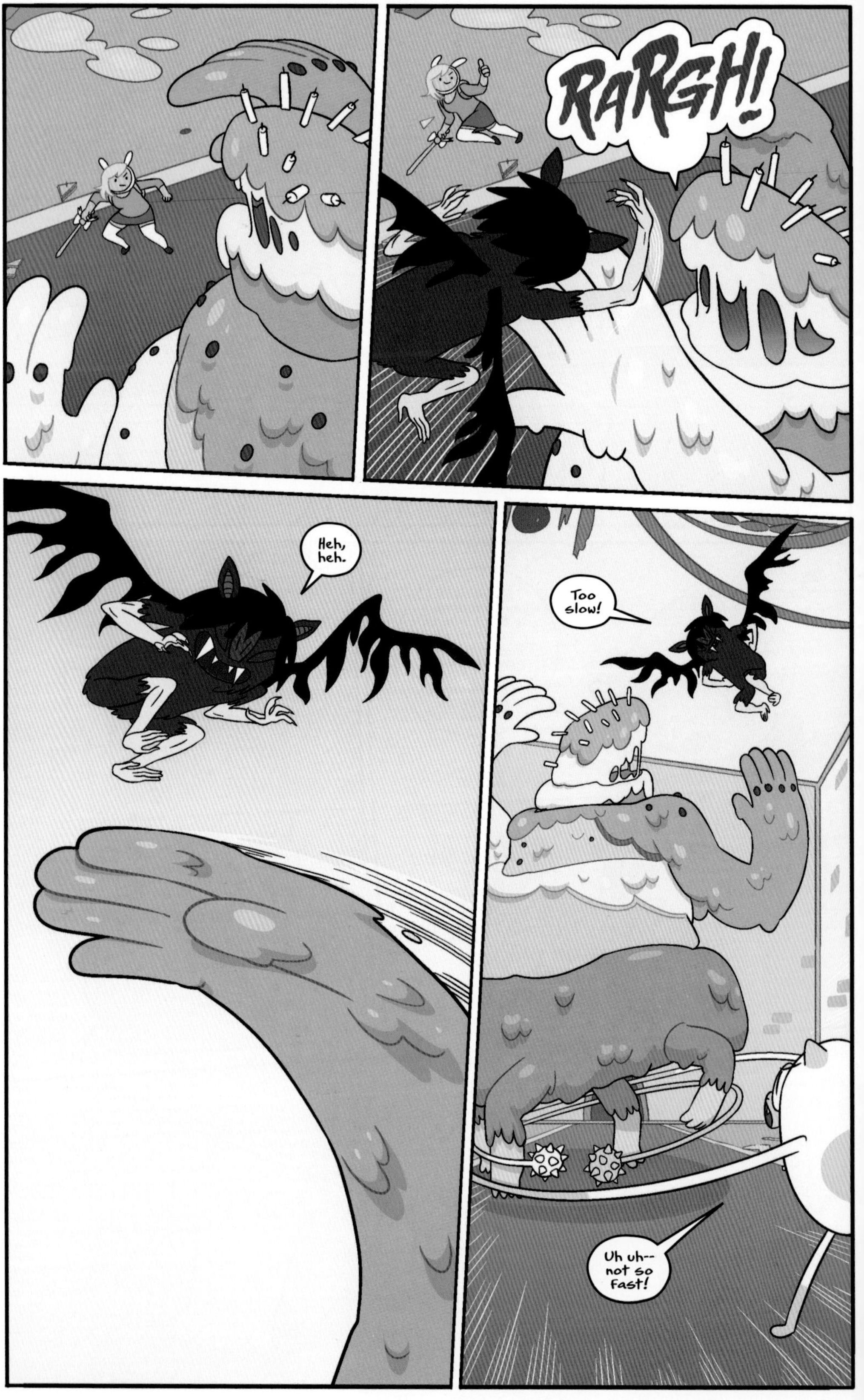
RARGH!!
Heh, heh.
Too slow!
Uh uh--not so fast!

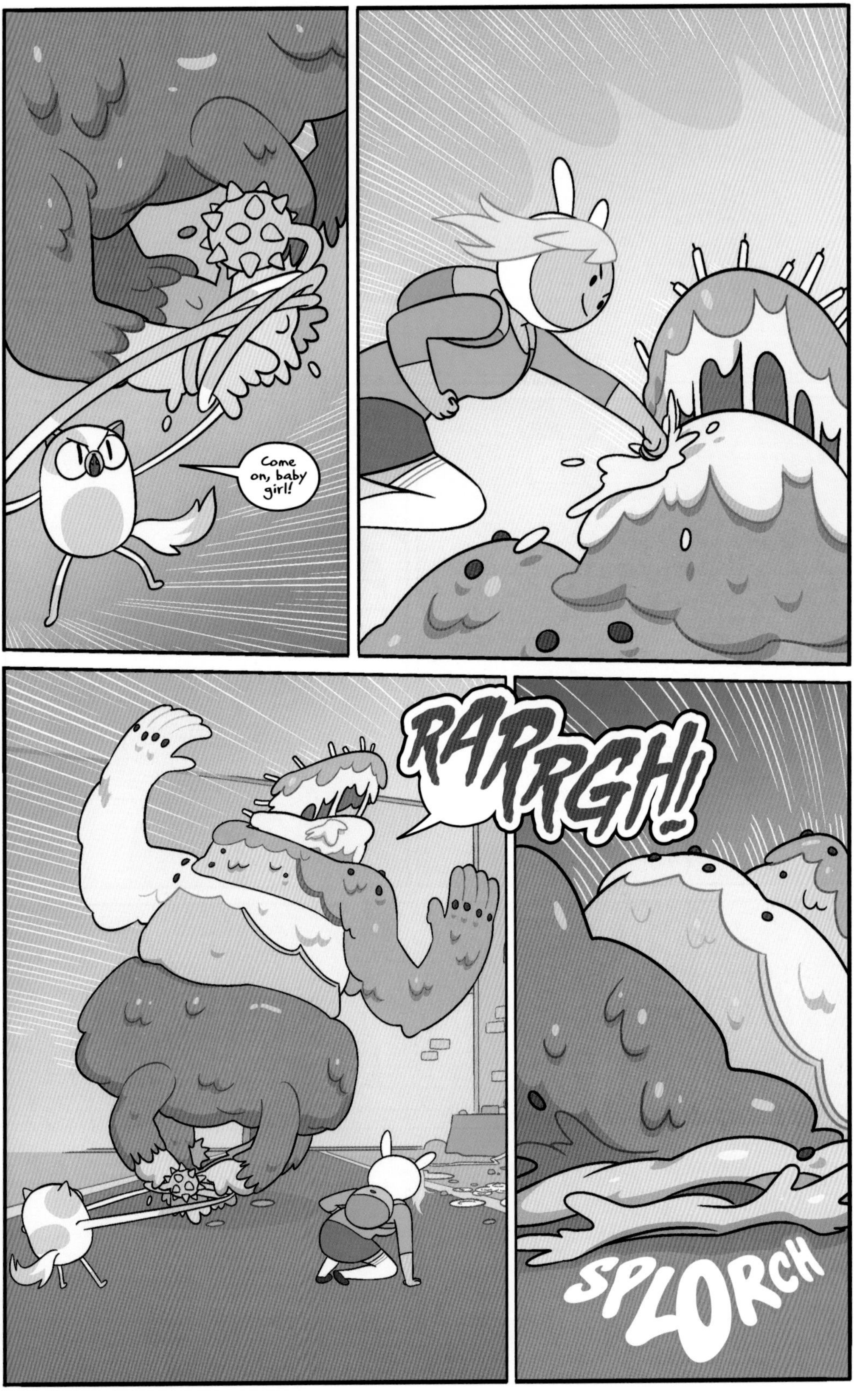
Come on, baby girl!
RARRGH!
SPLORCH

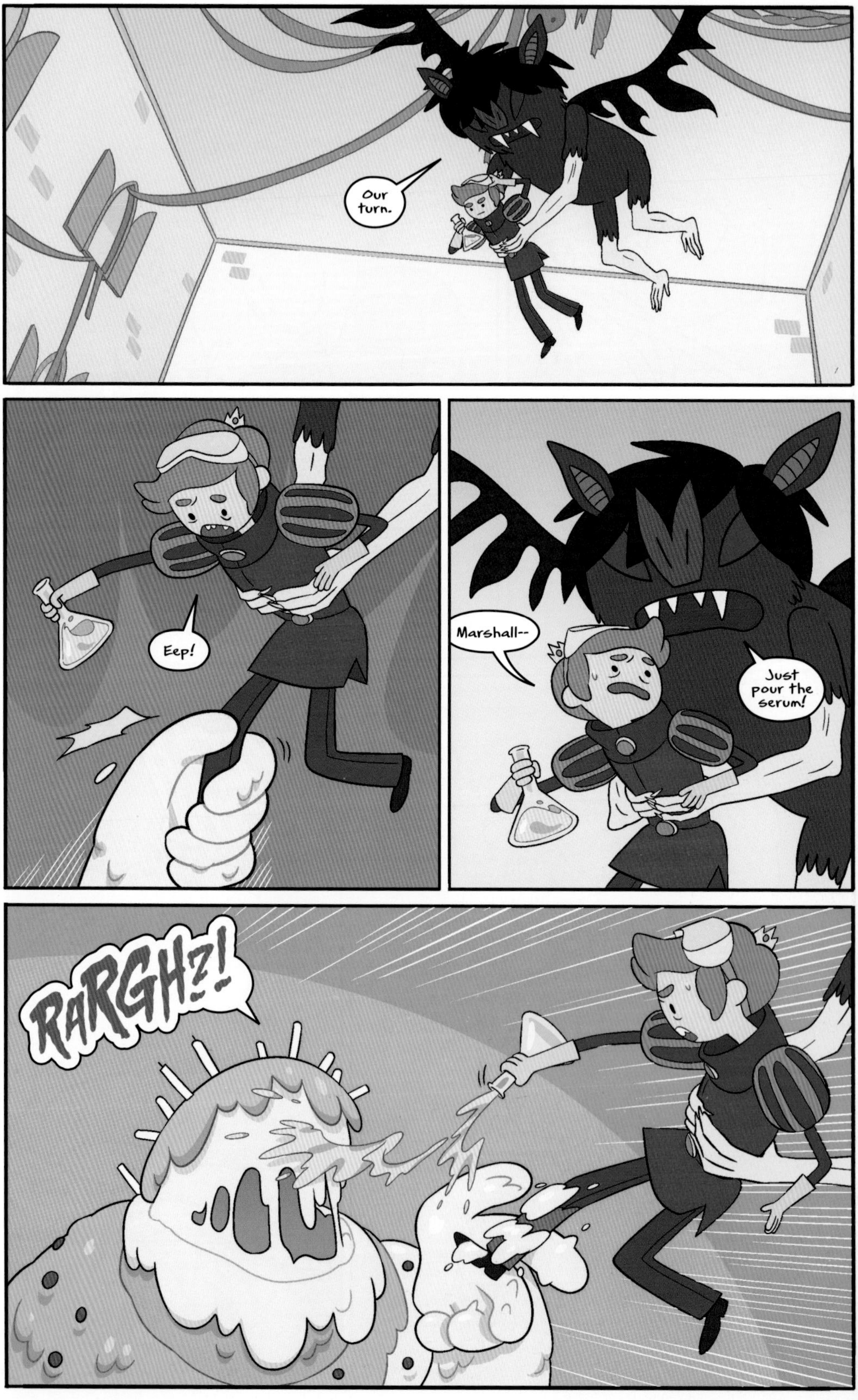
Our turn.
Eep!
Marshall--
Just pour the serum!
RARGHZ!

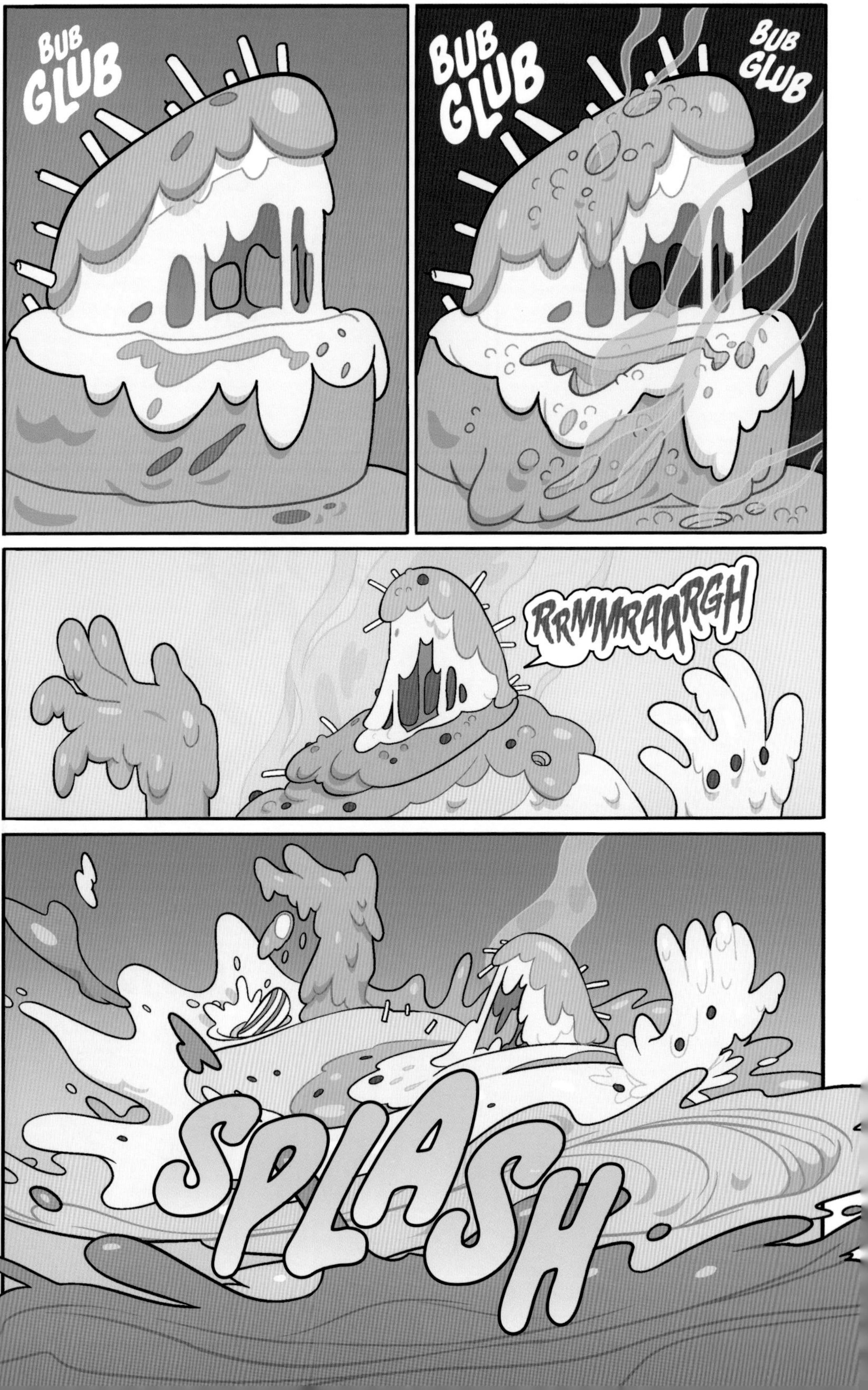
BUB GLUB
BUB GLUB
BUB GLUB
RRMMRAAARGH
SPLASH

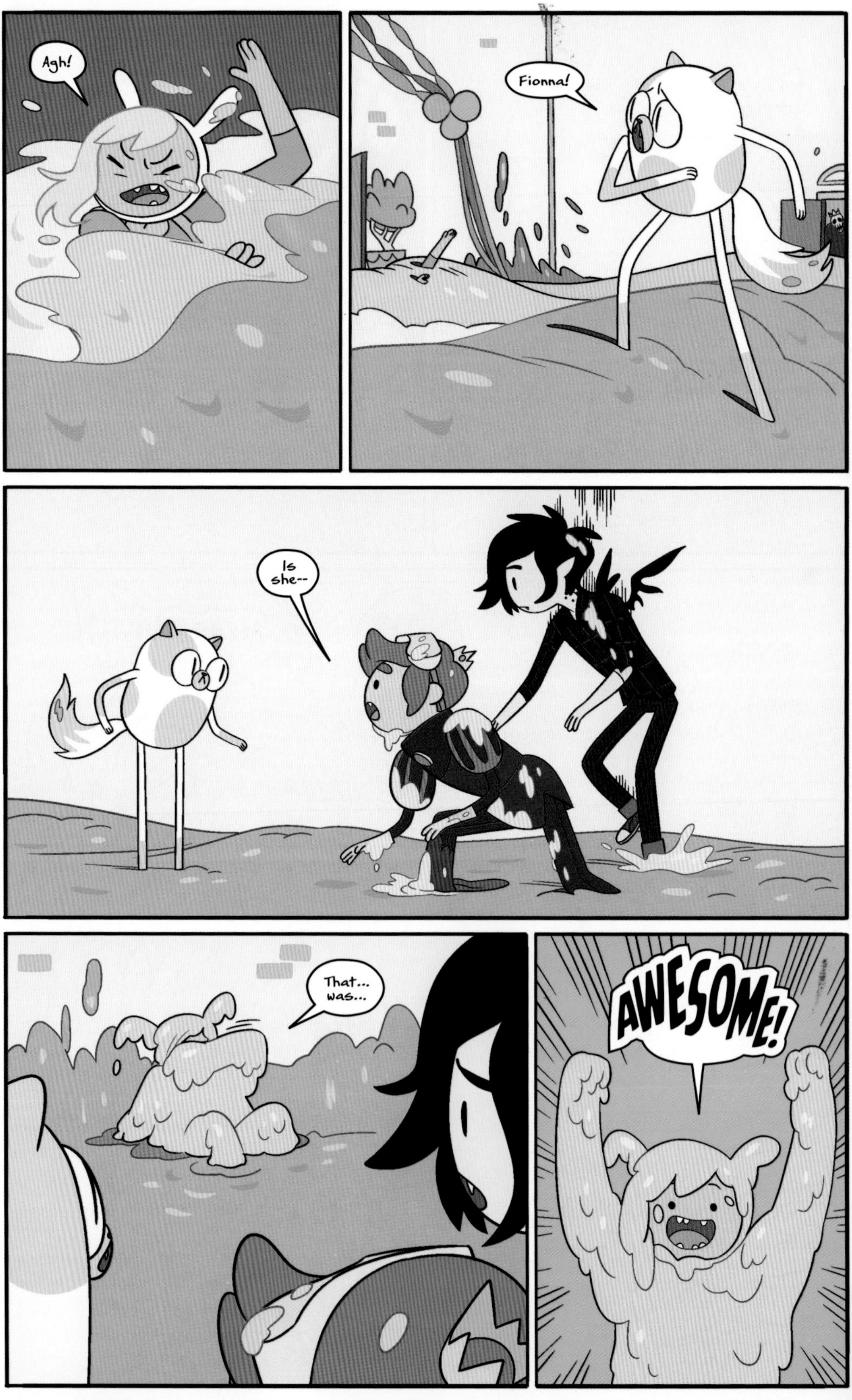
Agh!
Fionna!
Is she--
That... was...
AWESOME!

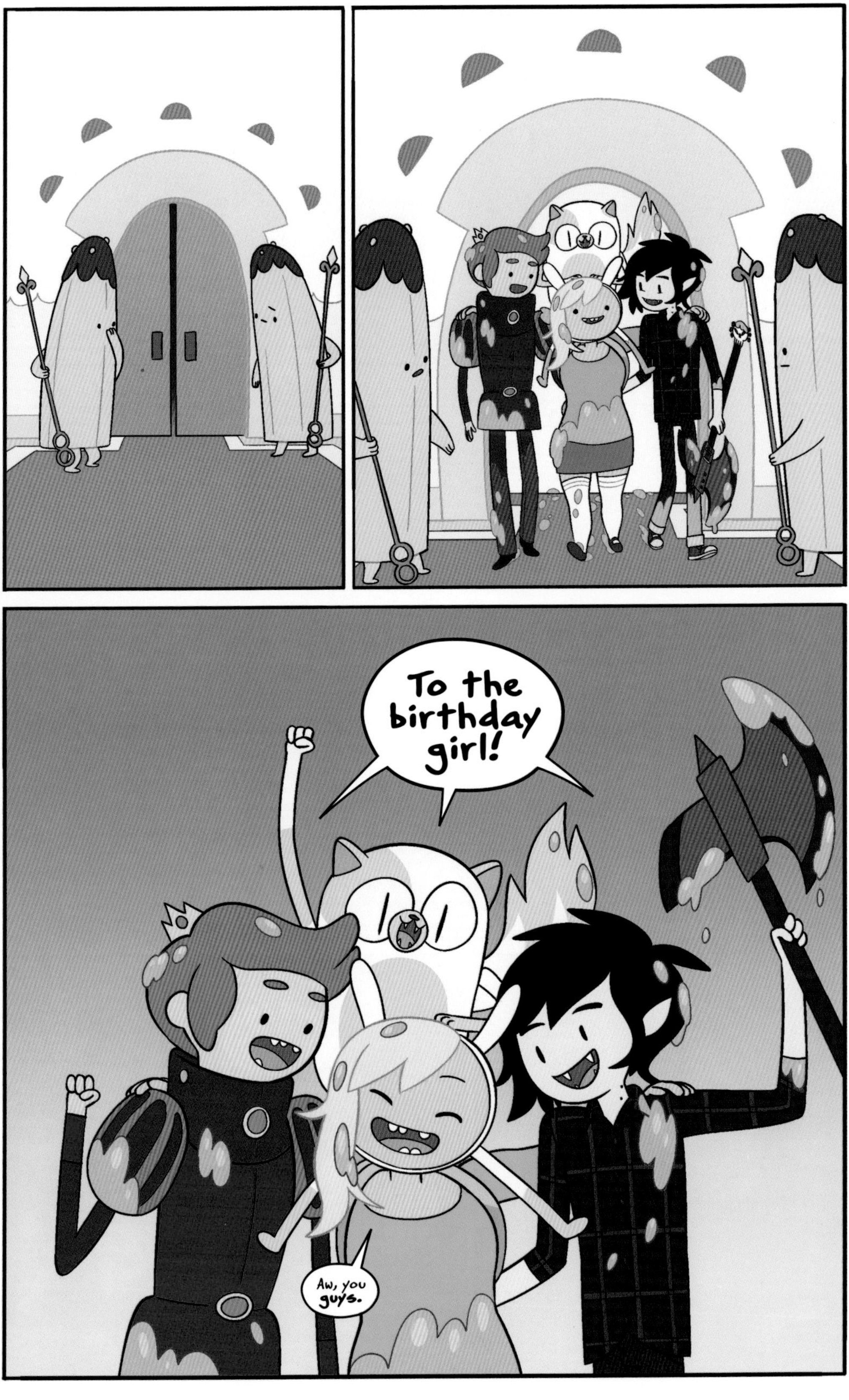
To the birthday girl!
Aw, you guys.

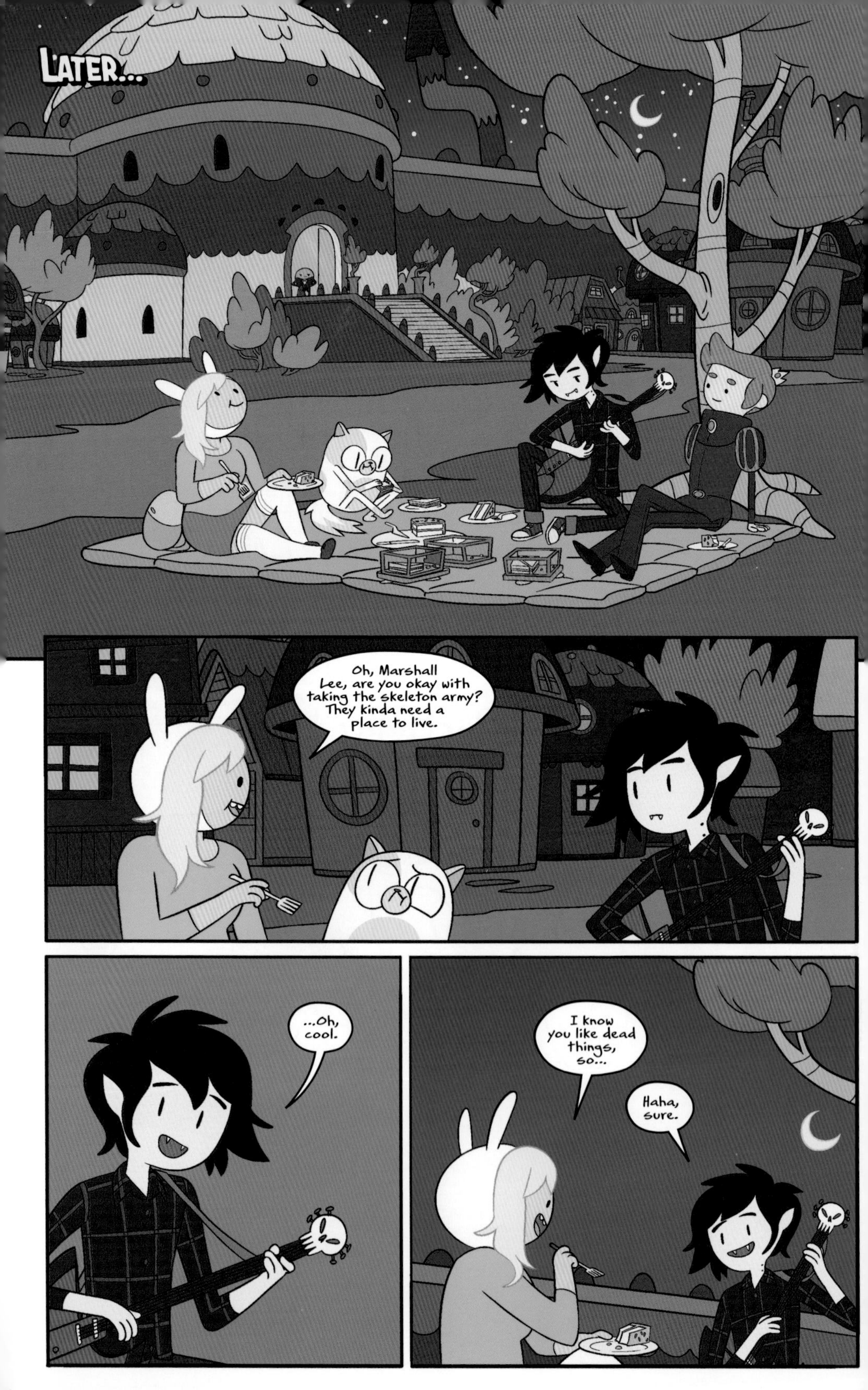
LATER...
Oh, Marshall Lee, are you okay with taking the skeleton army? They kinda need a place to live.
...Oh, cool.
I know you like dead things, so...
Haha, sure.

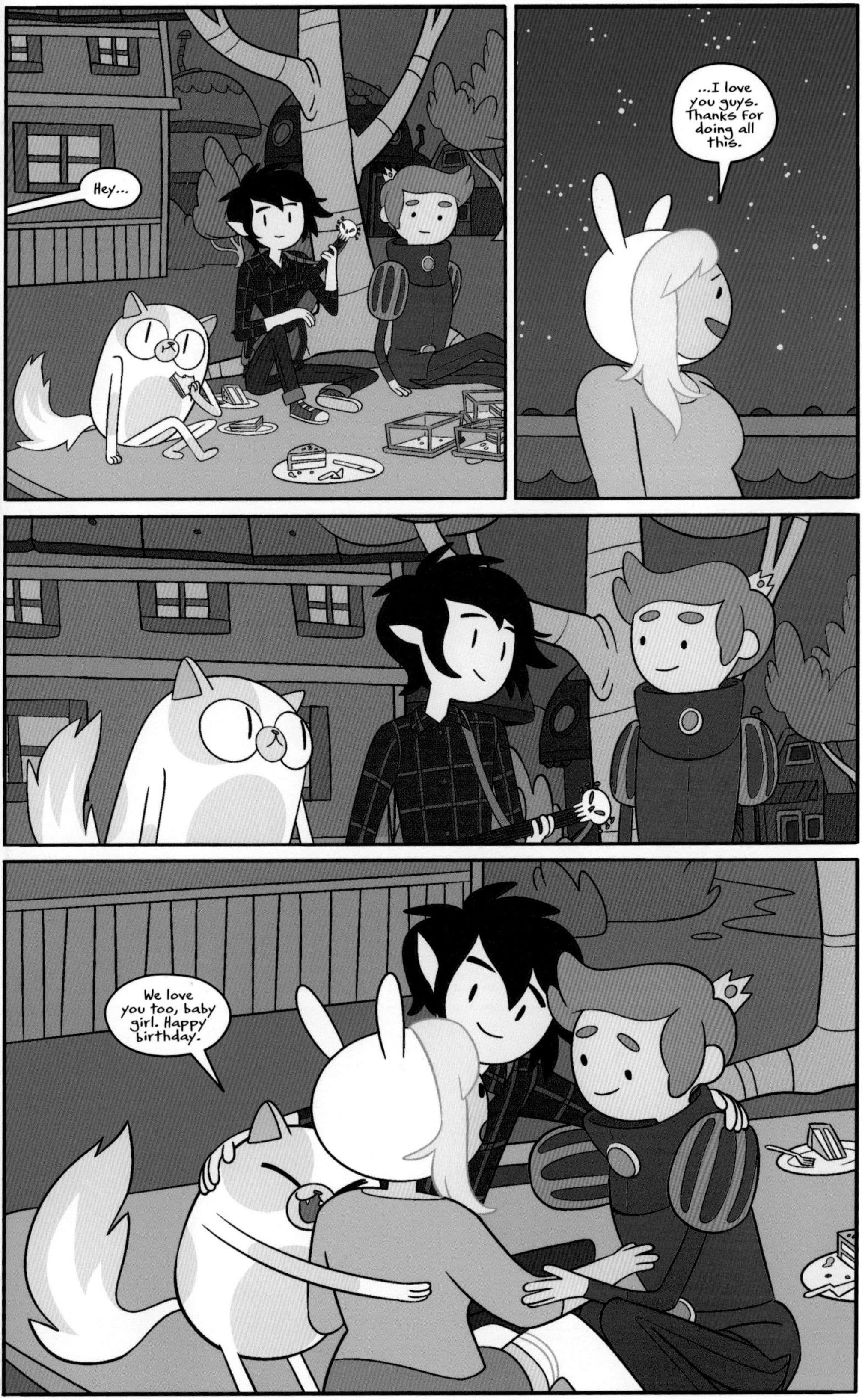
Hey...
...I love you guys. Thanks for doing all this.
We love you too, baby girl. Happy birthday.

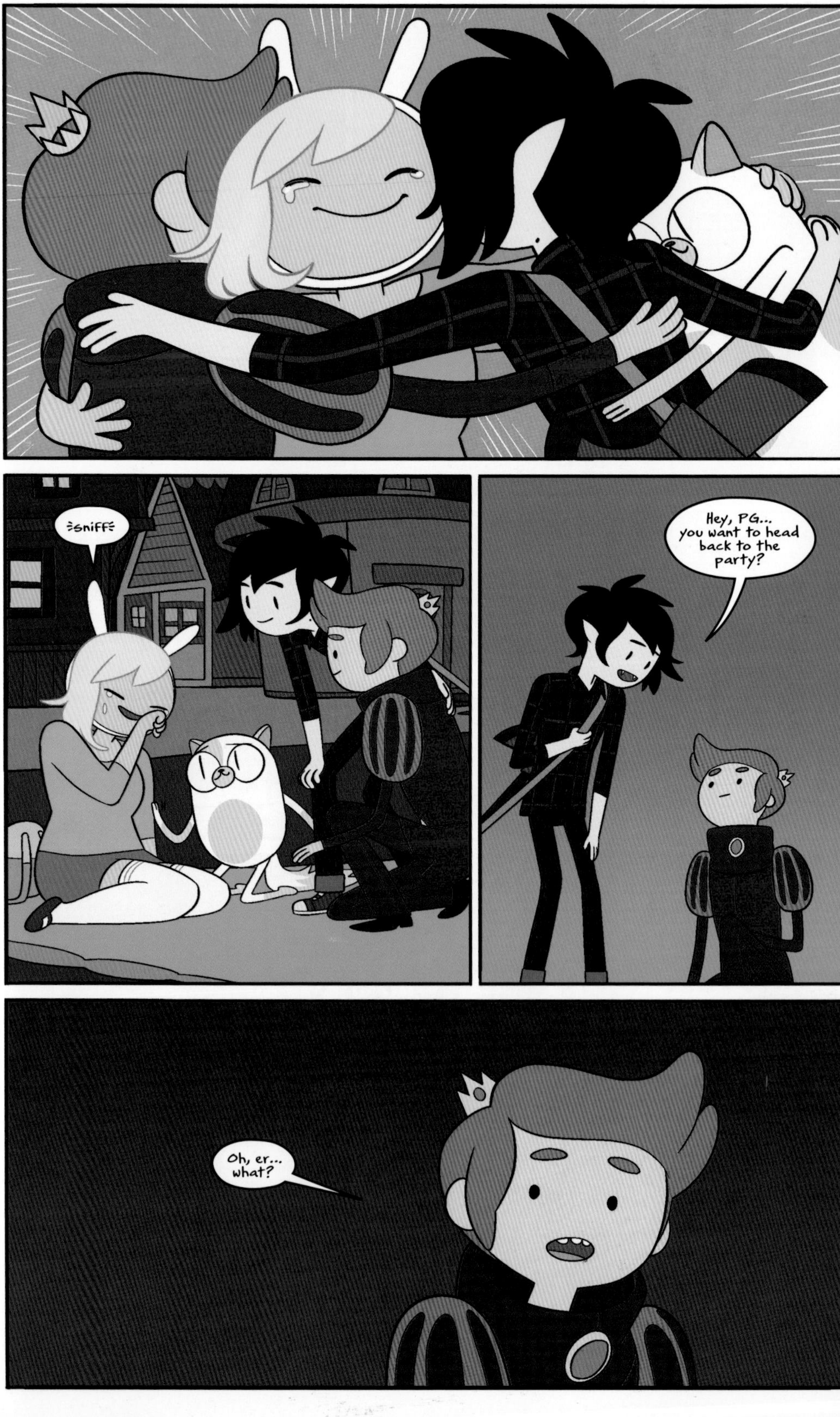

sniff
Hey, PG... you want to head back to the party?
Oh, er... what?

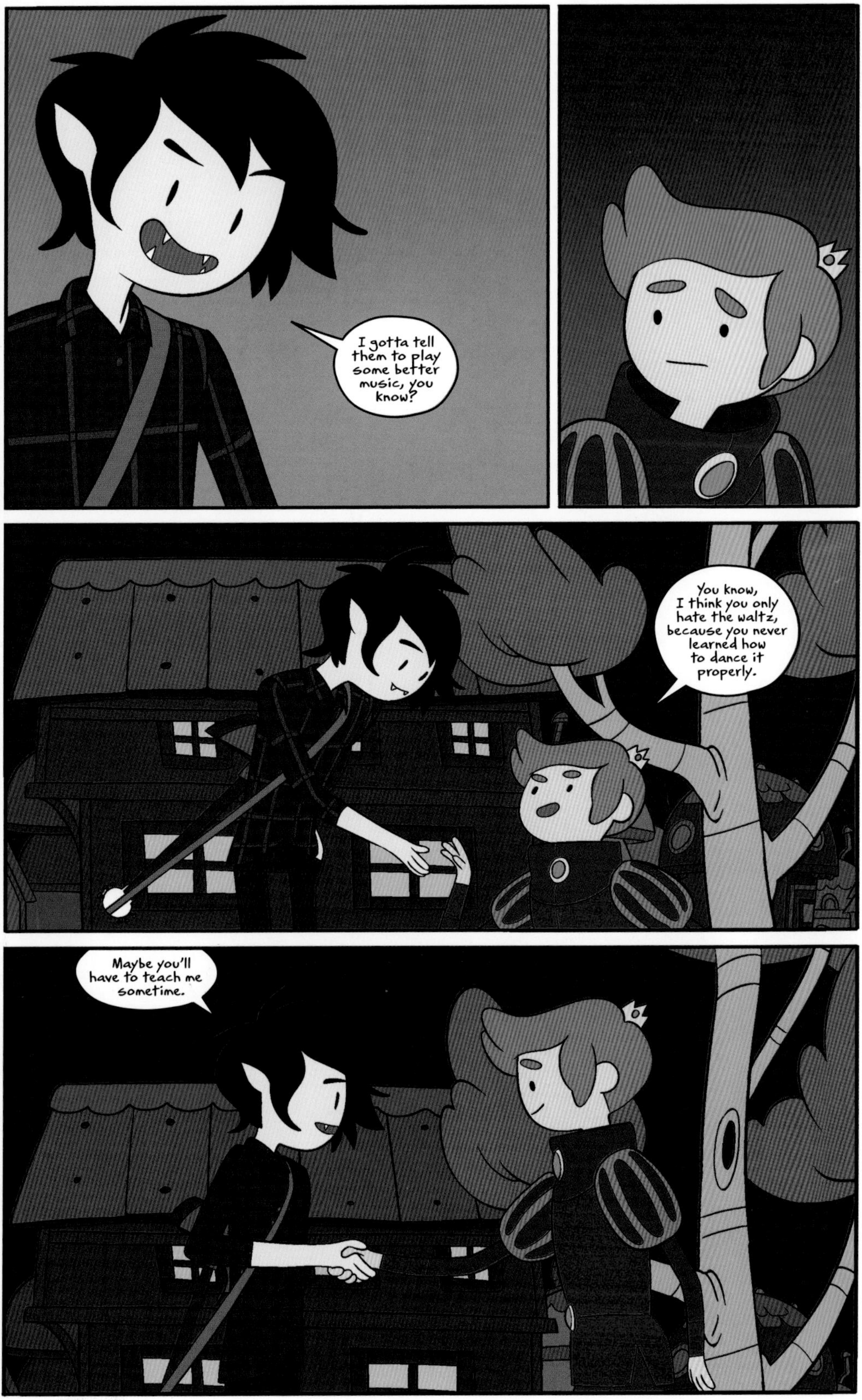
I gotta tell them to play some better music, you know?
You know, I think you only hate the waltz, because you never learned how to dance it properly.
Maybe you'll have to teach me sometime.

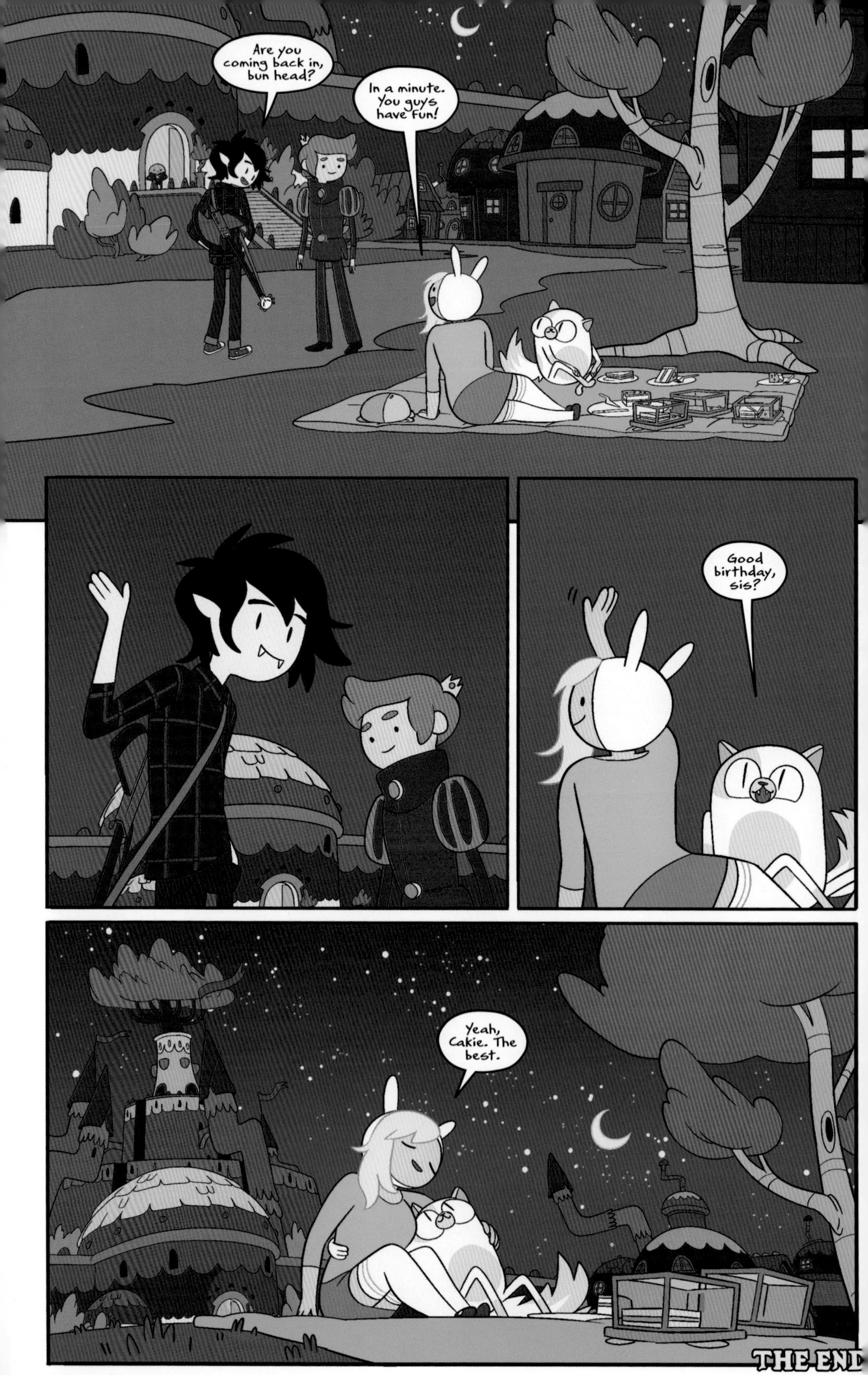
Are you coming back in, bun head?
In a minute. You guys have fun!
Good birthday, sis?
Yeah, Cakie. The best.
THE END

DISCOVER MORE
ADVENTURE TIME

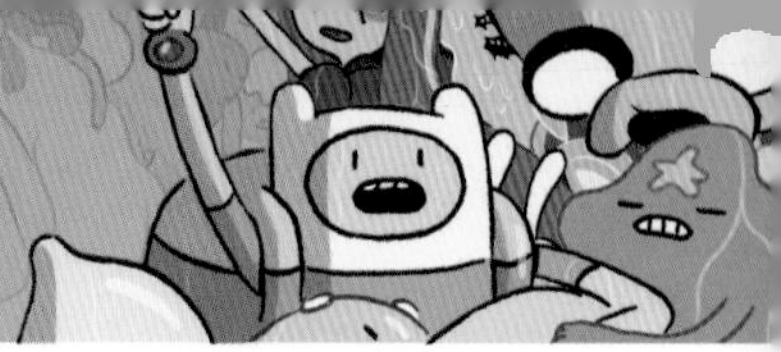

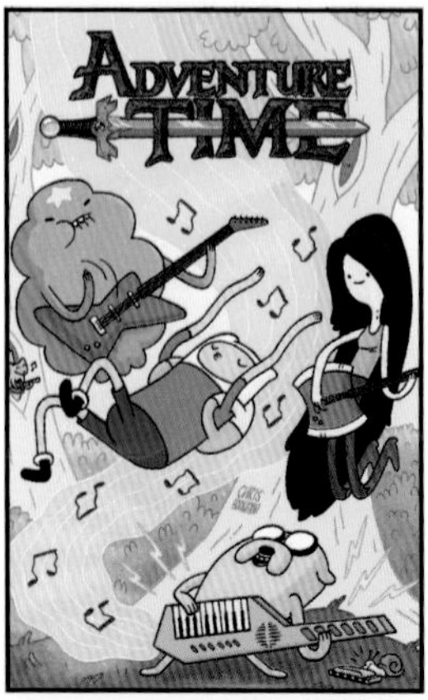

ADVENTURE TIME

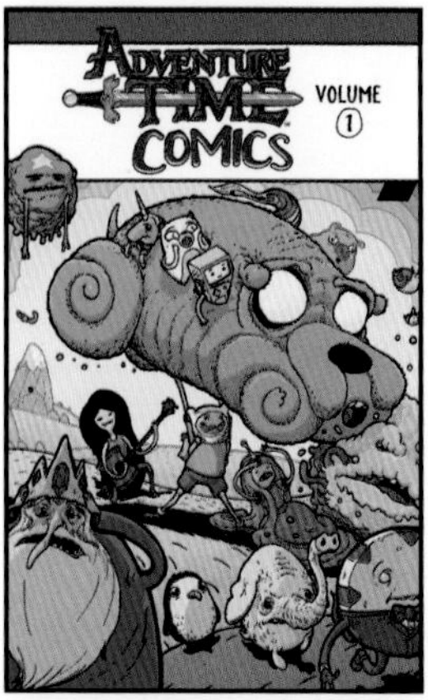

ADVENTURE TIME COMICS
VOLUME 1

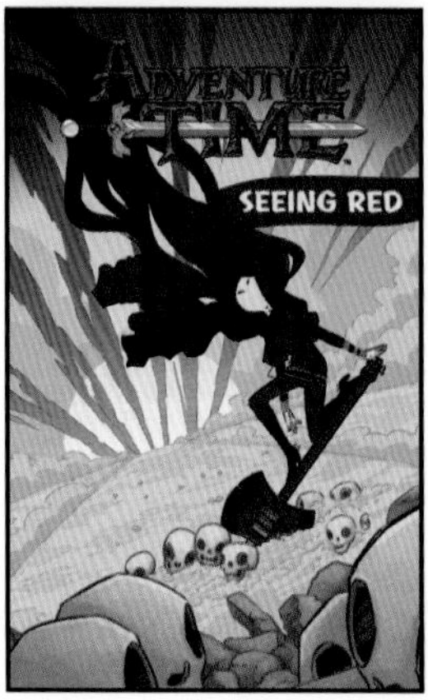

ADVENTURE TIME
SEEING RED

Adventure Time

Volume 1
ISBN: 978-1-60886-280-1 | $14.99 US

Volume 2
ISBN: 978-1-60886-323-5 | $14.99 US

Volume 3
ISBN: 978-1-60886-317-4 | $14.99

Volume 4
ISBN: 978-1-60886-351-8 | $14.99

Volume 5
ISBN: 978-1-60886-401-0 | $14.99

Volume 6
ISBN: 978-1-60886-482-9 | $14.99

Volume 7
ISBN: 978-1-60886-746-2 | $14.99

Volume 8
ISBN: 978-1-60886-795-0 | $14.99

Volume 9
ISBN: 978-1-60886-843-8 | $14.99

Volume 10
ISBN: 978-1-60886-909-1 | $14.99

Volume 11
ISBN: 978-1-60886-946-6 | $14.99

Volume 12
ISBN: 978-1-68415-005-2 | $14.99

Volume 13
ISBN: 978-1-68415-051-9 | $14.99

Volume 14
ISBN: 978-1-68415-144-8 | $14.99

Adventure Time Comics

Volume 1
ISBN: 978-1-60886-934-3 | $14.99

Volume 2
ISBN: 978-1-60886-984-8 | $14.99

Volume 3
ISBN: 978-1-68415-041-0 | $14.99

Volume 4
ISBN: 978-1-68415-133-2 | $14.99

Volume 5
ISBN: 978-1-68415-190-5 | $14.99

Volume 6
ISBN: 978-1-68415-258-2 | $14.99

Adventure Time Original Graphic Novels

Volume 1 Playing With Fire
ISBN: 978-1-60886-832-2 | $14.99

Volume 2 Pixel Princesses
ISBN: 978-1-60886-329-7 | $11.99

Volume 3 Seeing Red
ISBN: 978-1-60886-356-3 | $11.99

Volume 4 Bitter Sweets
ISBN: 978-1-60886-430-0 | $12.99

Volume 5 Graybles Schmaybles
ISBN: 978-1-60886-484-3 | $12.99

Volume 6 Masked Mayhem
ISBN: 978-160886-764-6 | $14.99

Volume 7 The Four Castles
ISBN: 978-160886-797-4 | $14.99

Volume 8 President Bubblegum
ISBN: 978-1-60886-846-9 | $14.99

Volume 9 The Brain Robbers
ISBN: 978-1-60886-875-9 | $14.99

Volume 10 The Orient Express
ISBN: 978-1-60886-995-4 | $14.99

Volume 11 Princess & Princess
ISBN: 978-1-68415-025-0 | $14.99

Volume 12 Thunder Road
ISBN: 978-1-68415-179-0 | $14.99

kaboom!™
A BOOM! Studios Imprint

AVAILABLE AT YOUR LOCAL COMICS SHOP AND BOOKSTORE
WWW.**BOOM-STUDIOS**.COM

CN CARTOON NETWORK

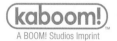

DISCOVER MORE
ADVENTURE TIME

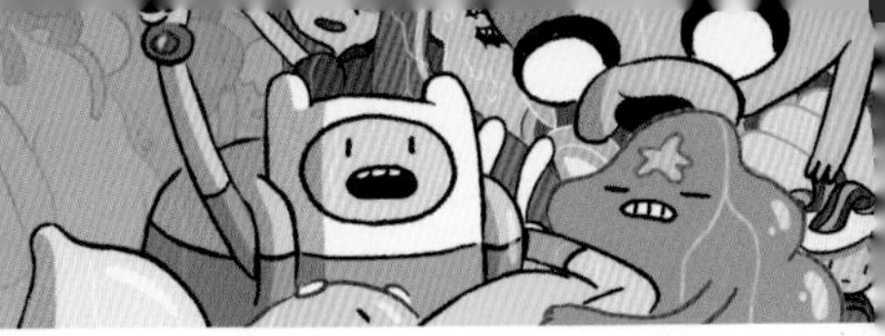

Adventure Time: Islands OGN
ISBN: 978-1-60886-972-5 | $9.99

Adventure Time Sugary Shorts

Volume 1
ISBN: 978-1-60886-361-7 | $19.99

Volume 2
ISBN: 978-1-60886-774-5 | $19.99

Volume 3
ISBN: 978-1-68415-030-4 | $19.99

Volume 4
ISBN: 978-1-68415-122-6 | $19.99

Adventure Time: Marceline & the Scream Queens
ISBN: 978-1-60886-313-6 | $19.99

Adventure Time: Fionna & Cake
ISBN: 978-1-60886-338-9 | $19.99

Adventure Time: Candy Capers
ISBN: 978-1-60886-365-5 | $19.99

Adventure Time: The Flip Side
ISBN: 978-1-60886-456-0 | $19.99

Adventure Time: Banana Guard Academy
ISBN: 978-1-60886-486-7 | $19.99

Adventure Time: Marceline Gone Adrift
ISBN: 978-1-60886-770-7 | $19.99

Adventure Time: Fionna & Cake Card Wars
ISBN: 978-1-60886-799-8 | $19.99

Adventure Time: Ice King
ISBN: 978-1-60886-920-6 | $19.99

Adventure Time/Regular Show
ISBN: 978-1-68415-166-0 | $19.99

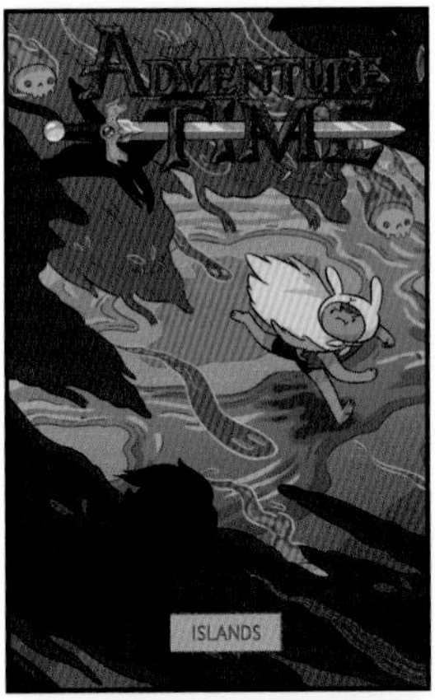
ADVENTURE TIME
ISLANDS

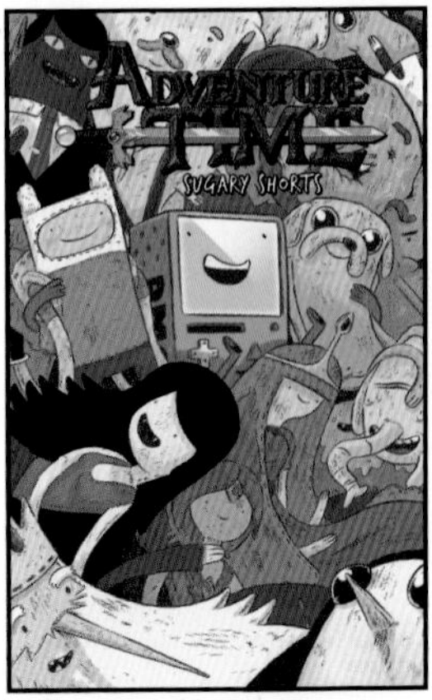
ADVENTURE TIME
SUGARY SHORTS

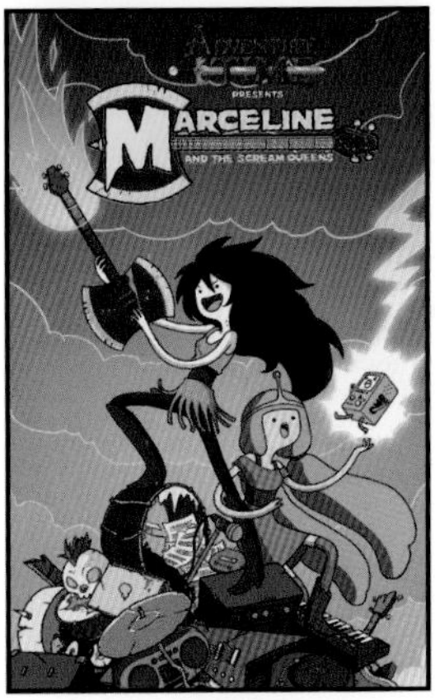
ADVENTURE TIME
PRESENTS
MARCELINE
AND THE SCREAM QUEENS

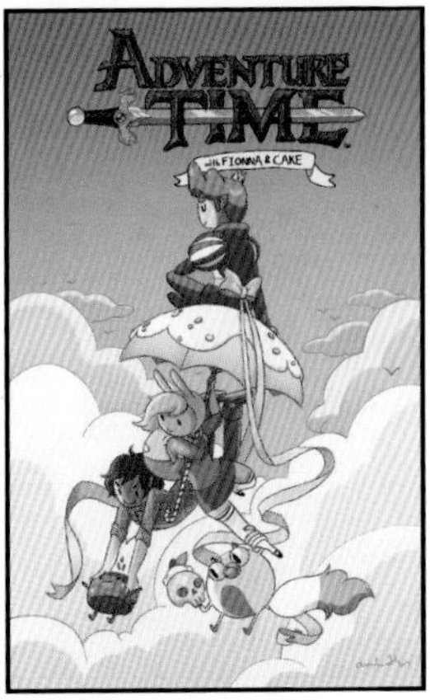
ADVENTURE TIME
with FIONNA & CAKE

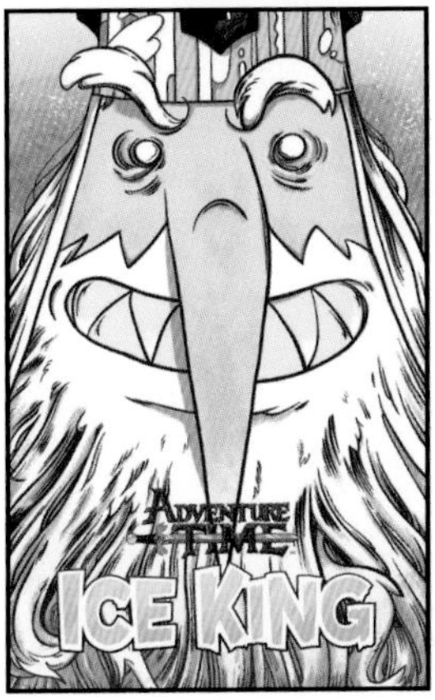
ADVENTURE TIME
ICE KING

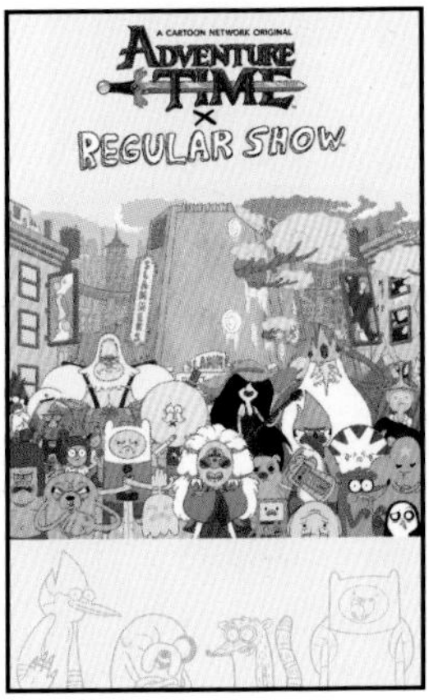
A CARTOON NETWORK ORIGINAL
ADVENTURE TIME
×
REGULAR SHOW

kaboom!™
A BOOM! Studios Imprint

AVAILABLE AT YOUR LOCAL COMICS SHOP AND BOOKSTORE
WWW.**BOOM-STUDIOS**.COM

CARTOON NETWORK.

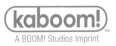

DISCOVER
EXPLOSIVE NEW WORLDS

Adventure Time
Pendleton Ward and Others
Volume 1
ISBN: 978-1-60886-280-1 | $14.99 US
Volume 2
ISBN: 978-1-60886-323-5 | $14.99 US
Adventure Time: Islands
ISBN: 978-1-60886-972-5 | $9.99 US

The Amazing World of Gumball
Ben Bocquelet and Others
Volume 1
ISBN: 978-1-60886-488-1 | $14.99 US
Volume 2
ISBN: 978-1-60886-793-6 | $14.99 US

Brave Chef Brianna
Sam Sykes, Selina Espiritu
ISBN: 978-1-68415-050-2 | $14.99 US

Mega Princess
Kelly Thompson, Brianne Drouhard
ISBN: 978-1-68415-007-6 | $14.99 US

The Not-So Secret Society
Matthew Daley, Arlene Daley, Wook Jin Clark
ISBN: 978-1-60886-997-8 | $9.99 US

Over the Garden Wall
Patrick McHale, Jim Campbell and Others
Volume 1
ISBN: 978-1-60886-940-4 | $14.99 US
Volume 2
ISBN: 978-1-68415-006-9 | $14.99 US

Steven Universe
Rebecca Sugar and Others
Volume 1
ISBN: 978-1-60886-706-6 | $14.99 US
Volume 2
ISBN: 978-1-60886-796-7 | $14.99 US

Steven Universe & The Crystal Gems
ISBN: 978-1-60886-921-3 | $14.99 US

Steven Universe: Too Cool for School
ISBN: 978-1-60886-771-4 | $14.99 US

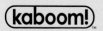

AVAILABLE AT YOUR LOCAL COMICS SHOP AND BOOKSTORE
To find a comics shop in your area, visit www.comicshoplocator.com
WWW.BOOM-STUDIOS.COM